BAGELS & SALSA

LARA REZNIK

CONTENTS

BAGELS & SALSA

By

Lara Reznik

PUBLISHER'S NOTE

Cover Design, Interior Formatting and Ebook Conversion:
Tosh McIntosh

**Printed and Published in the United States of America by
Enchanted Indie Press**

Print Edition v2.4.5
ISBN-13: 978-1-938749-38-4
ISBN-10: 1-938749-38-3

Digital Edition v2.4.5
ISBN-13: 978-1-938749-39-1
ISBN-10: 1-938749-39-1

ENCHANTED INDIE PRESS

For my husband Rudy, who inspired this unconventional love story. Through sickness and health, he is my true knight in shining armor.

EDITORIAL REVIEWS

BAGELS & SALSA

". . . Reznik draws on some elements of her real life in this novel and the humorous details of Jewish and Hispanic family life ring true, offered with a smattering of Yiddish and Spanish dialogue. The author tells a simple love story, but she structures the novel to provide a panoramic view of her characters. This is her second book featuring Laila as a protagonist. ... Reznik stays true to her theme of overcoming cultural differences. Overall, the story is well-paced, with scenes of excitement and danger." —*Kirkus Reviews*

★★★★★ "Another lovely read from Lara Reznik! *Bagels and Salsa* is a little bit sequel to Ms. Reznik's wonderful book *The Girl From Long Guyland,* but mostly a standalone delight about clash of cultures. As with all her novels there are also plenty of fun subplot twists and turns. I wanted more." — Barbara Gaines, Former Executive Producer of *The Late Show with David Letterman*

"Amid the constant string of ethnic slurs, Reznik balances the negativity with hilarious and light-hearted scenes—mainly centered on comfort food—that reflect the Hispanic and Yiddish cultures. Other nice additions are the Spanish and Yiddish comments and sayings that are heavily sprinkled throughout Reznik's plot. An engrossing intercultural read, *Bagels & Salsa* is well suited for romance enthusiasts." —Anita Lock, *Pacific Book Review* Star (Awarded to Books of Excellent Merit)

"Schmear and far: *Bagels & Salsa* is a bi-cultural love story set in New York and New Mexico She's got a saucy love story!" — James Harney, *Brooklyn Daily*

"One of the strengths of this satisfying serious novel is that it forces you to engage in it as it highlights the various challenges pertaining to the delicate dynamics of intercultural relationships. In addition, it is a narrative that intently observes a couple trying to keep their lives from spinning out of control by grasping hopefully at love." —Norm Goldman, *Book Pleasures.com*

★★★★★ "In the novel Bagels & Salsa, author Lara Reznik writes romantic suspense with serious and light-hearted moments . . .The author is a highly skilled writer, and there is a smooth flow to the story. She introduces many characters as the plot unfolds; some are positive and supportive of the new couple, while others are simply unpleasant, or even malicious. She also includes many twists and turns to the plot, and the reader cannot foresee the ending of the book. Her portrayal of the religious and cultural challenges that Eduardo and Laila face is enlightening, and the descriptions of the beautiful New

Mexico landscapes are gorgeous. Author Lara Reznik has written a fascinating and engaging fictional work in *Bagels & Salsa*. A very entertaining read!" —Deborah Lloyd, *Readers Favorite*

CHAPTER ONE
The Presentation

Laila

On the morning of July 29, 1977, as New York's blistering heat wave persisted, every woman in Manhattan was in a state of panic. The *Daily News* published a handwritten letter from a man claiming to be the gruesome .44 Caliber Killer. That specific day had been singled out in the letter as the date he planned to strike again. Some of my friends refused to leave their apartments. Others escaped to Fire Island or the Catskills, or retreated to their parents' homes in the suburbs.

I tried not to let the panic pervading New York City that stifling summer morning dictate my life despite the fact that July 29th was also the two-year anniversary of my disastrous nuptials to Julian Goldblatt or Jules Gold, the nom de plume he used on his hip late night radio show. Any reminder of my wedding day still made me cringe with rage and humiliation.

Admittedly, my anxiety was at an all time high as I parked my canary-yellow Chevrolet Bel Air, and fed coins into the meter at the curb. Fearful of the new threats from the Son of Sam, I opened my purse and eyeballed the .38 caliber pistol my father had slipped under the table last night at Ratners on Delancey Street, a kosher dairy restaurant, and the perfect choice for a vegetarian like me.

I looked in every direction before leaving the car to walk the two blocks to Morris High School, Pop's alma mater, but currently known as "one of the biggest, baddest high schools in the Bronx."

As I headed down the street plastered with graffiti, a toothless man smelling of stale booze and urine rolled up in his wheelchair. His face glistened with sweat. He held out a coffee can containing a few dollar bills and coins. "Can you spare some change, pretty lady?"

I held my breath and dropped a few quarters in the can.

"How 'bout a dollar? Surely a hot chickie like you can afford that."

Ignoring his request, I continued walking until I came across three Puerto Rican teenagers glaring at me. I half-smiled and crossed the street to avoid them.

The tallest produced a catcall as the other two made obscene hand gestures.

I tried to appear nonchalant as I moseyed on my way, but this sheltered girl from Long Island started hyperventilating. My stomach was already tied in knots at the thought of standing up in front of a full auditorium of people for my first speaking engagement ever.

"It's all a matter of confidence," Pop had said last night. "Just believe in yourself and you'll be fine."

My mother thought I was crazy to spend three years at NYU studying for my doctorate in sociology. "What kinda job are you gonna get with that degree? You could have been a *real* doctor for all the time and money you spent."

In a way she was right, but I'd followed my passion to study the science of social institutions and relationships, and had no regrets. Fortunately, I'd secured a part-time teaching job at Bronx Community College while still in graduate school. And, as luck would have it, my dissertation on the social phenomenon of America's teen pregnancies landed me a grant from the U.S. Department of Health. Since America's teen pregnancy rate was among the highest in the industrialized world, it was imperative to search for solutions to the epidemic problem.

My NYU advisor had arranged for me to join a panel of speakers at Morris High, a school rampant with teen pregnancies. Over dinner my father had offered to accompany me to his alma mater, but I'd turned him down. "I'm a big girl now, Pop."

Dressed like a professional grownup in a navy suit and matching high heels, I entered the buff-colored brick building with its elaborate limestone and terra-cotta trim. I had read somewhere that the school, built in 1904, was considered a masterpiece of neo-Gothic architecture.

The corridors reeked of Pine Sol and paste wax, with a touch of locker room jockstraps. The drab green paint was peeling off the plaster walls where metal lockers were attached in rows. My three-inch stilettos (which I now regretted wearing), clickety-clacked on fractured tile floors.

I teetered to the stage of the two-story auditorium with its elaborate balcony and masonry buttresses framing large arched Tudor stained-glass windows. The panelists were already seated on each side of a freestanding white screen as the school auditorium filled up with women and a sprinkling of men.

"Ms. Levin," said Flo Capuano, the moderator, a stocky woman who wore a skintight leather skirt and white go-go boots. "I was beginning to worry you wouldn't show."

I checked my watch. 8:55 a.m. . . . "You told me to be here at nine-thirty."

Flo's eyes protruded like an undernourished Pekinese.

"Didn't you get my message? We moved you up to . . . never mind. Thank God you sent your slides ahead of time."

I sat down in a folding metal chair, and rifled through my notes. As the auditorium lights dimmed, my stomach rumbled. I suddenly remembered my old message machine had been making weird clicking noises for days. Damn! How could I be so careless?

Flo stepped up to the podium and tapped the microphone. "Ladies and gentlemen, we're all here to discuss a serious problem facing our school and community. Our first speaker, Dr. Laila Levin, is an expert on the impact teen pregnancies are having in this country." She nodded at a man running a slide projector on a makeshift platform in the audience. "First slide, please."

I walked to the center of the stage to the sound of polite applause focusing on Pop's words about confidence. My first slide, a map of the United States, appeared on the screen. The areas in the country with the highest rate of teen pregnancies were crimson.

My lips quivered as Flo handed me the microphone and a wood pointing stick. I took a deep breath. "We face a challenging time in our country where—"

BANG BANG! Gunshots cracked through the air.

People in the audience ducked down and covered their heads.

Terrified, I backed into the screen and lost my balance. I braced myself with the pointer, but it snapped in half. Then, I felt a stabbing pain and the room began to spin around.

Next thing I knew, I was lying on the floor. The stink of floor wax filled my nostrils. The pain in my right shoulder was excruciating. My heart about stopped when I turned my head and discovered that part of my white blouse was soaked in blood.

The world ticked by in slow motion. I could hardly breathe. Was this the end? I hadn't begun to figure out the meaning of life. Wasn't I supposed to live to ninety-four like Grandma Levin? Voices around me sounded like a 78-rpm playing on slow speed. Someone said, "Is . . . there . . . a . . . doc . . . tor . . . in . . . the . . . room?"

Everything above me looked blurry as two men in dark uniforms whizzed by. Police? I opened my mouth to cry for help, but no words came out. Did anyone see me lying there?

Flo's garbled voice filtered through the microphone.

A tall man with curly black hair and a thick mustache knelt down next to me. The familiar aroma of Old Spice, Pop's cologne, permeated my senses. "I'm Dr. Quintana. I'd like to have a look at your shoulder."

"Okay."

He pulled out a pocketknife, ripped off the arm of my blouse, and cut my bra strap enabling him to apply pressure directly to my bleeding shoulder.

Was he really a doctor or some weirdo? I tried to push him away. "What are you doing?" The room stopped spinning and my normal breathing returned.

"You're going to have to trust me." He whipped out a white handkerchief from the back pocket of his pleated khakis and pressed it against the wound.

"You don't look like a doctor."

"Actually, I'm a cowboy." He smiled. His well-tanned face had a commanding presence. "You're a what?" Who was this man? Despite my apprehension, I had to admit he was rather good looking.

"That was a joke, honey. Well, a half-truth."

Lord, he had one irresistible dimple. "Don't honey me. How many bullets hit me?"

"Didn't you hear the moderator? It was just some kids shooting off firecrackers."

"You mean I wasn't shot?" The hairs on the back of my neck prickled. Was he saying everything was okay? I wasn't going to die?

"No, you lost your balance and fell down stabbing your shoulder on the sharp edge of the broken pointer stick. Four or five stitches and you'll be good as new."

"I can't walk in high heels. Big mistake wearing them today."

He grinned. "Worst case of stage fright I've ever seen."

CHAPTER TWO
ER

Eduardo

D r. Eduardo Quintana swished the curtain open to a small cubicle in the emergency room of the Bronx Lebanon Hospital. The young woman who'd fallen on the stage was propped up on pillows talking on the phone. He checked out her chart.

Patient: Ms. Laila Levin
Sex: <u>female</u>
Age: 28
Height: <u>5' 5"</u>
Weight: <u>112 pounds</u>
Religious preference: <u>Jewish-Buddhist-Agnostic</u>

Eduardo cracked a smile and made a note to ask her more about her unusual religious beliefs. Ms. Levin didn't acknowledge his presence as he stood by the bed waiting for her to get off the telephone. He considered returning later since he needed to check out other patients on his rounds. But instead of leaving, he broke hospital protocol and stood by her bed waiting for her to notice him. Why? He wasn't really sure.

There was just something about her. While she was an attractive woman with wild curly hair and vibrant green eyes, she was not a beauty in the classic sense. One ear stuck out through thick waves of reddish-brown hair, and her nose was a bit large for her thin face. New York was filled with *mujeres bonitas,* and he'd certainly dated his share of pretty women in the two years he'd lived in Manhattan. It never ceased to amaze him that when he'd added the letters MD to the end of his name, ladies flocked to him like heifers to a prize bull. Yet there was something about this woman that interested him. Her vulnerability combined with feistiness perhaps?

Ms. Levin continued to chat endlessly, ignoring his existence.

A nurse stopped in the room. "Mr. Silvio is waiting for his prescription."

"Tell him I'll be there in a minute."

The nurse shook her head and scrambled out the door.

Eduardo grabbed the phone from Miss Levin's hand and placed it back on the receiver.

Her green eyes pierced his armor. "What do you think you're doing?"

"I've got other patients that need me."

"You could have said something rather than—never mind, this shoulder hurts like hell."

"It will hurt for a few weeks, but you'll be okay as long as you avoid public speaking."

"You've got quite a sense of humor for a cowboy." A faint smile appeared on her pouty lips. "What were you doing at a presentation on teen pregnancies anyway?"

"I come from the teenage pregnancy capital of North America. I'm setting up a practice there and looking for solutions."

"You're leaving New York?"

"Don't worry. There are plenty of other *caballeros.* I understand John Wayne has a penthouse on the Upper East Side."

"I'll keep that fact in mind. You know, smart boy, you ruined my bra."

"Sorry, I'm adding it to my collection. Hottest little honey I ever roped, grounded, and tied in under a minute. Where I come from that's something to be proud of."

"Where do you come from? Rednecks R Us?"

"Oh, no. That's the *gringo* side of town. I live a little farther out." He was having fun, and liked that she brought out his sense of humor.

They stared at each other. Eduardo felt an awkwardness but also a strange familiarity.

"So seriously, Dr. Quintana, where are you from?"

"A small ranching town in New Mexico."

"No kidding. Where in New Mexico?"

"Does it really make a difference?" He hadn't met one person in the two years he'd been in Manhattan even remotely familiar with his home state. When he'd filled out a rental application for his apartment, his landlord thought he was from a foreign country.

"I spent a few years at UNM," she said.

"Seriously?"

"Why would I lie?"

"I don't know, Ms. Levin. Maybe you'd like me to ask you out." He regretted the words the second they came out.

"Don't flatter yourself."

"You're right. I don't even know why I said that. Please forgive me." It had been way too easy for him with women the last few years. This one was different.

"I forgive you, Dr. Quintana."

"Please call me Eduardo."

"If you start calling me Laila, we have a deal."

"Laila, would you consider having dinner with me one night?"

"I'm not looking to get involved."

"Neither am I. I'm leaving in a month."

The skin between Laila's brows buckled. "A month?"

"More or less."

"Hmmm. Can you agree to a platonic date?"

"No problem. How about Saturday?"

"I promised to babysit my niece and nephew," she said. "How's Sunday?"

"I work the late shift Sunday. Monday?"

They shook on it. But he held onto her hand an extra few seconds and felt a strange current between them. Static electricity? A weird connection of some type? *Ridiculo.* It had been too many years since he'd had such feelings.

AT 35, EDUARDO HAD JUST COMPLETED HIS RESIDENCY AT Columbia Medical Center and was working a shift in a tough neighborhood hospital in the Bronx. He had been forced to delay college and medical school for seven years to help out his *familia.*

As a teenager, Eduardo had big dreams that were all crushed the night of his senior prom. He had taken his high school sweetheart to the Bull Ring, the best steakhouse in Santa Fe, with a diamond ring stashed in his tuxedo pocket. A whole year's savings of mending fences for his uncles had been used to pay for the ring.

Violet's waist-length black hair shimmered in the candlelight. Her body was as flawless as the heart of the diamond he had purchased for her. "You'll never believe what happened to me today, Eduardo."

"Something good, I hope."

"I got a phone call this afternoon from a division supervisor at TWA. She says I have all the qualifications to make a great stewardess. *La mirada, las maneras y buena visión*, looks, manners and good vision. It's a bonus that I know *español*. Unbelievable! I leave for Chicago next week for training."

Eduardo felt sharp pains in his chest. He inhaled, and then slowly let out his breath before responding. "When did you apply?"

"They were interviewing over spring break at the Sunport. Surely, I told you about it."

"No, that's when you shared the other news."

Her lower lip quivered. "The miscarriage."

"Yes." While he'd initially been upset about her pregnancy, he'd embraced the idea of becoming a young father. When she'd told him she'd lost the baby, he was crushed beyond words. Now there would be no baby and no Violet.

She blinked. "It's done with. Be happy for me."

Clasping his hand on the box hidden in his jacket, his voice grew husky. "Ah, sure. Have a great life."

He felt blindsided on the silent drive from Santa Fe to Española High School. How could she do this after everything they'd been through together? He'd loved Violet since they'd rode ponies as children while their mamas gabbed and rolled tortillas in the kitchen.

When they arrived at the prom, he swallowed his pride and a shitload of beer in the schoolyard with his friends.

Strangely, Violet acted like everything was the same

between them. She clung to his body when they slow-danced, and kissed him passionately as the lights dimmed. Two hours later, between the beer and Violet's hot kisses he felt somewhat better.

Then, his sister Carla showed up at the gymnasium with a white-strained face. "Papa's had a heart attack. You need to come to the hospital."

The next few weeks were a blur. At one point, his father was at death's door, but he fought ferociously like the Marine he'd been in World War II.

As Papa slowly recovered, Eduardo kept the ranch afloat through some difficult times. Inwardly, he'd regretted missing out on college and his calling to become a doctor. In high school he'd believed he had a charmed life. The oldest and only son in a tight-knit Hispanic family, he was *el hijo que no podria hacer nada malo*, the son who could do no wrong. An A student, captain of the football team, and boyfriend of the smartest and prettiest girl in Española, he'd envisioned becoming a physician with Violet at his side.

Now, after seventeen years, his life was finally on the right path . . . well, at least the doctor part. He had lost track of Violet years ago and hadn't looked back. Although he'd known his fair share of women, none had evoked the strong feelings he'd once had for her. It was like something had died inside of him that night at the Bull Ring. Yet he wanted to have a family more than anything in the world. *Familia* was everything. Had he just not met the right woman? Or was he holding back his feelings out of fear of getting hurt again?

CHAPTER THREE
LaLa Land

Violet

Ira clawed at her clothes like an animal. First, the halter-top, exposing her big tatas. Then, her jeans which rode low on her hipbones.

Violet Sanchez closed her eyes and waited for him to be done. It would only take a few minutes. She'd been to this rodeo before.

Diez. If he didn't get done soon, she'd be late for her pedicure.

Nueve. She hadn't heard from Larry in three days. Would she have to do him again to get that dumb thirty-second role in the new Superman movie?

Ocho. Mama was coming for a visit. Ira would have to move out while Mama was here, and he wasn't happy about it. After all, it was *his* apartment. Violet moaned, "Oh my God!"

Ira swept a long strand of black hair from her face. "Baby, you dig this? Want some more?"

"Absolutely. You're the best." She examined herself in the mirrors covering every wall in his bedroom. Svelte as ever. Her breasts, sizable as they were, hadn't sagged one bit. Her jet-black hair still ran down her shoulders like rainwater. Or so said her high school sweetheart, Eduardo, in a poem he'd once written about her. Where was he now, she wondered?

Siete. Ira's back and shoulders were covered in ringlets of inky-black hair. He was sweating like a Polish pig. Ugh! She couldn't stand him anymore. He hadn't come through for her with even one shitty commercial in over a year. That's why she was double-dicking Larry.

Seis. But Larry was married and she had no one else lined up to replace Ira Krazinski. He provided her with a free pad and all the powder she could put up her nose in trade for a little kinky sex a few nights a week. At least he was quick . . . a total asset in a man.

Afterwards, she and Ira sat eating grapes on two stools in the galley kitchen of his small Santa Monica apartment. It was *un lugar muy malo*, a crappy place, pee-stained shag carpet, low ceilings, and a view of the A&P parking lot. But having an address in Santa Monica was prestigious to leave with producers after auditions. It showed them she'd already achieved some level of success. Image was everything in LA.

Ira let out a series of loud farts.

Violet wrinkled her nose in disgust. "You better restrain yourself when Mama is here."

"Of course, sweetcheeks." He slapped her ass. "Can you hustle up some dinner?"

"Whatever you say, hon."

Ira gave her a once over. "You know I'm crazy about ya?"

It was true. As bad as Ira was, at least he truly cared for her. In this phony town one needed someone they could count on. The idiot had even proposed. Not a chance in hell did she plan to accept, but she would put him off as long as possible.

Violet fried up *papitas y huevos* with ranchero sauce. She missed the fresh red and green chiles she'd grown up on in New Mexico and hoped Mama would bring some with her from Sabinal. Her mother had only been to California once in the eight years Violet had lived there. She'd been furious at Violet for not picking her up at the airport. It didn't matter that Violet had arranged for a stylish Lincoln Town Car limousine to pick her up. This time Mama had insisted, "*Quiero que tu me enquentras en el aeropuerto.*" She wanted Violet to pick her up at the airport. No limos, no cabs, not even Ira would do.

But the traffic was hell, the parking even worse, and Violet was not the best of drivers. The endless lines of coke had made her paranoid whenever she drove on the Santa Monica Freeway. Sadly, she'd totaled the Chevy Malibu that Daddy had left her, and had recently caused a couple of fender benders in Ira's old black Cadillac. Last time, she'd hit a parked Mercedes in Venice and miraculously escaped the scene without anyone seeing her.

Ira was fuming, nonetheless.

"Calm down," she'd said. "There's already a dent in the passenger door."

"That's not the point. Plus it's bad juju to hit a poor schmuck and leave the scene."

"Would you have preferred to pay for the damage to the Mercedes?"

"Thank God you wasn't driving the Porsche."

He'd never let her drive the silver Porsche, Ira's pride and joy and the last relic from the time when he'd been a successful agent to famous celebrities. Those were the days he talked about between lines of coke and daily doubles at the racetrack —the days, unfortunately *before* they'd met. Ann Margaret, Jacqueline Bisset, Goldie Hawn, Julie Christie—or so he said —all had been his clients. Ira claimed he'd jumpstarted their careers and then they all dumped him. *Right. Sure they did.*

Violet placed two paper plates of eggs and hash browns on the cracked Formica counter where Ira sat reading *Variety*. His balding head, pathetic comb-over, and hairy back grossed her out. How had she Violet Sanchez—child beauty contest champion, prom queen, TWA stewardess, aspiring actress with exotic good looks, great boobs and real talent—ended up here in this dump with Ira Krazinski? Her rising star had fallen, and even she had to admit it was time for Plan B. The only problem was that she had no clue what that plan would be.

CHAPTER FOUR
The Girl From Long Guyland

Laila

I'd tried to persuade Dr. Quintana, Eduardo, to let me go home, but he insisted I spend the night at the hospital. In addition to the stitches in my right shoulder, I had a mild concussion from the fall. He ordered for my transfer to a semiprivate room on the seventh floor. Fortunately, the other bed in the room was unoccupied.

My mother charged into the room an hour later, her arms filled with Macy's bags. She burst into tears when she caught sight of my shoulder in a sling. "*Oy gevalt*, look at you. My poor *sheina meidala*, pretty girl. Thank God, I was already in the city." She kissed my cheek, and then wiped the smudge of cherry-red lipstick off my face with her finger. "And of all days, on your anniversary."

"You promised not to bring that up anymore." I made a mental note. When July 29 rolled around next year, I planned to stay in bed.

"Then stop acting like you're dead. You never go anywhere . . . refuse to date. It's not normal for a girl your age."

"Maybe I should see a therapist."

"No daughter of mine needs a shrink. What you need is a matchmaker."

"Give me a break." My mother didn't believe in her daughters seeking psychological help. God forbid we might discover that *she* was at the root of our problems. Ironically, my sister, Rachel, married and living Ma's Jewish American Princess dream in Great Neck, had secretly been in therapy for more than a year.

My mother fixed her gaze on me. "I'm worried about you, honey. It's been two years. When are you gonna snap out of this depression?"

"I'm not depressed." A big fat lie and the reason I, too, was considering seeking a therapist. "Just because I'm not dating . . ."

As if on cue, my father, a silver-haired man of sixty, entered the room gasping for breath. A former New York City firefighter, he still looked trim and muscular. Thank God for Pop. I could always count on his support when my mother's behavior advanced from inquisitive to inappropriate. This occurred more often than not.

I stretched out my good arm for a hug. "Oh, Pop!" The numbing medication had begun to wear off and my shoulder pulsated with pain.

"I came as soon as I heard. Bumper to bumper the whole way on the Long Island Expressway."

Ma waved her arms at him. "Hello, Elliot. Your wife is here too, you know."

"Sorry, dear." He brushed her lips with a quick kiss.

My mother's brows met at sharp angles as she turned her attention back to me. "When are you gonna get serious about your life?"

"Finishing my PhD and getting a federal grant isn't serious?"

She shook her head. "This is no life. You're almost thirty."

Ma exaggerated everything. "I just turned twenty-eight."

"You're just wasting time, Laila."

"Well, it's my life. I spent seven years getting my degrees, thank you very much. Why wouldn't I use them?"

"Esther Goldberg's nephew, Stevie, just broke his engagement. He's an accountant, you know."

"Wonderful. Maybe he can do my income tax return next year."

Pop chuckled. "Right now Laila needs TLC, not pressure from you, Evie."

My mother never let up. She'd had an agenda for my sisters and me from the minute we were born. Strike that. From the minute we'd been conceived. Ma had been a stay-at-home mother like most women of her generation. I'd come to find out she'd always wanted to be an actress. When my sisters and I left home, Ma began dressing in tight stretch pants with long silk blouses and dangly gold earrings. She landed an agent who found her bit parts in TV commercials. One day, she dyed her hair black with a white streak down the middle claiming her agent had said it would make her look exotic. Personally, I thought it made her look like a skunk. Her given name had been Ethel, but she officially changed it to Eve after the 1957 movie, *The Three Faces of Eve,* about a woman with multiple personalities. Ironically, apropos for my *mchuge* whimsical mother. She even asked my sisters and me to stop calling her "Ma" and refer to her as Eve.

I strained to make conversation. "How was your audition yesterday?"

"Forget the audition. Kmart has this tagline, 'Shaving prices to the bone.' They want a woman to shave her head on national TV. Can you imagine?"

"Sounds like it's right up your alley. And national TV, too. Don't they pay a premium?"

"I have my standards—"

"I know, Mother, ah, Eve. You won't eat dog food or appear in commercials about sanitary napkins, vaginal sprays or douches."

"A director at Kimberly-Clark begged me to be a part of its New Freedom Pad commercials. That woulda been very lucrative, but I turned it down."

Dr. Quintana poked his head in the room and nodded at my parents. "I can come back."

"Ah, maybe it would be best." Geez, did I dare subject him to my mother? Only a good idea if I wanted him to head for the hills.

"No, come in," said Ma. "We want to know everything."

My father extended his hand to Eduardo. "Elliot Levin."

Eduardo gave him a firm handshake.

Eve peered over at me. "You need to brush your hair, Lai. It's a mess as usual."

"It looks great to me," Eduardo said.

I nodded at him. "Thank you." Two points for a man who stood up to Eve.

My mother flashed him one of her fakey smiles that caused her cheeks to plump up. "You like girls wild and loose like my Laila's hair? What about her *pulkes*?"

Dear God, keep me from strangling her. "Welcome to the Levin family circus, Doctor."

CHAPTER FIVE
The Date

Eduardo

Laila's mother gaped at Eduardo like she was inspecting lamb chops at the butcher shop. "So what was a nice doctor like you doing at my daughter's presentation?"

The gaudy woman decked out in kilos of gold jewelry reminded him of someone, but he wasn't sure whom.

Laila shot her mother a hard look. "It's really none of your business."

He touched Laila's hand. "It's okay." Then he turned to Mrs. Levin. "I'm starting a practice—"

"Quintana. Is that Puerto Rican? Cuban perhaps?" Her mother was a trip.

"Oh, for godsakes," Laila said. "Can you just leave, Ma? He needs to examine me."

Her mother looked like she'd swallowed a hairball. "Oh my God! Are you taking off your clothes?"

Laila winked at Eduardo. "Just my bra."

He tried to keep from laughing.

Her father put his arm around his wife. "Let's go, Evie. You're embarrassing Laila as usual."

Mrs. Levin's eyelids flickered. "I just—"

"I'll call you later." Laila kissed the air. "Love you, Mother."

Mr. Levin's eyes connected with Eduardo's as they headed to the door. "Take good care of my little girl, will you, Doc?"

"You can count on that, sir."

"Make sure she gets some rest," added Mrs. Levin as her husband gripped her elbow and steered her from the room.

"I've stopped apologizing for my mother," Laila said when they were gone.

He liked her parents despite her mother's quirkiness. "Your folks really care about you."

"I know. But my mother treats me like I'm still twelve."

It suddenly dawned on him who Mrs. Levin reminded him of—not her eccentric looks but her overbearing personality. "When it comes to her *niños*, my mother acts like a mama bear too."

"Then we have something in common, Doc."

Eduardo grinned. Oddly enough it appeared that they did. "We're still on for dinner Monday, right?"

"Of course."

It surprised him how much he was looking forward to it.

ON MONDAY AFTERNOON EDUARDO STOOD IN THE emergency room reception area agonizing over where to take Laila for dinner. Even though he'd lived in New York for two years, he had survived on hospital cafeteria food, takeout pizza, and street vendor hot dogs. He rarely treated himself to a meal at one of the city's finer establishments unless he had a date, but nothing out of the ordinary came to mind. He wanted to take Laila somewhere special.

After searching the Yellow Pages for an hour, he enlisted the help of his favorite nurse, Rita, an older Puerto Rican woman who'd taken him under her wing. Her narrow face was partly hidden by wispy brown ringlets. "A dinner date? First tell me something about *la chica*."

"If you promise not to announce it over the system."

She gave him a disarming grin. "*Tu sabe major que eso.* You know better than that, Doc." Everyone gossiped and poked fun at each other in the old Bronx hospital's ER. It was how they dealt with the daily trauma of blood, guts, burn victims, heart failure, broken bones and everything in-between.

"*Ella es especial*, okay? Cute woman with a PhD. Grew up in Long Island."

"That *chica* you treated for stitches the other day?"

"*Sí.*"

"*Déjamelo a mí.* Leave it to me. I'll even make the reservation and send a message to *su chica*. Seven o'clock should give you plenty of time to change and hail a cab. Tell the driver you're going to Sardi's. He'll know exactly where it is."

At 6:15 an ambulance pulled up with a man who needed an emergency appendectomy. The doc on the evening shift was running late so Eduardo had no choice but to perform the surgery. Afterwards, he sprinted up to the men's locker room and quickly changed into a Western-style sports jacket, bolo tie, and Tony Lama boots.

The plan was to meet Laila at the restaurant. Damn. Not only was he already twenty minutes late, but he'd also forgotten to inquire how expensive the restaurant would be. He had a hundred-dollar bill in his wallet, yet was clueless as to whether that was enough.

When Eduardo stepped into Sardi's, the mouthwatering aroma of sizzling steaks and poultry greeted him. Red-leather upholstered booths, Persian-style carpeting, and caricatures of famed celebrities covered the walls. Jimmy Durante, Clark Gable, Humphrey Bogart and Lauren Bacall represented decades of New York theater and Hollywood film history.

The maître d' whisked him to a table where Laila sat reading a paperback. She closed the book, stood, and gave him a warm hug.

He caught a delightful whiff of rose-scented perfume as he embraced her, careful of her tender shoulder. The simple black dress she wore emphasized every corner and angle of her slender figure. "Sorry, I'm late . . . a last-minute patient."

"No problem. Your nurse friend Rita called to let me know you'd be late. I took the liberty of ordering us wine."

"*Estupendo*. I like a woman who can take charge. How's the shoulder?"

"It hurts a lot. I've never had stitches before."

"Those high heels looked treacherous."

She jiggled her foot in front of him. "Don't worry, I'm wearing my Birkenstocks tonight."

Eduardo laughed at her wide flat shoes that didn't do justice to the sexy silk dress. He tried not to stare across the table.

Laila talked about her work, speaking with a passion he'd rarely heard from women he dated. Then she turned the tables and poked into his past.

It took a couple of rounds of Chardonnay for him to loosen up and speak about the things that mattered to him. His plans to go back to Sabinal and make a difference in the community. His love of the ranch and his *familia*. As he gazed at her impossibly curly hair, he could picture her as a little girl in pigtails. A cheerleader in high school for sure. "Tell me something about you besides your work."

She crinkled her eyes. "I was a hippie in the late sixties."

"Drugs, sex, and rock 'n' roll?"

She laughed. "You know what they say. If you remember the sixties, you weren't there."

"Is that when you became a Jew-Bu-Agnostic?"

"Hey, I was in excruciating pain when I wrote that. And what are your beliefs, *Señor*?"

He considered the question. "You might call me a Cowboy Catholic."

"Got me there."

"When I was a *niño,* Mama and my sisters would go to church on Sundays while Papa and I stayed on the ranch and prayed for rain. Papa called the raindrops 'pennies from heaven.'"

"I spent a lot of time with my pop growing up too." She leaned back in her chair. "Now that you've met my mother you can understand why."

"It appears you come from a close knit *familia.*"

"At times, maybe too close."

He arched a brow. "How do you mean?"

"My mother never lets up."

"In what way?"

"You know. Getting married, having children."

"What's wrong with that?"

"Frankly, a lot of men in New York are commitment phobic."

"Shortsighted if you ask me." He knew the type. A couple of residents at the hospital bragged about their conquests and claimed they'd never settle down. It made no sense to him.

"Too bad you're leaving."

"I'm beginning to think that myself. Or maybe I've had too much wine."

"Would you consider staying in New York?"

"That would be impossible. Although with a few more glasses of *vino* you might convince me to do anything."

"I sincerely doubt that. You don't appear to be a man who acts on a whim."

A waiter, dressed in a red tuxedo jacket and black pants, appeared with a pad in hand. "My name is Gustave and I'll be your server this evening. Can I take your order, Madam?"

Laila opened her menu and glanced at the contents. "I'll have the Fruitwood Smoked Salmon with Classis Garniture, and Spinach Cannelloni au Gratin for my main course."

"And you, sir?"

Eduardo read the menu but wasn't familiar with much. "I'd like a steak, medium rare."

Gustave wrinkled his nose. "The Steak Tartare, or perhaps the Grilled Sirloin with Horseradish Whipped Potatoes."

"Hmmm."

Gustave tapped his pen and reopened Eduardo's menu. "Why don't you just point at something?"

Eduardo clenched his jaw and continued to study the menu. He noticed the Grilled Marinated Center Cut Pork Chops, but wasn't in the mood for pork.

Laila touched his hand. "We can go somewhere else."

"No, no." Eduardo pointed at an entree on the menu. "I'll have the Rocky Mountain Oysters."

Gustav arched an eyebrow. "Do you know what those are, sir?"

"Calf balls." Eduardo made a point to say the words loudly.

People at the surrounding tables began to laugh and gawk at him. It didn't faze him one bit.

The waiter swiftly collected the menus. "A real delicacy, sir."

"I grew up on a ranch. I guess that makes us connoisseurs."

Laila smiled. "Touché. You are one of a kind, Doctor."

He gave her his best toothpaste commercial smile. "Is that good or bad?" He honestly didn't know if he'd embarrassed her by his boldness.

Laila drained the last of the wine in her glass. "It's quite good. But you're leaving New York so I guess it doesn't matter."

"What if I weren't leaving?"

She considered the question for so long he was afraid he'd been too forward. Perhaps she was feeling buyer's remorse before they closed the deal.

When she finally looked up at him, moisture glistened in her eyes. "It's been a while for me."

"How long?"

"Two years."

A woman like her didn't go without dating for lack of offers. She'd sidelined herself for some reason . . . a broken love affair most likely. "The guy must have been a jerk."

"That doesn't begin to describe him," she said.

"Give me his address and I'll break his legs."

She laughed. "But you're a doctor."

"That's the good part. After I break his legs, I can set them myself."

"You make it sound funny I'd rather not spoil tonight talking about him."

Eduardo recalled another spoiled night at the Bull Ring in Santa Fe so many years ago.

Suddenly, the room went dark. Everyone at Sardi's was screaming, shouting, and racing toward the exits. A twenty-five hour blackout earlier in the month had crippled the city. Was it happening again? Eduardo glanced out the window, noting the traffic lights and stores across 44th Street were still lit up.

"The Son of Sam," yelled a woman at the next table. "He's here. I know it's him."

"No reason to panic, Ma'am." Eduardo said. "It's probably just a breaker."

Laila clamped his forearm. "Maybe so, but let's get outta here."

They snaked through the dinner crowd toward the kitchen. Most of the customers were heading the opposite direction to the front door. A couple of flashlights in the kitchen provided a path of light. Eduardo spoke in Spanish to the two Puerto Rican dishwashers. "*Dónde está la salida?*"

They pointed a flashlight toward the back door.

"*Vámonos,*" Eduardo said, and they all ran out the exit to the alley.

He continued to grip Laila's hand as they raced down the street for at least three blocks and then stopped to catch their breath. There were people window shopping, eating in small cafés, buying hot dogs and kosher pickles from a street vendor.

They walked past a parked patrol car and Eduardo knocked on the passenger window.

The cop inside rolled it down. "Waddaya want?"

He told the officer about the blackout at Sardi's.

The cop pressed a switch on his radio "A possible 415 at Sardi's restaurant. Got anything on it?"

The voice on the speaker said, "Some problem with a breaker. It's been taken care of."

"Wow, you were right." Laila said. "You certainly are the guy to be with in a crisis."

The cop craned his neck toward the window. "It's all fixed if you guys wanna go back and finish your dinner."

"No way," Laila said. "I just wanna go home."

Eduardo reached out for her hand. Despite the warm weather it was ice cold.

Laila pointed at a food vendor peddling hot dogs and fresh pretzels on the street corner. The aroma filled his senses. "Wanna grab a bite to eat? I'm starving!"

"You betcha."

Laila started to laugh.

"What's so funny?"

"'You betcha?' You sound like a hick."

He smiled. "Surely you haven't mistaken me for a city boy?"

She cocked her head. "Forgive me for sounding like a New York snob."

"No problem. Let's eat." They walked up to the red-faced potbellied vendor. "Two dogs, please." He hoped the guy had change for a hundred-dollar bill.

"Just one. I'll have a pretzel instead," Laila said. "I don't eat meat."

"I'll try and remember that."

Afterwards, they headed back toward Sardi's and Laila pointed at a yellow Bel-Air parked at a meter down the street. "This is mine."

He stood silent for a few minutes gathering his thoughts. He wanted to make sure she got home okay but didn't want her to think he was too forward. Papa always said, 'If you don't ask, you don't get.' He stepped closer to her. "I'd like to see you home."

"You don't have to do that."

"I know. But I want to."

"Remember, this date is strictly platonic."

"*Sí, señorita.* I understand the rules."

CHAPTER SIX
Looking for Love in All the Wrong Places

Dave

Déjà Vu was a classy strip joint just down the street from the infamous Sardi's restaurant. Dave was a regular there. He would go at least three or four nights a week after work as a mail clerk in the Bronx . . . a lousy minimum wage job he'd had for twelve years. While Dave was only five-foot-four, he was damn proud of his muscular body. He spent three hours every day pumping iron in his tiny apartment behind the Happy Suds Laundromat in the Bronx. With his powerful physique, wavy brown hair and hazel eyes, Dave was a decent enough looking guy for a man in his early forties. But he stuttered every time he spoke to a girl, and feared they made fun of him behind his back. Or right to his face, like they did in high school. "Here comes D-davie B-berko J-jerko."

Dave felt a sense of belonging at the club. While his personal preference was brunettes with small boobs, the place was full of Lady Clairol blondes sporting gigantic silicone implants. But most of the girls greeted him by his first name and that made him feel important. Several nights a week he'd shell out ten bucks to have a girl do a table dance for three minutes. Then again and again and again . . . until his paycheck was gone.

Occasionally, after a couple lines of coke in the bathroom stall combined with many shots of Jim Beam, he'd tuck a wad of twenties into a girl's hands and ask if she'd come home with him. The chicks were polite yet always handed him back his money and saying, "It's against house rules."

Right. He wasn't no dummy. He observed the girls throw themselves at businessmen dressed in three-piece suits and wingtips. Surely, they "broke the rules" for those jerks flashing hundred dollar bills. Married guys out for a few laughs after work. Looking for a little nookie on the side.

The sad fact was Dave was still a virgin. He'd rather shoot himself than admit that to anyone. He'd only been on one date. One New Year's Eve his cousin Barney had asked Dave if he would take out his wife's sister who was visiting from Cincinnati.

Dave remembered her from Barney's wedding. "You're shittin' me. She's got a dogface and two tree trunks for legs."

"Beggars can't be choosy," said Barney.

"Whattaya mean? I got lottsa gorgeous chicks at Déjà Vu. You know, the club I t-told you about."

Barney rolled his eyes. "Just do me a favor. One night, okay?"

They all ate filet mignon at Keens Steakhouse on 36th Street. At the end of the night, he walked her to the front door, closed his eyes, and puckered up his lips, but she ducked and he kissed his cousin's storm door. Insult upon injury. Barney owed him big time for that.

What Dave really wanted was a wife. Not some slut like the chicks at the club but a gal with class. He had fallen in love once. A couple of years back he'd taken a class in sociology at Bronx Community College. The professor, Miss Levin, had all the qualifications he wanted in a wife. Wavy chestnut hair, curves in all the right places. He never spoke up in class, fearful of embarrassing himself with his ever-present stutter. But he appeared regularly during her weekly office hours and she'd spend at least thirty minutes reviewing the class material with him. He felt so comfortable around her he didn't stutter. Not even once. A true miracle! She was the one he'd been waiting for.

The aroma of her rose perfume alone would give him a hard on, but he kept that fact to himself by placing a book on his lap. After weeks of pretending he gave a shit about sociology, he finally got the nerve to ask her out. He'd showered, shaved, ironed a white shirt, and even bought himself a new pair of tan Dockers. But when he got to her office, she introduced him to her fiancé, some blonde asshole named Julian. Wrong-time-wrong-place Dave. The story of his sorry life.

Cherry, a six-foot tall redhead, interrupted his thoughts. "Hey, Davie boy, want a table dance?"

Although not his type, the red giant always made him feel good.

The deejay cued up Lynyrd Skynyrd's "Ain't No Good Life."

Cherry shook her booty to the music. Her face looked hard and distant.

Dave wondered what she was thinking about and touched her arm. "How 'bout you s-sit down for a m-minute." He was feeling especially lonely that night. "Get me m-my usual and whatever you w-want."

Cherry delivered a double shot of Jim Beam and a glass of Sangria then sat down next to him.

He took a crisp ten out of his wallet and handed it to her. It was the first time he'd paid any chick to just talk. He drained the bourbon and searched Cherry's eyes. "What's on your m-mind, sweetheart?"

She squinted. "Huh?"

"T-t-tell me something about yourself."

"My goddamn toilet is clogged. I tried using a plunger before work—"

"How 'bout something more p-p-personal?"

"Oh. Ah, let me see. I'm twenty-two and I wanna be an actress."

Ha, ha. He peered at the puffy bags under her eyes and the deep lines that fanned at the outer corner of each eye. The sagging skin on her neck. She was easily pushing forty, but Dave went along with her lie. At least she was friendly. "Tell me something you don't share with all the other g-guys."

She paused a minute. "I got twin girls. Just turned five last—"

"How 'bout something d-dirty?"

"Like what I'd like you to do to me in bed?"

Droplets of sweat flowed down Dave's forehead. His voice turned husky. "Yeah, l-like that."

She held out her hand for more cash.

He placed another ten-dollar bill in it.

"I'd let you smother me with kisses all over my body." The song ended, as she got more specific where those kisses would go.

He shelled out another ten dollars. Again and again until his wallet was empty. "If you give me your address, I'll f-fix your toilet."

"Really?"

"Swear to God."

She scribbled something on a cocktail napkin and stuffed it in his pocket.

Just then one of the bouncers approached them. "Are you soliciting, buddy?"

"No, ah—"

"Get the hell outta here. And don't show your mug here again."

"Yes, s-s-sir." He was mad as hell at himself as he stumbled out onto 44th Street. Did the bouncer really mean he couldn't hang out at Déjà Vu no more? It was like home to him . . . a place where all the girls called him by name. First name only, of course. No reason to get too personal. Dave could give a shit about the red giant's address. Maybe he should go back and hand the crumpled napkin over to the bouncer. Explain that he was just gonna fix her toilet.

As he reached in his pocket, he saw a woman with long brown hair rushing down the street with some dude. She had an ass on her that he wanted to get to know better. As they got closer, he realized it was *her*. Professor Levin! And the guy was not the blond fiancé he'd met in her office. No, this one had curly black hair.

Dave tailed behind them until they slipped inside a yellow Bel Air parked across the street from Sardi's restaurant. He pulled out a stubby pencil and pad from his pocket and scribbled down the license plate. His cousin, Barney, was a cop and owed him a favor.

CHAPTER SEVEN
The Affair

Laila

I unlocked the front door of the building and Eduardo walked me to the elevator, rode up with me to the fourth floor, and through the hallway to Apartment 4D.

Squeezing his hand, I spoke in a hoarse voice I barely recognized, "I'm okay now. Thanks for escorting me home."

"You're sure?"

"Yes." I leaned back against the wall in an attempt to put distance between us. Blood pulsated in my ears. "You're leaving what . . . in a month?"

"*Correctomundo.*" He placed his hands on either side of my face and stroked a lock of hair away from my cheek. Then he leaned down and kissed me.

I started to lose myself in the kiss then pushed him away. "What's the point? We had an agreement." I was flooded with feelings I hadn't had since Julian. Why now? And with a man who was moving 2,000 miles away.

"You're right. I'm sorry."

"It's just—"

"It's just what?"

"I-I like you."

Eduardo smiled. "I like you too."

That dimple. Oh, lord. I placed a soft kiss on his lips. We locked in an embrace and our hands began to explore each other.

"If you want to stop," Eduardo whispered, "Tell me now."

"No, I-I want . . . "

Eduardo slid his hands down my torso. I gripped his back, gliding my hands up to his neck and hair. He lifted my leg, pressed it against his hip, and kissed my neck and shoulders.

We banged against the door to my apartment.

"Laila!" shouted Mrs. Schneider, my next-door neighbor who also was Ma's distant cousin. She poked her head full of pink curlers out the door of her apartment. Then she stepped into the hallway dressed in her tattered robe, shook her head, and stomped back inside. No doubt she would be speed dialing my mother within seconds.

Eduardo and I entered the apartment and were greeted by my Aussie-mix, Brooklyn, and my white-and-orange cat, Zorro. I loved those animals like they were my children. "Girls, I'd like you to meet Eduardo."

After he petted Brooklyn's belly and stroked Zorro's fur, I bribed them with treats to retire to their pillow beds in the bedroom.

I felt a little tipsy. Well, maybe more than a little. He kissed me some more. Deep soulful kisses that made my whole body feel alive.

His face was so serious in the dim light of the small lamp in the living room. Then he ran his tongue down my neck. It had been more than two years. I didn't know if I should let him. Oh, but it felt so good.

He unzipped my dress.

I let it slide to the floor.

Then he undid the back of my bra. That fell off too.

He stared at me. "You are so beautiful."

"I bet you say that to all the girls."

"You're going to have to trust me."

"I-I'm trying."

He kissed my forehead.

I led him to the bedroom and pulled his shirt over his head. No surprise he was tan and muscular. I touched a deep scar on his shoulder with my finger. "How did you—?"

"For another time." He unzipped his slacks and slipped out of them, leaving on his boxers. "Do you have any body lotion?"

"Any what?"

"Some oil perhaps? I'd like to give you a massage."

"You're serious?"

"Of course."

I padded into the bathroom and came back with a bottle of Johnson's Baby Oil. Then I lit two rose-scented candles.

He rubbed my feet first. Slowly, like he had all night, feeling every bump and callous with his loving hands. Then he asked me to turn around and lie on my stomach. He continued massaging my neck and shoulders, spreading the oil like a professional.

"Where did you learn to give a back rub like that?"

"I worked nights in a nursing home where I gave back massages to the old people."

"Didn't the nurses do that?"

"Nope, only me. It helped with the patients' pain. Now, shhhh."

He continued to massage my body in silence. My back, my legs, my ass. Then he turned me over and moved his hands up my thighs and beyond.

I felt like I would melt away as he reached down to the floor for his pants and pulled a condom out of the pocket. "You came prepared."

He smiled. "A man can hope."

We both kept our eyes open as we moved together in unison. He had long eyelashes and a beauty mark on his cheek. His chest was damp with perspiration that shone in the candlelight.

He'd stop and withdraw himself then lick parts of my body where the oil glistened. Every nook and cranny of our bodies fit perfectly together. I could lie there forever with him. And then I felt more. Oh my God. It had been too long.

THE NEXT MORNING, I LAY CUDDLED WITH EDUARDO under my goose down comforter. I was sore, my lips felt chapped, and my whole body tingled. There was this overpowering sense of serenity. Had I ever felt this way before?

Next to the bed, Brooklyn and Zorro lay sleeping on their respective pillows.

By the grin on Eduardo's face, I knew without asking that he was experiencing a similar sense of tranquility. We lay quietly for a long while wrapped together in bed.

An hour or so later, Eduardo sat up and broke the magical silence. "That was incredible."

I smiled, having no words to describe what I was feeling.

He wrapped his arm around my shoulder. "You know what would make this day perfect?"

"Room service with caviar and champagne?"

"No," he said. "Green chile stew."

"What?"

"Mama makes the best in the world."

"It sounds hot?"

"Hot, but delicious. Like you."

"Does it have meat in it?"

"Of course."

"I'm a vegetarian."

"Ah, yes, I'll have to remember that." He kissed my neck.

I started to get turned on, then pushed him away. Reality began to rear its ugly face. Why had I slept with this stranger? "I shouldn't have let this happen."

"But we did," he said. "Haven't you ever done anything crazy?"

I thought about the question for a minute then climbed on top of him. I couldn't stop myself. "Oh, yeah. This is crazy!"

After we were done making love, Eduardo showered and dressed for work. "See you tonight?"

"Sure," I whispered then locked the deadbolts behind him. It all felt surreal. When he was gone, I took a luxurious bath in a dreamlike state. Last night had been the most sensual experience of my life. Only once had I experienced such passion with a man, and it wasn't with Julian. But that relationship had been jinxed from the start.

Eduardo and I never should have happened. He was leaving and I would ultimately be alone again. Just another relationship that was not meant to be. I hated to look at things from Eve's point of view. Yet I had to admit there was something wrong with the fact I was twenty-eight years old, with no marriageable prospects.

Brooklyn jumped up on my lap and stretched across it.

"You hungry, girl?" She was much too big for a lap dog, but no one had told her that. She whined and then barked at me. Zorro rubbed my leg with her head. I was so focused on my affair with Eduardo I had forgotten to take them for their morning walk.

I put on their leashes, rode down the elevator, and headed over to Central Park. Zorro acted more like a dog than a cat, and walked perfectly well on a leash. She had lived with me since I'd found her stranded in an arroyo in Albuquerque during college. If it weren't for that cat, I could never have survived what had happened on my wedding day.

But now all I could think about was Eduardo. I could smell his Old Spice like he was standing next to me. How stupid was I to let myself fall for this guy?

After an hour of walking the animals around the park, I headed back to the apartment to get ready for tonight's date. Should I break it off with him? I had grown accustomed to feeling alone. Now the solution to my loneliness had shown up at Pop's alma mater. But was changing my whole life for Dr. Eduardo Quintana the right choice? Damned if I do, damned if I don't.

CHAPTER EIGHT
The Reaction

Eduardo

Eduardo stood near the reception desk in the ER as a surgical team hurried by in scrubs and paper shoes. What was Laila doing right now? Should he call her? No, he didn't want to seem too eager. The sex had been amazing. Had he told her how special it was? He recalled rattling off some corny stuff before he'd left for work following a second round of lovemaking in the morning. He was consumed with thoughts about her. But where could their relationship go? All he knew was he had to see her again soon. Tonight.

"Dr. Quintana wanted in OR One," blasted from the PA system.

"Doctor, are you deaf?" asked the Puerto Rican nurse at the reception desk. "They've been calling you for the last five minutes."

He rushed to the OR and washed up.

"Where have you been?" asked the doc from the night shift who'd already removed his scrubs.

"Sorry." Eduardo had never let his mind wander like this before. "What do we have?"

"Acute alcohol poisoning. Patient's girlfriend dumped him here a few hours ago and split. He passed out at the front desk. Nearly OD'd. I've inserted a tube into his windpipe and put him on a drip. He's ready for a stomach pump."

Time to put Ms. Laila Levin out of his mind and get to work.

NINE DAYS LATER, EDUARDO STILL FOUND HIMSELF daydreaming about Laila at work. They'd seen each other every night. She'd pop into his head for no apparent reason. She made him think about things he hadn't thought about— environmental issues, women's rights, religious beliefs. She was passionate about so many things.

If he had to say what he loved most about her, it was that she made him laugh. He'd focused his whole life on hard work at the ranch, getting through college and medical school, and taking care of the *familia*. He'd never thought of himself as "too serious," but now he was learning how to have fun. During the day, he couldn't stop thinking about her. Afternoons at work dragged on endlessly as he awaited their evening dates.

But Laila and he were worlds apart. She was a New York girl. If they were to have a relationship, she would have to come home with him to Sabinal. What were the odds of that? And even if she did come, would she be happy there? Long Island Jewish girl living in the boonies of his beloved Land of Enchantment.

Yet she'd attended college at the University of New Mexico. She'd seen the beauty of the mountains and mesas. The whole thing smacked of some fatalistic meant-to-be life changing reality. Eduardo didn't believe that events were predetermined and inevitable. Or were they?

He needed a game plan. When they got together tonight, he would ask her to accompany him to New Mexico. After work, he stopped at Argo Electronics on Canal Street and bought Laila a small tape recorder and some Spanish language tapes. While his family all spoke English, it would be useful for her if she planned to work with teens. He smiled to himself as he thought about the expression on Mama's face when he arrived home with Laila Levin.

CHAPTER NINE
The Invasion

Laila

I just couldn't help myself. For more than a week, I'd wanted to break it off, but every morning after Eduardo had spent the night he'd smile and say, "See you tonight?"

My response, "What time? How about dinner at my place?" Or, "I'll grab some Chinese and bring it home."

He often brought a bag of groceries and cooked for me. Cheese enchiladas, shrimp fajitas or grilled salmon tacos.

I made him my specialty, spinach lasagna and my norm of brown rice and vegetables. Eduardo claimed he didn't miss the lack of meat. He even said he felt better on a vegetarian diet.

It was a sunny New York afternoon when I reached my apartment after jogging with Brooklyn in Central Park. A stranger, wearing a black leather jacket and aviator glasses, gave me a once over as I entered the building. He also gave me the creeps. *Could he be the Son of Sam? Don't be ridiculous.*

I double-checked that the building door slammed shut behind me before darting over to the rows of mailboxes and keying mine open. Then I emptied the contents and shuffled through the envelopes, which were mostly bills.

Someone tapped my damaged shoulder not once, but twice. I winced at the stab of pain that shot down my arm as I whirled around to confront my attacker.

"Laila?" said Mrs. Schneider, dressed in a flowered housecoat. "Did I hurt you?"

I let out a breath. "No, you just startled me."

She grinned revealing one front tooth crossed over the other. "Got yourself a cute new *boychik*."

"Thanks." Although Mrs. Schneider was my mother's third cousin, I remained on a formal name basis. The old lady had been calling Eve regularly since my first night with Eduardo. She served as Ma's personal private investigator, reporting the details of my life. It was a tradeoff I'd made for Mrs. Schneider's help obtaining the rent-controlled East Village apartment.

My mother had called numerous times all week, but I either had not picked up the phone or had stonewalled her questions about "a new boyfriend." I smiled at Mrs. Schneider whose back seemed more hunched over than usual. "Do you need anything at the store today?"

She crinkled her eyes. "I hate to be a bother, sweetheart. I made you return the coffee last week 'cause it wasn't the right Folgers."

"It's never a bother, Mrs. Schneider."

"Well, maybe just some milk. Two percent. No, one percent. Make it skim. Just a pint. And lettuce, the leafy green, unless iceberg is on sale."

I stood patiently listening. "Why don't you write a list and leave it under my mat? I won't be going out until later."

Mrs. Schneider pinched my cheek. "You're a doll. My daughter, Shelly, now she just up and moved to New Jersey. No help at all to me. Your mother is a lucky woman to have you."

"Thank you. Let me help you back to your apartment."

After a cup of Lipton's tea with Mrs. Schneider, I returned to my apartment, turned up my stereo, and began dancing to the Eagles' *Hotel California*. Brooklyn pranced behind me, followed by Zorro. Dancing was my favorite way to unwind, and the animals loved it too.

All at once, the phone rang and the intercom buzzed. I grabbed my cordless phone praying for it to be Eduardo. When I heard my sister's voice, I tried not to sound disappointed. "Hey, Raach. Hold on a minute." I clicked the button on the intercom and said hello.

No answer.

Back to my sister. "Sorry, someone pushed the intercom but didn't respond. So, what's up with you?"

"Forget me. How's it going with the doctor?"

"Fine. On the other hand, it's going nowhere. Remember he's leaving." I walked to the kitchen and found a biscuit for Brooklyn. Then I poured milk in Zorro's bowl.

"Look, I'm standing here with a mop in my hand," said Rachel. "The kids are snacking on Oreos and milk. Long Island is b-o-r-i-n-g. The most exciting thing in my life right now is Maya's appearance on *Sesame Street*."

"What are you talking about?"

"The Children's Network held auditions at her preschool and she was selected for a short segment with Big Bird."

"*Mazel tov.* Ma must have wet her pants when you told her."

"Are you kidding? She's already talking about acting and voice lessons, ballet and tap, a future for Maya at Juilliard."

"She's certainly changed since we were kids."

Maya was crying in the background.

"Shhh," Rachel said. "I'm trying to talk on the phone."

"Let me speak to her." I adored my niece. With brown

curly hair and enormous green eyes, she was a three-year-old mini-me.

A few seconds later, Maya said, "Hi, Auntie Lala."

"I'm so proud of you, honey."

"Me too."

I laughed. "You're proud too."

Rachel interrupted. "Say bye to Auntie Lala,"

I smacked my lips. "Big kiss to you."

"Bye, bye." Maya made a kissing sound and then Rachel returned.

"Okay, dear sister. What's up?"

I walked back to the living room and plopped down on the couch. "He may be the one. But he's headed back to New Mexico."

"Why don't you go with him? You loved it out there in college."

"Sabinal is not exactly Albuquerque. It's like miles from anywhere. I can't even find it on a map. The closest place is a town called Española. Ever hear of it?"

"Sure I have," Rachel said.

"Right."

"Look, if *you* don't go, I will."

"You sound like Ma."

Rachel cleared her throat. "Ma's not happy—"

"About me running off to New Mexico. Déjà vu? Do you remember when I went out there for college?"

"You were crazy back then. She had good reason to worry about you."

I smiled as I recalled my mother meeting Chris and Ben when I'd brought them home to West Meadow. Chris was my college boyfriend, and Ben was his best friend. But it was Ben

I thought I was in love with. A complicated scenario that didn't end well. "We both know she won't be a happy camper."

"That's saying it mildly. Oh my God, William, be careful! Hold on." Rachel shouted.

When she returned to the phone, I asked her what happened.

"Will banged his head on the Singer." My sister's fancy sewing machine had been a big splurge but not near as big as her husband's new red Camaro. She made all her kids' clothes and they looked like they came from Bloomingdale's or Lord & Taylor.

"You need to hang up?"

"His head's still attached. So confide in me, Sis."

"How do you know for sure? I'm so gun shy after Jules." I rarely said his name out loud.

"I don't think you ever *really* know. Sometimes, even now I—"

"You what?"

"Lately Bob's been coming home later and later. With pretty lame excuses I might add."

As Rachel talked, Brooklyn ate her biscuit, nudged Zorro from the milk bowl, and slurped it up.

Zorro hissed. Then the intercom buzzed again. So much for peace. "Rachel, are you saying—?"

The intercom continued to buzz. I pressed the button and the distinctive nasal voice of Eve filtered through my apartment. "Laila, it's me. I had an audition close by."

Right. No doubt my phone excuses had stopped working. "Hold on, Ma." Brooklyn was barking at the hissing Zorro. I shouted to the dog. "Stop that!"

"Stop what?" Eve yelled.

"I'm talking to Brooklyn. Why don't you use the key I gave you?"

"Do you think I'd be standing here with my arms full of packages if I had it?"

"Okay, I'll buzz you up." I turned my attention back to my sister. "Are you still there, Rachel?"

"Bob says he has to work—"

"Don't jump to any conclusions."

"I'm telling you, Laila. Something's really wrong. We were so young when we got married. If it hadn't been for Will—"

The phone made a clicking noise. "Hang on, the other line." I pressed the hook for Call Waiting. "Eduardo!" My ears filled with the sound of my heart pounding in my chest. "No, nothing special. Can you hold a sec?" I pressed the phone hook for call-waiting as the buzzer rang again.

The three-ring Levin circus had invaded apartment 4D. "Rachel? I have to call you back."

"Don't forget. I live vicariously through you, babe."

I clicked the phone back to Eduardo. "I'll be right with you. Sorry to keep you on hold."

I pressed the intercom button. "You can open the door, Ma."

"Is this a bad time?"

"Frankly, it's a horrible time."

"Sorry, I can call you back," said Eduardo.

"Oh, Geez. I was talking to my mother, not you." I sat on the couch, exhausted. Brooklyn jumped on my lap and licked my ear. Zorro followed, nudging out the dog. "Come on guys . . . get off of me."

"What guys?" said Eduardo.

"Can I call you back?"

"I'm with patients most of the afternoon."

Was he putting me off? No, *he* had called me. I had to stop being paranoid. "Can you come over tonight around seven?"

"How many guys?"

I smiled. "You idiot, I'll see you later?"

"You betcha."

That silly expression. Get used to it, Laila. I hung up the phone as the intercom buzzed again.

"Are you calling your mother an idiot?" The button had gotten stuck and Ma was eavesdropping.

"I thought you were on the way up."

"I am now. And you better tell me what's going on with you, Laila."

Great. The last thing I needed right now was an interrogation by Eve that would do the FBI proud!

CHAPTER TEN
The Doctor

Eve

Rings of perspiration sullied the underarms of Eve Levin's hot pink silk dress after fifteen minutes of searching her Dolce & Gabbana crocodile purse for the apartment key Laila had given her to use "in case of an emergency." Now the dress was ruined. She was furious at herself for wearing such a stupid ensemble during a heat wave, as well as leaving the damn key in one of her many other pocketbooks.

Her arms were full of shopping bags from a sale at Macy's on 34th Street. But the sale was not why Eve had taken the Long Island Railroad to Manhattan. She needed to find out what was going on with Laila. Every time she called her daughter for the last ten days, she'd deflected her questions with, "He's just a friend, Ma" or, "I'll tell you when there's something worth a headline on your front page." Expert evasion.

Laila hated her to pop in unannounced, but Eve couldn't ignore the daily phone calls from Doris Schneider any longer. She would have come sooner . . . right away, but she was in the middle of redecorating their Long Island home. While Elliot let her spend an obscene amount of money, he was no help at all.

When Eve stepped out of the elevator on the fourth floor, she stood in the hallway debating if she should stop to see Doris first. She had no idea who her daughter was dating and feared the worst. A creep, a bum, or *oy vey*, a Negro? Laila was colorblind for sure. No, Doris would have told her if the guy was colored . . . black.

Eve detested not being in control. She was grateful her eldest, Rachel, was married and settled in Great Neck, and her youngest, Amby, was engaged to Sheldon, a nice dental student at the University of Buffalo.

Laila wasn't even on the program. She hadn't dated since her wedding debacle. Eve was forbidden to discuss what had happened that day. The three girls all stuck together on this topic like they did on everything else. A united front against their mother. How unnatural was that?

Eve decided against wasting time with Doris, scrambled down the hall to Laila's apartment, and banged on the door. "It's me, honey."

She heard the clicking sound of deadbolts opening. Three deadbolts, like her daughter lived in Fort Knox. This was no way for a girl to exist. What was wrong with her?

When the door finally opened, Eve dropped her shopping bags, gave Laila a smooch, and then wiped the lipstick from her cheek.

Laila winced. "How was Macys?"

Eve plopped down on Laila's overstuffed sofa. "Let's cut to the chase. Who is he? You *shtupped* him, didn't you?"

"God, I hate that expression."

"He's not Jewish I presume?"

"If you must know, he's Latino," Laila said.

"Wait a minute. That doctor at the hospital."

"Bingo. He's from New Mexico."

"Now that's a weird coincidence."

"So it seems."

The temperature in the room suddenly felt stifling. "You're not considering moving out there again."

"No worries. He hasn't asked me yet."

"Yet?"

"We'll see what happens, Mother."

"What would you do there?"

"I could work on my grant. The town he comes from has the highest per capita of pregnant teens in the country. I checked it out at the library."

"You're serious?" Pain gripped her chest again. Heart palpitations?

"It feels right with Eduardo."

"Right as with Julian?"

"You're not allowed to talk about that, Ma."

Even her husband, Elliot, was in on the conspiracy to keep that part of Laila's life sealed. It had cost them thousands of dollars for the wedding reception yet her *meshugana* husband would put his hands over his ears if she dared even mention that day. "Can you at least bring this Eduardo out to the house for dinner?"

"I'll ask him."

Eve felt her blood pressure rise. She reached inside her handbag and remembered she had left the bottle of Valium in her red leather Gucci bag along with Laila's key. Damn. While she wanted Laila to find someone and be happy, some Latino from New Mexico was not what she had in mind. On the other hand, at least she could tell her friends that he was a doctor.

CHAPTER ELEVEN
The Decision

Eduardo

Eduardo arrived at Laila's apartment with the tape recorder and Spanish cassettes. He also brought a bottle of Chardonnay, a bouquet of roses, a gourmet doggie biscuit, and a squeaky rubber mouse. As he stood in the doorway, he began to doubt the wisdom of asking her to go to New Mexico with him. Considering they'd spent less than two weeks together, it was downright insane. It wasn't that he had misgivings as to whether he wanted her to go. He'd certainly been around the block a few times and knew what he wanted in a woman. But he feared perhaps she might feel rushed, and panic at the boldness of his proposal.

But what was the alternative? Stay in New York? That was never an option. Delay going back to home? He'd already given notice at the Lebanon Hospital and committed to taking over Dr. Lopez's practice in Española. Most of all, Mama would be devastated if he didn't come home now, after he'd promised her. She was counting the days.

Laila's dog barked as she unlatched the multiple deadbolts, then pushed open the door with a welcoming smile and a kiss that hinted at more. She looked hot in a tight black tank top and a pair of Levis. Her wavy brown hair flowed down past her shoulders. He'd dreamed of her all day, and seeing her again didn't disappoint. Would there be time for sex before dinner? *Whoa, cowboy. You need to slow down.*

The aroma of fresh garlic and oregano sifted through from the kitchen.

"Hope you're hungry."

He handed Laila the roses. Then he tried to kiss her again but she moved her head and his lips landed on her hair. It smelled like fresh mint.

The dog, Brooklyn, jumped up on him.

Eduardo petted her head as Laila placed the roses in a vase.

The cat rubbed against his leg.

He gave each of the animals the gifts he'd brought for them.

Brooklyn dropped the dog biscuit and snatched the rubber mouse from Zorro.

The cat hissed.

Laila pointed a finger at them. "Stop it, you two."

Eduardo looked the Aussie in the eye. Dogs always liked him. Although at the ranch, animals never came inside the house. "Come on, Brooklyn, that toy's for cats."

The dog tilted her head, dropped the rubber mouse, and dashed back to her biscuit.

"Unbelievable." Laila pointed at the couch. "Have a seat and I'll get some glasses for the Chardonnay."

A few minutes later, they clinked crystal glasses and sipped the wine slowly.

Laila moved closer to him. "How was your day?"

His heart was pounding like a high school boy on his first date. He contemplated her question. It had been a tough day, but nothing unusual for his job in a big city emergency room. "They brought a guy in with three stab wounds in his chest."

"You saved his life?"

"It was a team effort."

"That's wonderful. I wish—"

"That I'd be happy here in Manhattan."

"If I'm to be honest. Yes."

"My parents sacrificed so much for me. I have to give something back."

Laila nodded. "I understand."

They sat gazing at each other.

"Why don't you come with me?" He cupped her chin with his hand. "We need to give this relationship a try."

"I can't leave my work and this rent-controlled apartment."

"You can bring your work to New Mexico."

"Yes, I checked the stats on teenage pregnancies in the library."

He grinned. "So you're already considering it?"

She flushed. "Guilty. But I-I'm scared."

"Of what?"

"What if I hate it there?"

"I won't chain you to the stove."

"I've never followed a man anywhere."

Eduardo placed a gentle but lingering kiss on her lips.

She pushed him away. "You're trying to confuse me."

"Look, you wouldn't just be going there for me. If you've checked the stats you know it's the perfect place for your research."

"I almost failed Spanish in high school."

He opened the bag from Argos and handed her the tape recorder and Spanish tapes.

"It appears you've covered all the bases."

"When I want something, I don't leave things to chance."

Just then, Brooklyn climbed onto his lap with the cat toy in her mouth.

Zorro scrambled up after her.

Eduardo looked down at the animals. "You two are going to have to behave if you're coming to New Mexico."

The dog dropped the toy then the cat trotted off with it.

"See? The girls want to come." He started to kiss Laila again but she bolted from the couch.

Something smelled like it was burning.

"My sauce!" She raced to the kitchen with the animals and Eduardo tracking behind her. "It's ruined." She looked up at him with wet lashes. "Now you're gonna think I'm totally incompetent in the kitchen."

He kissed her neck. "I can cook."

"So what do you need me for?"

He grinned. "Sex."

"Half the women in Manhattan would have sex with you. There's got to be more."

"I know this is crazy. I've been telling myself that for the last couple of weeks. But I do believe there are times in life when you just have to grab at opportunity."

Laila sighed. "I've been thinking the same thing."

"We'd make a great team working on this teen pregnancy project."

"That's true."

"And you're beautiful and smart. And your *nalgas* . . . hmmm." He placed both hands on her ass.

She giggled and then playfully smacked his hand.

Eduardo gazed into her green eyes. "Laila, I-I think I'm in love with you."

She shook her head. "I thought this only happens in the movies."

"Me too."

"Okay."

He furrowed his brow. "Okay, what?"

"I'll come with you."

Eduardo kissed her lips and undid the top button of her blouse. As he reached to undo the next button, a loud noise interrupted the mood.

The cat had jumped from a chair to the counter, leaped across to the stove and had knocked down the pot with the burnt sauce. She and Zorro stood together licking the remains of the dinner from the floor.

Laila yelled at them as the phone rang. She picked up the receiver and smiled at Eduardo. "Mother?"

Eduardo could hear Mrs. Levin's nasal voice through the phone. "Bring him over tomorrow night."

"Don't set your heart on it," Laila said. "He may have to work."

"Tell him to take the night off."

"Goodbye, Mother." Laila hung up the phone and looked over at Eduardo. "I don't want you to feel pressured—"

"No worries. I'll see if I can switch shifts with one of the other docs." He would figure out a way. Eduardo liked that *familia* was as primary to Laila as it was to him. Everything was falling into place. She had repeatedly told him how much she loved New Mexico. Although a city girl, Laila enjoyed hiking and biking and had even ridden horses in sleepaway camp. Surely, she would love the ranching life.

That night, Eduardo told her about Violet. "I'd known her my whole life. When she moved away, well, it about broke my heart." It was so long ago but he'd never shared this information with anyone before. Papa knew, but they didn't speak about it. "And you? Have you ever been in love before?"

She picked at a cuticle on her thumb. "There were a few guys in college. Do you have a problem with that?"

"Not at all. Who? I mean . . ." He searched for the right words. "You said you've been hurt by someone."

"Yes," she gulped. "He cheated on me."

"I'm sorry. For what it's worth, I think the guy was a fool."

"I appreciate you saying that."

"You can spare me the details."

She squinted. "I appreciate that too."

There was a part of him that really wanted to know, but he could sense by her pitiful expression it was too painful for her to discuss it any further. Did it really matter? After so many years of hard work and sacrifice, his dream of working as a doctor and settling down in Sabinal with the woman he loved was very close to coming true. He was not about to risk that.

CHAPTER TWELVE
The Confession

Laila

I did not share my ultimate shame and humiliation with Eduardo. After all, he said I could spare the details. But it did cause the memory of Julian Goldblatt to flood through my mind. I nearly drowned just thinking about it.

Jules and I had been an item for almost three years before he'd popped the question. He was one of those handsome, successful New York commitment-phobic men, so his proposal came out of left field. We were spending a typical Saturday night at my apartment, eating takeout Chinese with chopsticks from the white cardboard boxes. My favorite movie, *Casablanca*, was playing on *Saturday Night at the Movies*. The picture began to get fuzzy as Ingrid Bergman boarded the plane with her husband Lazlo.

I stood up and adjusted the rabbit ears of the small portable television. The movie resumed just as Humphrey Bogart walked off in the fog with Captain Louis Renault.

"Isn't that the most romantic ending?"

"It certainly has inspired me," Jules said. Next thing I knew, he went down on one knee. "I want to marry you, Laila. Whaddaya say?" He pulled out a diamond ring from his pocket and handed it to me.

At first I thought it was some kind of joke. "You're kidding, right?"

Creases fanned from the corner of his piercing blue eyes. "No, I'm dead serious."

No mention of the word "love" should have been a clue. But then I'd never pressured Jules to do anything, let alone get hitched. At twenty-six years old, I was in graduate school at NYU and felt no need to rush into the whole marriage bit. Looking back, I think that was part of my allure to him.

As far as Eve was concerned, Jules was the catch of the twentieth century: a wealthy Jewish stockbroker who also happened to be one of the heirs to Manischewitz. Yes, *that* Manischewitz.

But none of that impressed me. I liked the side of Jules that played basketball with underprivileged kids Saturday mornings and worked the midnight shift as a deejay at an alternative radio station. He'd often dedicate love songs to me at 2 a.m. It was no secret that groupies hung out at the radio station in the wee morning hours.

"I've had my share of women," he'd said when we began dating. "You're the one and only for me, Lai."

For some insane reason I believed him. Ha ha ha. Famous last words.

We were an odd match. By 1975, being a feminist hippie might be considered passé but it still was how I identified myself. I wore my hair long and parted in the middle, and dressed in maxi skirts and a pair of cowboy boots I'd bought during college in New Mexico. I was a cheap date, happy to spend nights cuddled on the couch, frequenting an off-off-Broadway theater, or a foreign film.

Jules, on the other hand, dressed in three-piece suits and wingtips. He had thick blond hair, a cleft chin, and a jawline that could chisel marble. His favorite pastime was hanging out at exclusive clubs on the Upper East Side with his Harvard roommate, Winston, and his wife Jillie. She was a model, so thin and gold-blonde stunning, that I felt like the Goodyear blimp whenever she looked in my direction. Fortunately, that wasn't often. Usually, she ignored me while pretending to understand the stockbroker babble her husband and Jules talked incessantly about over vodka martinis.

Later, I discovered the reason for Jules' proposal. The major portion of his trust fund would only become available when he married. The night before our wedding, Jules handed me a prenuptial agreement. At the time, I didn't even know what it was. I read through the paperwork and glared at him. "Why get married if you don't think it's going to last?"

He kissed my forehead. "I didn't want it. Dad shoved it in my face last night and said it was part of the trust agreement." Then he explained the deal about receiving the money and handed me a pen.

Without further hesitation, I signed the papers. What did I really care? I wasn't marrying Jules for his money.

I never asked for an extravagant wedding, but my parents spent a small fortune on the reception at the legendary Huntington Town House. This was right after Pop had made a tidy sum with a stock investment. Since my mother had been poor her whole life—first as a child of the depression, then married to a NYC fireman—she planned to use my wedding as a vehicle to show the world that Eve Levin had finally made it. She would prove that she was more than up to the task of rubbing shoulders with the heirs to the Manischewitz fortune.

There must have been 500 guests at the reception. A smorgasbord of delectable hors d'oeuvres, bottles of expensive champagne, an open top-shelf bar, ice sculptures, a sit down dinner of filet mignon, (which I skipped), an emcee, two bands, even a Don Rickles wannabe comedian. It was supposed to end with fireworks, which it did, but not the kind that light up the sky.. . .

Following Rabbi Nobel's blessings, Jules stomped on a wine glass, and everyone shouted *mazel tov.* Friends and family lifted us each up on chairs and paraded us around the ornate ballroom. We danced to the *hora.* I had more than my share of champagne.

The night ticked on as little kids danced with their parents, and grandmas took off their shoes and rolled down their compression stockings. At midnight people began to disperse. Kiss-kiss, hug-hug to relatives as they retrieved their coats and mink stoles (even though it was July), and handed me envelopes stuffed with cash and checks.

"Say goodbye for us to Jules," Uncle Irving said as I accompanied him and my Aunt Irene to valet parking.

"Whatta catch," my aunt said. "Give his brother Lori's numba, okay?"

"Sure thing," I said. My cousin Lori was a forty-year-old lesbian who lived in New Zealand.

It had been some time since I'd seen Jules, and I wanted him to thank the guests as they headed home. I walked the perimeter of the ballroom, but he was nowhere in sight. Then I asked his friends still gathered at the bar, but none of them had seen him in a while.

After checking the lobby, I wandered into the groom's quarters where I opened the door to many future nightmares. There was my new husband *schtupping* his best man's wife. Yes, I hate that word. But it describes exactly what my husband of four hours was doing to the beautiful Jillie as her long flaxen hair pooled around her shoulders. He was about to penetrate her size two body when I barged into their private party.

"Oh my God!" I shouted. Then I screamed at the top of my lungs.

Once a fireman, always a fireman. Pop was the first responder. Then my sister, Rachel, appeared, followed by at least five other guests.

Jules and Jillie scrambled behind the heavy velvet drapery. His voice sounded muffled from behind the drapes. "This isn't what it seems."

"Of course not," Pop said. "But if you come out of those curtains, I'll flatten your face."

The bystanders left the room. Rachel pushed me out behind them. "I'll drive you home."

Both sisters sat up with me all night in my apartment. I wasn't even sure if I loved Julian, but the embarrassment and shame of his betrayal made me nauseated.

My sister Amby pulled out a joint from her purse. The three of us laughed and cried until a patch of sun sifted through the blinds in the living room.

At nine o'clock my parents arrived at my apartment. Pop said he'd spoken to his attorney, Mel Spencer, who'd happened to be at the wedding reception. Who hadn't been there? Mel assured Pop there'd be no problem having the whole thing annulled.

"Totally, the thing to do," said Amby.

"Like it never happened," said Rachel.

Eve was unusually quiet. She'd brought a platter of bagels, lox, and cream cheese, which she placed on the old metal trunk I used as a coffee table.

I felt astonishingly better surrounded by my family.

Everyone agreed my life would go on just fine once the paperwork for the annulment was completed.

Everyone that is except for Eve. Her eyes twitched as each family member reaffirmed I should end the marriage. "Maybe you should reconsider," she finally said.

"What!" Pop said. His eyes bore a resemblance to the headlights of my Bel Air.

"Reconciling with Julian," Ma said. "Has she even spoken to him?"

"You're kidding?" Rachel said.

"Well, *I* spoke to him this morning," Eve said as she fanned herself with a napkin. "That's what Julian wants."

"Kid me not," Rachel said. "Who gives a flying fuck what *he* wants. He's humiliated my little sister."

Eve smeared cream cheese on a bagel. "Look at the big picture. Jules admitted to me it was a big mistake. A huge mistake. One he would never make again. He'd had way too much to drink. He confessed he'd even smoked marijuana."

Amby rolled her eyes. "That must have been why he did it, Ma."

"No excuse," Pop said. "What kinda way is that to start off a marriage?"

Eve began clearing the dishes from the coffee table. "Just give it some consideration. No rush to make a decision."

"You're just thinking of that Manischewitz fortune," Rachel said.

Ma winced. "You girls always presume the worst of me. I'm thinking about what's best for Laila."

"I bet he was upset," I said. "He won't see any of the trust fund now."

Pop glared at my mother. "I can't believe you'd want Laila to even consider a reconciliation."

"It's just . . ." Ma began.

"It's just what?" Amby said.

Ma shrugged. "This is a chance for Laila to have it all. I'm not saying what Jules did wasn't terrible. But if he's truly contrite—"

"You're totally insane!" I shouted. What was wrong with her? All she could think about was all that money. Did she honestly believe I could forgive Jules' indiscretion? I flew into my bedroom and slammed the door.

As I lay in bed with my comforter over my head, I could hear my family arguing in the living room. Everyone gave Ma hell. I wasn't sure but I thought I heard her crying. After a while, I fell asleep.

When I awoke, Rachel was standing next to the bed. "We made Ma agree never to say another word about last night ever again."

Amby entered the room with a grin on her face. "I just told Jules to drop dead. He's called at least a dozen times."

That was almost the end of the story. After my sisters left, Jules called another six or seven times. Finally, I answered the phone and agreed to meet him for coffee.

Unshaven, his cheeks looked sunken, his thick blond hair stood straight up like a porcupine. "I don't expect you to understand," he said as he fondled a cheese Danish. "Jill and I have been in love for years. I couldn't marry her for the obvious reasons."

"Let me guess." I said smugly. "Great grandpa Manischewitz didn't want a *shiksa.*"

He looked down at his black high-top sneakers. "There

was a stipulation in the trust agreement that the spouse had to be Jewish."

When he glanced back up, I locked eyes with him. "How long has the affair been going on?"

"That's just the thing. There was no affair. We haven't been together since I broke it off years ago and she married Winston on the rebound. Married him to hurt me. You don't know how much I've suffered."

"Sorry I didn't bring my violin."

"Here's the thing. I now realize it was all a mistake. I was drunk and . . . Laila, can we give this marriage a try?"

I threw my coffee in his face and bolted from the restaurant. If I hadn't liked my coffee with plenty of cream and sugar, he'd have been scarred for life. But instead, it was me who was scarred with endless nightmares, loss of sleep, and total loss of interest in dating anyone again.

A year later, I bumped into Jules while jogging in Central Park. Not just a *year* later, but on July 29, the anniversary of our ill-fated nuptials. He looked thin and drawn. Wiry stubble covered his chin and his hair was thinning in the front. I wouldn't have even recognized him if he hadn't stopped me.

"Laila, how are you?"

"I'm okay," which was about my state at the time. Numb described it better but I wouldn't share that with him.

He pointed at an empty park bench. "Got a minute?"

I glanced at my watch as if I actually had somewhere to be. "I can spare a few."

The clouds above us drifted by in shades of white and grey. The grass smelled freshly mowed. I looked at the man who had caused me so much pain. Cost my parents thousands of dollars. The embarrassment of everyone they knew, everyone I had ever known. Eve had invited the world to that wedding.

Jules looked like a sad, pathetic stranger, and not someone who'd been the centerpiece of a year's worth of nightmares.

"What do you want to talk to me about?"

"If you must know, Jillie left Winston and we tried to make it work. Rabbi Nobel gave her lessons and she converted to Judaism."

"So you're together?"

"Unfortunately, there was a problem. The fine print of the will specified that the girl I married had to be born a Jew. Her Conservative conversion was not acceptable. It appears my great-grandpa believed in a very Orthodox tradition. There was a possibility of starting the conversion process over again with an Orthodox rabbi, but no guarantee it would get past the executor, Mr. Rothman, also an Orthodox Jew."

I had to hold down the giggles. "So you broke it off?"

"No, she did. Winston took her back, and they moved to L.A."

"Back to square one. Still looking for a nice Jewish girl?"

"It doesn't matter anymore."

I arched my eyebrows. "Because?"

"I've been cut out of the will. There's some stipulation about staying married."

"The annulment. Doesn't that make it like you were never—"

"Not to Mr. Rothman. "I'm out." My brother and cousins get it all."

I almost felt sorry for him. But not quite.

His blue eyes looked somber. "Laila, what if you and I? I mean then I would still be—"

"Not a prayer." I stood and jogged off.

The nightmares ended.

Exactly one year from that day, I thought I'd been shot at Morris High School, then rescued by one Dr. Eduardo Quintana.

CHAPTER THIRTEEN
Mama's Coming to LA

Violet

Violet was livid when she saw Ira sitting on the couch reading the *Los Angeles Times* in a torn white undershirt and boxer shorts. "Is that what you're wearing when Mama gets here?"

"I thought you didn't want me here when your mama arrives."

"She mustn't know we're living together. But I'd like her to meet you. We need to leave for LAX in, like, thirty minutes."

"Okay, baby, I'll change. But I'm not sure how we're gonna hide us living together."

She went into the bedroom and retrieved a white shirt from his closet that she had pressed with a lot of starch just for the occasion. When she returned to the living room, she handed it to him. "We've been talking about this for weeks. You said you'd ask your buddy about staying with him while Mama was here . . . that guy I've never met."

"Diesel? That ain't gonna happen."

"Do you care about me anymore?" She forced out a tear. "I haven't had any work in months."

Ira stood, put on the shirt, and kissed her cheek. "Don't be ridiculous. I've spoken to six producers just today. Nobody's looking for a Mexican chick right now."

"I'm not Mexican, I'm Hispanic. Big difference. My family's been in the states centuries before your Polack ancestors showed up at Ellis Island."

"Mexican, Hispanic, you're thirty-four years old. Your window for making it as an actress has just about closed."

"You told me I could pass for twenty-four. Were you lying?"

"Of course not. You're still the most gorgeous chick I've ever seen."

The sound of loud pounding on the front door interrupted their argument. Violet glared at Ira. "Who's that?"

"No idea."

The door tore open. "Ira, my man, you got my money?" A beefy dude, wearing a white shirt unbuttoned to his navel showcasing a beer belly and three gold chains, entered the room.

"Soon, Diesel, I swear to God."

Violet held out her hand to him. "Nice to finally meet you, Diesel."

Instead of shaking Violet's hand, he punched Ira in the nose.

"Oh my God!" Violet screamed.

Blood ran down Ira's face and stained the collar of his white shirt. "Hey, man, that hurt."

"It was s'posed to hurt, asshole."

Violet started to cry.

Ira patted her hand. "I'm okay, sweetheart. Diesel and I just got a little matter to clear up."

Violet rushed into the kitchen, returned with paper towels and handed them to Ira. What the hell was going on? They needed to leave for the airport in twenty minutes. Mama would never forgive her if they were late. Ira would have to change his shirt. No time to iron another one.

Two more strangers walked through the open front door.

One was as fat as a pregnant whale, while the other was thin with pus-filled zits dotting his face and neck. The skinny one pulled out a pocketknife and pointed it at Violet. "You never mentioned you got a chick with such nice tits."

"Leave the chick out of this." Ira said. He glanced at Violet. "Go into the bedroom and shut the door."

She headed toward the bedroom but the fat guy grabbed her arm.

Ira's face puffed up. "Let go of my girl! I'll have the money tonight."

The fat dude made no move to let go of her arm.

"Please, Diesel," Ira shouted. "Tell your goon to leave my girlfriend out of this."

Diesel shrugged. "How do I know you'll have the money tonight? You've been bamboozling me for weeks."

Ira let out his breath. "I've got a Porsche." He pulled out the keys from his pocket and dangled them in front of Diesel.

Diesel grabbed the keys. "Now you're talking."

Minutes later, the thugs scrambled out of the apartment with the title and keys to Ira's Porsche, and an unequivocal warning from Diesel. "That car is just a down payment. You still owe me fifteen grand. If it ain't delivered by tomorrow, you and Miss Mexico are toast. *Capiche?*"

Ira swallowed. "Loud and clear."

Violet checked her watch. "We have to get to the airport."

Ira mopped his forehead with the paper towels. "What are you talking about?"

"Mama. Her plane is landing any minute. If we leave right now, we can meet her in baggage claim."

"We gotta get out of Los Angeles, sweetheart."

"I don't understand."

"The fifteen grand. I don't have it. Diesel won't be so generous tomorrow."

"But—"

"There's no buts. Pack your suitcases. We'll take a cross-country trip in the Caddy. Anywhere you wanna go, but we gotta leave yesterday."

"What about Mama?"

"Hmmm." Ira scratched the bald spot on his head. "I got an idea. You've always said your Mama wants you back in Mexico, right?"

"New Mexico, idiot, not Mexico. It's a state."

"Yes, I meant that. Anyhow, I'll drop you off at the airport and you can tell Mama you wanna go home, back to the *casa* in *Nuevo* Mexico. Change her return ticket and buy yourself one with my credit card." He handed her a plastic card from his wallet.

She examined the card with the letters VISA on it. "When did you get one of these?"

"Never mind. Just get on a plane. I'll drive out and meet you there in a few days."

MAMA'S FACE WAS WHITE AS THE DAINTY GLOVES SHE wore while standing alone at Carousel 5 with a burgundy Samsonite suitcase parked next to her. Everyone on the flight had already left the area. Violet knew her mother was furious the second she saw her.

"How could you do this to me?" Mama said. "I waited at the gate for half-an-hour. Then I came down here and waited another hour."

If Mama knew the reason, she'd drop dead of a heart

attack like Daddy had. Instead of sharing the truth, Violet said, "I have the best news for you, Mama."

Her mother puckered up her lips. "It better be *bueno*."

"I'm coming home to Sabinal with you."

Mama hugged her. "You're serious? When are you leaving?"

"Now, Mama. I'm going to change your return ticket and we'll fly back to Albuquerque together."

"Right now? But I'm tired. I've been flying for six hours. Had to change flights in Houston and—"

"It's now or never," Violet said. "If we wait, Mama, I may change my mind."

"Well," Mama said. "*Es el plan de Dios.*"

"Yes, Mama, it's God's plan."

"You'll never guess who's coming home too."

Violet couldn't care less. There was no one in that two-horse town she was interested in. "You're right. I'll never guess."

"Eduardo," Mama said smiling. "You do remember him? And he's a doctor now. He's been working in New York but he's coming home to Sabinal. He bought Doc Lopez's practice in Española."

"Really? I had no idea he'd become a doctor." Violet thought about her high school sweetheart and wondered if he was still as good looking as she remembered.

CHAPTER FOURTEEN
Nouveau Riche

Eduardo

The next night, Eduardo drove with Laila to Long Island to have dinner with her parents. He wasn't looking forward to breaking the news that he was taking their daughter to live in New Mexico. Usually the *viejas* adored him, but Laila assured him her mother would not be easily won over to a man who planned to take her daughter 2,000 miles away.

They sat in rush hour traffic for hours on the Southern State Parkway. Laila squeezed his hand as they inched along. "I warn you now. My mother has no boundaries."

"Sounds like my mama. Don't say I didn't warn you."

"She can't be as bad as Eve."

Eduardo laughed. "I'll bet the ranch she will give your mother a run for the money."

"You're on, big guy."

"Why do you call your mother Eve?"

"It makes her feel younger."

"Okay."

"I'll also caution you about their house. Think classic *nouveau riche*. Eve spent a fortune redecorating it."

"Your father's a retired New York City fireman? His pension can't be that big."

"A few years ago, he made a bundle in the stock market when the oil prices shot up overnight."

"That's quite impressive."

"Don't ask, or he'll talk your ear off about it."

"But I'm genuinely interested."

Laila smiled. "You've been properly warned."

Mrs. Levin opened the front door dressed in a figure-hugging red dress that clung tenaciously to her plump curves. A weird stripe of white hair ran down the middle of her scalp. Had he not noticed it when they first met at the hospital?

Multiple bangle bracelets clanged as she reached out to shake Eduardo's hand. Then she changed her mind and awkwardly hugged him. "It's so nice to meet you again, Doctor."

A toy poodle snapped at his feet.

Mrs. Levin pointed at the dog. "Stop that, Golda!" She peered up at Eduardo. "I'm so sorry, Eddie."

Laila shook her head. "Eduardo."

"Eddduardo."

He extended his hand so the poodle could sniff it but the dog kept yapping. Then he remembered he had an extra dog biscuit in his pocket that he'd bought for Brooklyn. He fished it out, tossed it across the room, and Golda shot out after it. "Nice to see you again too, Mrs. Levin."

"Call me Eve."

Eduardo handed her a bouquet of roses.

"That's so sweet. I'll get a vase from the kitchen."

He looked around the room. A stone fountain with a fake stone Greek baby peeing blue water stood as a centerpiece in the living room and clusters of gold leaves hung on the walls.

Eve returned with the roses inside a clear cylinder vase. "Come sit down. Have a pig in a blanket."

He had no idea what a 'pig in a blanket' was, as he and

Laila sat on one of the two oversized, zebra-striped couches in the living room.

Eve primped her hair and sat across from them in a La-Z-Boy. "Did Laila tell you I'm an actress? Bit parts mainly. You know . . . commercials, soaps. I used to do off-Broadway years ago."

"Mother had a very promising career when she was young," Laila said.

Eve batted her lashes at him. "I gave it up for Laila and her sistas."

"We appreciate you sacrificing your career, Ma," Laila said. "Just wish we didn't have to hear about it every time we see you."

Eve waved her hand dismissively and turned her attention back to him. "You know my son-in-law, Bob, is a doctor, too. A chiropractor. Do you think they're *real* doctors?"

She eyeballed Eduardo as he carefully chose his response. "They play an important role in the medical profession."

Eve grinned.

He assumed that meant he'd answered correctly. It became evident that Eve was keeping a mental scorecard of his responses.

"And Laila's a doctor too. Well, if you call a doctorate in sociology . . ."

Laila rolled her eyes. "Where's Pop?"

"He'll be home any minute."

There was a thorny silence. Eve looked at Eduardo with question marks written all over her face. "So how do you like our home? We've just done a major renovation."

He glanced around at the flamboyant decor. "I see where Laila gets her great sense of style."

Eve smiled. "We're gonna get along just fine."

The roaring sound of a motorcycle interrupted the polite conversation. It seemed out of place for the conventional Long Island suburb.

Laila put her arm around Eduardo's shoulder. "That's Pop. He bought himself a Harley last month."

"My husband's gotten a little *fakokta* since he retired," Eve said.

Laila lowered her gaze. "Why shouldn't he enjoy himself?"

"You always take your father's side."

Mr. Levin entered the room dressed in jeans, a white T-shirt, and a helmet. One thing for sure, Laila's parents were full of surprises.

Mr. Levin shook Eduardo's hand. "Welcome to our home. Can I get you a drink? Scotch, vodka, a beer perhaps?"

"Whatever you're having, Mr. Levin."

"Call me Elliot. You'll love my infamous amaretto sours. I'm making some for the ladies too."

"Sounds great."

When her father was out of earshot, Laila whispered, "Sip your drink slowly."

"Huh?"

"Pop's mixed drinks are about as good as my cooking."

Elliot returned with the cocktails and handed each of them a glass. Then he raised his hand in a toast. "*La chaim.*"

Eduardo raised his glass. "*La haim.*"

"No, it's *l'ch-h-aim.*" Eve said. "You have to say *ch-h-h* if you're gonna be part of a Jewish family."

"For chrissakes, we're not getting married, Ma," Laila gasped. "I'm just going to New Mexico with him."

Pop's mouth fell open. "You're going where?"

"You barely know each other," Eve said in a strained voice.

"We're in love," Eduardo said. "And Laila can continue her work out there."

"How will you live?" Pop said.

Eduardo told them that he had bought Doc Lopez's medical practice, and he would help Laila with her research on teen pregnancies. "My intentions are honorable," he said looking her father in the eye.

"So you're getting married?" Eve asked.

"We just met a few weeks ago. But I assume in time if things work out, we will marry."

"This is a smart *boychik*. Have another pig in a blanket." Eve passed him the platter filled with miniature hot dogs wrapped in pastry, as well as tiny meatballs with toothpicks stuck in them. He took a small china plate from the coffee table and filled it with the hors d'oeuvres.

Eve held the tray up to Laila.

"You know I haven't eaten meat in years, Ma."

Elliot threw his hands up. "Your mother has a short memory." He turned to Eduardo. "So what does your father do?"

"He's a cattle rancher."

Eve shook her head. "What will a rancher think of a Jewish girl who doesn't eat meat?"

"It's not a problem," Eduardo said.

Her mother glared at him. "Do your parents speak English?"

"Of course," Eduardo said.

Laila's mouth was drawn tight. "Twenty questions are over, Ma."

"Just one more." She smiled at Eduardo. "Are you circumcised?"

"Oh my God!" Laila's hands flailed about like an upended turtle. "Damn it, Ma, you've crossed the line once again."

Elliot shook his head. "Why are you embarrassing her like this?"

"Eduardo needs to know what's involved if he decides to convert to Judaism."

Laila stood and grabbed his hand. "It's time for us to leave."

Eduardo's eyes widened. He had to admit that Eve could give Mama a run for the money.

CHAPTER FIFTEEN
Rachel's Crisis

Laila

I was scheduled to leave with Eduardo for New Mexico in less than two weeks. My to-do list was growing by the minute.

Check: Purchased plane ticket with money Eduardo insisted on giving me.

Check: Went to the vet to get the girls current on their shots, and purchased pet carriers for the flight.

Check: Placed ad in the *Times* for someone to sublet the apartment. Since it was rent controlled, I'd already had five calls.

Check: Borrowed two large suitcases from Rachel.

A few nights later, Eduardo had to work a double shift so I used the opportunity to sort through ten years of my wardrobe. Much of it still reflected my old hippie days: long skirts, Levis and T-shirts, including my prized original from Woodstock.

Around midnight, Brooklyn began barking furiously, followed by a loud hammering on the front door. I couldn't imagine who'd be stopping by unannounced so late. Mrs. Schneider never stayed up this late. Had Eduardo gotten off early from work? But he had no way to enter the building. The visitor had to live here. Unless . . . it was an intruder.

A lump mushroomed in my throat. This type of paranoia was another good reason to leave New York. I grabbed the .38 from my purse that Pop had left with me "just in case." Then I looked through the peephole. To my surprise, Rachel stood slumped against the wall holding Maya in her arms. Will stood at her side. Both kids were dressed in their pajamas.

I quickly unlatched all the locks and opened the door.

My sister's pale haggard eyes looked out from reddened lids. The bones of her chest stood out of her sundress. When had she gotten so skinny?

The kids dashed inside followed by my sister. "I'm so sorry to barge in on you." She held up the building key. "Remember you gave me this when you moved in."

My nephew and niece chased down Brooklyn who was only too happy to play with them.

"Say hello to Auntie Lala," Rachel said.

"Hi Auntie," the kids said in unison as they ran toward the bedroom where I stashed toys for them in a large wicker box in the corner. A few minutes later, Maya reappeared. "Look what I found." She held up a stuffed bunny rabbit. "Is he new?"

"Mr. Bunny. No, he's quite old. He was mine when I was your age," I said. "Nana dropped him off here a few weeks ago."

"When she turned your old bedroom into an exercise studio," Rachel added.

Maya held the rabbit to her face. "I love Mr. Boonie. Can I keep him?"

"If you promise to take good care of him."

"I promise." She looked at Rachel. "Where's Daddy?"

Rachel's voice was choked up. "Daddy . . . went on a trip. He misses you and Will very much."

"When is he coming home?"

"Soon," Rachel said.

"Come give me a hug, and go play with Mr. Boonie in the bedroom," I said.

Maya hugged me and then ran off with the stuffed bunny cradled under her arm. When she was out of earshot, tears streamed down my sister's cheeks.

I handed her some tissues from a box on the coffee table and noticed how bloodshot her eyes were. "What's going on?"

She plopped down on the couch. "I don't know where to begin."

"Start with why you're here at midnight with two little kids?"

"I've been driving around for hours with them asleep in the back of the car."

"Because?"

"When I got home this afternoon, a man was posting a FORECLOSURE sign on our front door."

"What? It must be a mistake."

"I thought so, too. But after speaking with our mortgage company, I've discovered Bob hasn't made a payment in six months."

"Where is the SOB?"

"Supposedly, he's at a chiropractors' conference in Chicago."

"Have you gotten a hold of him?"

"He's not registered at the hotel where he said he'd be. After some detective work, I discovered there is no chiropractic conference in Chicago this week."

"That's strange."

"Long story short, his receptionist called this afternoon and said her paycheck had bounced. She was totally freaked out. I went to the office and the two of us searched his desk."

"And?"

"We found an itinerary from a travel agent. Two first class plane tickets to Miami for Mr. and Mrs. Bob Morris only the woman's first name was Gigi, not Rachel."

"*Gigi,* as in Ma's favorite movie?"

Rachel jutted her chin forward. "They're staying at the Fountainbleau."

"The bastard's taking her to the place you spent your honeymoon?"

"And there's more bad news. I went to the bank. All our savings are gone."

"*Oy.* At least Mom and Pop can help you out."

"Promise me not to say anything to them."

"Of course. I'll help you get through this. I've put away a couple of grand."

"You'll need that for New Mexico," Rachel said.

"I won't leave you at the mercy of Ma."

Rachel had been the rebellious one in high school. She ran around with a crowd of hoods and fell hard for Bob Morris, a James Dean wannabe who wore his hair slicked back in a ducktail and dressed in tight Levis and pointy black boots. His saving grace with my parents was the fact he was Jewish.

The summer of Rachel's senior year of high school, she discovered she was pregnant. She had just returned from freshmen orientation at Boston University. Eve invited Bob's parents over for brisket and a week later Rachel and Bob had a shotgun wedding in our backyard.

Bob got a business degree and then went on to chiropractic school, while Rachel obtained her "MRS" and stayed home with baby William. After Bob graduated, he accepted a job working for a chiropractor in Great Neck and later opened his own practice. By then, Maya was born, and my mother had gained a firm grip on my formerly defiant sister.

It only took Eve ten hours before appearing on my doorstep together with Pop. After all, she had her own private eye living next door. "You need to move to West Meadow with us" were the first words out of her mouth to Rachel. Even Pop thought it a mistake for her and the kids to stay in my charming one bedroom East Village apartment. In New York, "charming" is a euphemism for tiny. The apartment was barely 600 square feet.

"I'm not moving in with you, Ma," Rachel said.

"Then don't expect any money," Eve said in an agitated voice. "What are you gonna do? You have no job skills. You shoulda gone to college."

"Are you serious? *You're* the one that encouraged me to marry Bob."

"Encouraged? For crissakes, you were pregnant. What other choice did you have?"

Rachel started to open her mouth then closed it again. She glanced over at the kids who were playing with Brooklyn on the couch and had missed my mother's insensitive remark.

"Why would you bring that up?" I asked a clueless Eve and then patted Rachel's hand. "We'll manage. Between my grant and teaching job I can keep us all afloat."

My mother's face flamed red. "You girls always stick together. What about the doctor and your move to New Mexico?"

She had me there. "I can always go later," I said.

Ma locked eyes with me and smiled. "Are you sure about that?"

Touché, Eve.

MY SISTER REGISTERED WILL AT A LOCAL PUBLIC SCHOOL and placed Maya in the Peanut Butter & Jelly preschool a few blocks from my apartment. While I'd rather die than admit my mother was right, it turned out she was correct about a few things. For one, Rachel's lack of education and job experience proved to be a major liability.

"All I know how to do is cook, clean and sew," Rachel said when I tried to help her put together a résumé. Her home cooking didn't qualify her as a chef, and the mere thought of my sister cleaning houses or hotel rooms was too depressing to consider. Sewing was her only real job skill. She had created most of the kids' clothes on her fancy Singer machine, and she was quite talented.

On Sunday we combed the classified section of the *New York Times* in search of seamstress jobs. There was one at a dry cleaner in Jamaica, Queens, and one in a factory in Harlem. Both were located in what Pop termed as "iffy neighborhoods." Neither job paid much more than minimum wage.

The following week, we changed strategies. At Eve's insistence, the Levin sisters had all taken typing classes in high school. It had been her Plan B for us if we didn't finish college and become teachers, and/or nab a rich Jewish husband. To Ma's credit, the *Times* had two columns of office job opportunities.

Every morning, Rachel dressed up in my navy suit and matching pumps, and checked out secretarial jobs. Most of the positions required typing and steno skills. Rachel could type but not nearly the required 75 words per minute, and had no experience other than typing Bob's college term papers. One of the interviewers had to explain that stenography had nothing to do with geography, in which Rachel had received an A during high school.

Every night, she'd come home with a long face and aching feet. After a quick dinner, she'd spend hours working on an outfit for Maya's appearance on *Sesame Street*. The show was scheduled for Friday. The same day I was supposed to fly to New Mexico with Eduardo.

"You should go," Rachel said. "I refuse to let you miss out on this opportunity for me."

"If it's meant to be, Eduardo will wait until you get more settled."

"What if Ma's right?" She verbalized my worst fears. "Have you told Eduardo you're not leaving with him?"

"Tonight. We're having dinner at Anton's. Despite what Ma has predicted, it shouldn't be a problem."

EDUARDO AND I SAT IN A RED LEATHER BOOTH AT Anton's, a small pizza parlor we'd frequented on numerous dates. We jointly devoured the Veggie Special smothered in Mozzarella cheese.

"This pizza is the best," he said.

"Won't you miss all this incredible New York food?"

"Wait until I introduce you to some real Mexican fare in Española."

I cleared my throat. "I-I won't be getting on the plane on Friday, but . . . I will come as soon as Rachel finds a job."

The color left his face. "Right. Sure you will."

His reaction startled me. He'd been so supportive of me helping out my sister. "How can you doubt me?"

"Why doesn't Rachel move in with your folks?"

When I tried to explain that Rachel couldn't live with Eve —that it would be mental torture for any of us to live with my mother—his eyes glazed over, and the corners of his mouth turned down. "My sister Kiki and her kids live with my folks. What's the big deal?"

"Your mother is not Eve."

"I told you. Mama's got her own set of *problemas*."

"Really, like what?"

"What does it matter if you're not coming to New Mexico?"

"You're putting words in my mouth, Eduardo. I just need time—"

"A week, a month, a year?"

I shrugged. "My grandfather settled in America and worked for two years to save the money for Nana to come over from Russia."

"*Bien por él.*"

"What?"

He shrugged. "Good for him."

I'd never seen this side of Eduardo. He was especially upset that I couldn't provide him a date. While I continued to stay over at his furnished studio the next few nights, a cloud hung over our relationship. On Wednesday morning, he said that he didn't want to spend his last night in New York with me.

"You can't be serious," I said.

"What's the point? Besides I'll be staying in a dive close to the airport."

"The point is, you don't believe I'm coming out to New

Mexico later. How can you doubt that?"

He shrugged. "I want to believe you, Laila. But I can think of a million reasons why you might change your mind."

Wednesday night Eduardo called me from a motel near LaGuardia. "I guess this is goodbye."

Tears stung my eyelids. "Can't I come over?"

"I'll see you when, and *if*, you get to New Mexico."

"Why are you so negative?" Damn if Eve hadn't been right about this.

When I hung up the phone, I tried to put myself in Eduardo's shoes. Was it possible that like me, Eduardo was vulnerable too? That girl in high school must have hurt him terribly.

But I'd told my sister she could count on me, and I wasn't going back on my word. Rachel put the kids in bed early, and uncorked a nice Merlot as we watched *Baretta* with Robert Blake.

The crime show was suddenly interrupted by the voice of David Brinkley. "We interrupt your regularly scheduled program to bring you this very important announcement. David Berkowitz, a twenty-four-year-old postal employee, was just taken into custody and charged with being the Son of Sam, the serial killer who has terrorized New York City for more than a year, killing six young people and wounding seven others with a .44-caliber revolver. Berkowitz generally targeted attractive young women with long brown hair."

Rachel drew her hand across her throat. "You are aware, Sista, you fit the profile of Berkowitz's victims to the tee."

"It's crossed my mind more than once."

CHAPTER SIXTEEN
Sesame

Laila

At 6 a.m. Friday morning, I stood in the kitchen flipping buttermilk pancakes. My temples pulsated with a major headache as a result of tossing and turning all night with major doubts about my decision *not* to go to New Mexico with Eduardo. Was helping out Rachel and the kids just an excuse? Or were there deeper reasons that kept me from moving to the Land of Enchantment with him?

Mrs. Schneider, who arrived at my door carrying her own coffee mug, interrupted my thoughts. She sat at the table, and I poured her a cup from the decanter of my drip coffee pot. "Isn't today the day Maya's on *Sesame Street*?"

"Yes, Rachel's getting her dressed right now."

A few minutes later, Rachel appeared dressed in my navy suit, followed by Maya, who pranced about in a starched white dress with each of the Sesame characters embroidered on it. Her curly hair was tied up in a ponytail with a big red ribbon.

"You look beautiful," I said. Rachel had made the dress from scratch just for the occasion.

Mrs. Schneider sat at the kitchen table sipping her coffee. She held up her mug. "Can you pour me a warm-up? This is a *bissel* cold."

I filled Mrs. Schneider's mug with fresh coffee and served up the pancakes to everyone. After breakfast, I walked Maya and Rachel to the elevator and gave them each a big hug. "Good luck."

"Don't forget to wake Will up at 7:30," Rachel said. "And remind him to take his lunch box."

Fifteen minutes later, there were several thuds on the front door. "Open up," shouted Rachel.

She raced into the bedroom and returned with Mr. Boonie in her hands. "Maya won't go anywhere without him."

"You left her downstairs by herself?"

"Of course not. She's sitting in a taxi with Eve."

"I didn't know Ma was going with you."

"Sorry, I forgot to mention it. She called last night and practically begged me. What could I say?"

"Two letters, N-O. If it were me—"

"Right, Laila."

MRS. SCHNEIDER AND I SAT SIPPING CONSTANT Comment tea in the kitchen, when Rachel and Maya returned home shortly after noon.

Maya ran up to me for a hug, and then scrambled back to the bedroom with Brooklyn.

Rachel smiled. "It was quite a day. Maya was terrific, of course. But you'll never guess what Eve did."

"Let's see. She got a part in a nude horror movie on the top of the Empire State Building?"

"Nope, although I grant you that's a good guess."

"She found Bob and beat him to a pulp?"

"She helped land *me* a job on *Sesame Street.*"

"No kidding?"

"One of the producers had made a big deal about Maya's dress. After the show, Ma went to talk to him. Next thing I know he's asking me to work in the costume department."

"Wow, that's fantastic."

"The pay's not great but it's a start."

I hugged her. "I'm so happy for you."

"And Eve has even offered to pay for the kids' sitter. So between the job, this rent-controlled apartment, and with a sitter covered, I think I can make it."

My mother was a complicated woman. In the end, she helped Rachel cut the cord and live her life on her own terms.

"So now there's no excuse for you not going to the Land of Enchantment with Eduardo," Rachel said.

"Yeah there is. I'm scared. Look at what happened the last time I fell in love."

"Despite everything that's happened to both of us, I still believe there are some good men out there."

"Like Pop," I said.

"Exactly." Rachel looked at her watch. "What time is his flight?"

"One-thirty, if I remember correctly."

"If you hustle, you can still make the plane. Pack a suitcase, and I'll take care of the reservation."

"One suitcase won't cut it."

"I can ship the rest of your stuff next week."

"What about Brooklyn and Zorro?"

"You've already bought pet carriers."

"I guess I'm out of excuses."

Mrs. Schneider began to cry.

I put my hand over hers. "What's the matter?"

"Who's gonna take care of me when you leave?"

"Don't worry," Rachel said. "You can count on me."

WHEN I STEPPED INTO THE YELLOW CAB, I COULD barely breathe and rolled down the window to get fresh air. As an old truck cruised by, noxious exhaust filled the cab and made me cough uncontrollably. Was this an omen? Should I grab the animals' carriers, and head back to the safety of my rent-controlled apartment?

The cabbie, a short young man with a fluff of curly red hair atop a balding skull, twisted his head around. "Where you going, lady?"

In between coughs, I said, "Sabinal."

"Where the fuck is that?"

A new round of coughing commenced until I felt like I might choke. You'd think the cabbie might offer me a drink or something so I didn't die in his cab.

Instead he checked his watch unsympathetically. "I don't got all day."

Brooklyn licked me through her crate. Magically, the coughing stopped. I shot a hard look at the cabbie. "LaGuardia." *Asshole.* I was reminded there were many things about New York I would not miss.

CHAPTER SEVENTEEN
Rain, Rain Go Away

Dave

Dave woke up Thursday, with a major hangover from the countless shots of Jim Beam and lines of coke he'd snorted the night before. The capture of the Son of Sam was all over the news. Dave couldn't believe all the things he had in common with the serial killer. Their names were so similar (David Berkowitz vs. Dave Burke), and both worked for the United States Post Office. And like Dave, Berkowitz desired women with long brown hair. What were the chances? Maybe he should take over for him. Yeah, how cool would that be?

But Dave had never hurt anyone in his life. Besides, now that he'd found Miss Levin, his one true love, he lost all interest in other women. He repeated her first name out loud over and over again, day and night. "*Laila, Laila, oh, pretty Laila.*"

After work, Dave rode the subway to her East Village apartment. It was a classy building just like her. Double stone pillars stood on each side of the entrance, and the windows had white-leaded borders. He'd been there a few times now, spending hours hanging out in a pair of aviator sunglasses and a black hooded sweatshirt.

As he stood outside the red brick building, grey clouds appeared and a few raindrops splashed on his face. He pulled up the hood of his sweatshirt and wondered if he'd ever see Laila. Had she moved? His temples throbbed at the thought that he may have lost her forever. Miss Levin. Where have you gone?

Thunder crackled in the sky, followed by streaks of lightning, and then a heavy downpour. Dave crossed the street to take cover under the awning of a restaurant. He was soaking wet by the time he got there. Under his breath he sang, "Rain, rain go away, come again some other day," reminding him of another day when he'd sung that song a long time ago. A menagerie of disjointed images filled his head . . .

Mommy romped around their small Bronx apartment in her ruby robe. "Be a good boy, Davie, and go ride your bike for a while," Mommy said.

Uncle Bernie tossed him a quarter. "Go get yourself an ice cream cone, son."

Mommy's good boy always did as he was told. When he arrived home too soon from the store, Mommy was making loud noises inside the bedroom. Dave peeked through the keyhole and saw Uncle Bernie on top of her. They were both naked and it looked like he was hurting her.

Cupcake, Mommy's toy poodle, started to bark.

Mommy grabbed her robe, lunged out of bed, and yanked the door open. She slapped Dave across the face. "Bad boy, Davie. Whaddaya doing here? I told you to ride your bike. Now leave this house." She marched back inside the bedroom and slammed the door behind her.

Seven-year-old Dave climbed on his red Schwinn bicycle another uncle had bought him for Christmas. He drove around in the freezing drizzle until his hands were numb, and his feet felt like two blocks of ice.

By the time he returned to the duplex, he was ice cold and drenched to the bone. He opened the door and snuck inside.

Water dripped all over the entry. His hair, his clothes, and even his ears were filled with water. He was terrified that Mommy would be mad at him.

But when she saw him, she gave him a hug. "My poor Davie." She pulled out an old wool blanket from the hall closet and handed it to him. "Take off your clothes so you don't drip water everywhere; then come into the kitchen."

He did as told.

Mommy handed him a mug of hot cocoa with tiny marshmallows on top.

Uncle Bernie sat at the table drinking a cup of coffee. He glared at Dave. "Whaddaya say when someone gives you something, boy?"

Dave's lips quivered. "Th-thank you, M-m-mommy." He stuttered for the first time.

According to the information Barney had given him, Miss Levin lived in Apartment 4D. Dave desperately wanted to slip inside the building and knock on her door. He believed if he could only speak to her, he would win over her heart. The rain finally stopped and the sun poked out from behind some clouds.

A woman with butter-yellow hair tied back in a ponytail strolled up to the heavy glass doors of the building while holding an umbrella over herself and a couple of yapping kids.

Perfect.

Just as he'd hoped, the door remained a half-inch open behind the little girl. As he stuck his fingers inside and pulled on the door, an old woman with a shopping cart full of packages yelled at him. "No tailgating, young man? That's the rules."

"Ah, sorry, m-ma'am. Can I h-hold the door for you?"

"Rachel!" she hollered. "I need your help."

"Be right there, Mrs. Schneider." Blondie turned around, dashed back to the front door, and held it open for the old lady. She glared at Dave in his hoodie. "Who are you?"

"I know everyone in the building," the old lady said. "And I never seen this *schlemiel* before."

Dave scowled, turned away, and scuttled down the street muttering to himself. Damn. He was back to square one. Would he ever reconnect with the one woman who could fulfill all his dreams? And what if he found her and she rejected him?

CHAPTER EIGHTEEN
The Flight

Eduardo

He looked out the window of the airplane at a magnificent aerial view of New York City's skyline that included the Empire State Building, the World Trade Center, and the Statue of Liberty. Living in Manhattan for the last few years had been an experience of a lifetime. But Eduardo was ready to go back to the Land of Enchantment, the land where his ancestors had lived for three hundred years.

In the end he thought that Laila would come with him. While he respected her devotion to her sister, he doubted she'd come to New Mexico in the future. Would he ever find someone to share his life? The thought plagued him. He knew the majority of women in the northern New Mexico area did not have the education or sophistication of the women he'd been dating during college and medical school. Sadly, many of the girls where he grew up had dropped out of high school pregnant.

With the whole row on the TWA jet to himself, Eduardo stretched out and decided to take a nap. Just as he was drifting into sleep, someone tapped his shoulder.

"*Perdone, señor. Esta occupado este asiento?* Excuse me, sir. Is this seat taken?"

He looked up and had to blink a few times to take in the sight before him. "*Yo no puede creer. Es un milagro.*"

Laila grinned. "Something, something, it's a miracle?" She craned her neck and kissed him.

A stewardess approached with a wry smile on her face. "Excuse me, Miss, you need to take your seat."

Laila sat down next to him in the vacant aisle seat. Should he pinch himself? "I thought Rachel needed you."

"It's a long story."

He listened to Laila's explanation about how she'd come to her decision to join him. "What about Brooklyn and Zorro?"

"I hope it's not a problem with your *familia*. They're in cargo."

"No *problema*. We have lots of animals on the ranch." Eduardo wanted to hold Laila and never let go, but he settled for her resting her head on his shoulder and clasping her hand in his lap. He hadn't slept well ever since she'd told him she wasn't going to New Mexico. But now, all of a sudden, he had a hard time keeping his eyes open. That is until the plane hit a storm with major turbulence.

CHAPTER NINETEEN
Nuevo Mexico

Laila

A seasoned flyer, the sudden turbulence didn't bother me. Pop, a former U.S. Air Force captain, always said to think of it as bumps in the road.

I touched Eduardo's hand. "Are you okay, honey?"

He had squeezed his eyes shut and was gripping the armrests with his fingernails. "I'm fine."

"You're sure?"

He clenched his jaw. "I'm trying to sleep. Why don't you listen to those tapes I bought you?"

I put on a headset and pressed the button on the small tape recorder. "Lesson one, *Hola señor. Como estás?*" Repeat.

The airplane stopped in Dallas, where most of the people got off. Fewer than twenty passengers remained on the plane for the last lap of the flight to New Mexico.

When we made our final descent into Albuquerque, Eduardo said, "Switch seats with me." He pointed at the view of a mountain range. "That's the Sandias. And over there to the west are mesas."

I checked out the mountains, mesas and the sprawling desert city with its pastel-colored stucco homes glowing in a spectacular sunset. Hues of rose, saffron, crimson and malachite radiated through the blue sky. Slices of paler tints encircled the horizon. The color infused the grooves and saddles of the mountains and deepened to a potent magenta. "It's been so long since I've seen a sunset like this."

Eduardo grinned. "Welcome back to New Mexico."

"I'm going to love it."

His father stood at the gate as we entered the Sunport. A tall man with deep creases in his forehead, he was dressed in worn cowboy boots and Wranglers. He took off his Stetson and his bushy eyebrows curled up like two caterpillars.

Eduardo introduced us.

"Hola, Señor Quintana." I said in greeting. *"Como estás?"*

"I'm fine. Welcome to New Mexico," he said. "Please call me Ramon."

I smiled. *"Gracias, Ramon. Nuevo Mexico es muy bueno."*

"Laila," said Eduardo grinning. "My father is speaking to you in English."

"I'm so sorry." What a fool. I was so nervous I hadn't even noticed he was speaking English.

"I'll leave you two to get acquainted while I head to the restroom," Eduardo said.

Ramon insisted on taking my carry-on bag. "I want to thank you for making it possible for Eduardo to return home."

"You're giving me too much credit, Mr. Quintana, ah, Ramon. Eduardo would have come home without me. In fact—"

"Come home, yes. Stay home, I'm not so sure."

"I don't understand."

"Did Eduardo tell you about my heart attack the summer he graduated high school?"

"I don't recall him mentioning it."

"He gave up a full academic scholarship to manage the ranch while I was recovering. Then we had a drought and financial problems. Eduardo kept us above water for the next few years by negotiating with the bank and selling off some property. Those were very tough times."

Eduardo had told me he'd delayed college. Now I knew why. It appeared there were many things I didn't know about him.

In a few minutes, Eduardo joined us at baggage claim. We stood there awaiting our luggage, and the crates carrying Brooklyn and Zorro.

"So how's the ranch?" Eduardo asked.

Ramon squinted. "We could use some rain. Cattle prices could be better."

"Same as always, then."

"I'll go get the truck," Ramon said.

As our flight's luggage descended down the chute to the carousel, an airline representative hand-delivered the two crates with Zorro and Brooklyn. I quickly unlatched the cages and hugged each animal in turn before putting on their leashes.

Brooklyn pulled on her leash, eager to get outside, while I held Zorro in my arms.

After my luggage arrived, we walked outside where Ramon was waiting in an old Chevy pickup. His eyebrows inched up when he saw the animals.

"Give me the girls," Eduardo said. "I'll take them for a quick walk."

When he returned a few minutes later, he began placing them in their crates in the back of the pickup.

I gulped. "They can't ride back there!"

"On a ranch, animals are treated like animals," Eduardo said. "They ride in the back."

Who was this man? I stood there paralyzed.

Eduardo quickly realized his mistake. "Papa, we have a problem."

A few minutes later, we began the journey to Española with each of us holding an animal. We had barely left the airport when Zorro leaped from Eduardo's hands, and blasted around the truck like a crazed tiger. Then Brooklyn bolted from my hands chasing Zorro, who jumped on Ramon and scratched his cheek, drawing blood.

"Zorro, bad cat!" I yelled. "I'm so sorry, Ramon. The flight in cargo must have really spooked my girls out."

In the end, Eduardo rode in the back of the pickup with the animals. I waved at him through the cab window every so often as the truck rambled down Central Avenue past the University of New Mexico where I had attended college. It all looked quite familiar as we entered the freeway heading north on I-25.

Ramon and I conversed quite well. He was surprisingly easy to talk to, a trait Eduardo had inherited from him. I spoke about my family and my research. It was dark by the time we reached Española. The city consisted of old buildings, a K-Mart, two beauty salons, a car dealership and a body shop. A few vehicles were parked at a Dairy Queen and another half-dozen at a local bar called Martina's.

I recalled driving through this town in a snowstorm back in 1970. At age seventeen, I was a naive college student who'd been tricked into transporting a suitcase back to the East Coast for some drug dealer boyfriend. It felt like another lifetime and I chose not to mention it to Eduardo. The only good that had come from the whole adventure was that I finished up college in the Land of Enchantment, a place I'd fallen in love with and where I was now returning. It reinforced my belief that many of life's events are not random.

Ramon turned into an Exxon, killed the engine, and stepped out of the truck.

Eduardo hopped out of the back of the pickup, unscrewed the gas cap, and placed the nozzle in the truck's tank. He looked up at me. "How ya doing, honey?"

"I'm fine." I stepped down from the cab, stretched my legs, and took the animals for a short walk behind the Exxon. Then I filled the dog and cat bowls with water and changed Zorro's shoe-sized litter box.

The gas station attendant who wore a work shirt that said "NESTER" on the pocket, walked up to Ramon. "*Como estás.* How come you ain't coming to poker no more?"

Ramon shook his head. "After last month, the wife won't give me back the checkbook."

Nester chuckled. "She's got you by the *huevos,* eh?"

I listened to the conversation with amusement. Nester patted Eduardo on the back and then headed over to another pickup that had just pulled into the station. As I stood waiting for the gas tank to fill up, the reality of Española sunk in. Had I just made the biggest mistake of my life? I glanced at Ramon. "What do people do here for entertainment?"

"There's lots of church activities," he said. "Of course, Sabinal is another twenty miles north."

My eyebrows flickered. "You mean *this* is the big city?"

Eduardo smiled. "I told you we lived out of town."

"No worries. We have lots of things to do in Sabinal," Ramon said. "Dances and *matanzas.*"

"What's a *matanza?*"

"It's when we kill a pi—"

"Never mind, Papa," Eduardo said. "It's a party, a kind of potluck."

"And we butcher a—"

Eduardo gave his father a stern look. "*Nada mas!*"

"You might want to join Sylvia's quilting bee," Ramon said. "They meet on Tuesdays."

"Tuesdays, great." I turned to Eduardo. "Is there a good pizza joint in town?"

"It depends what you consider good."

"How about a kosher deli?"

A CLOUD OF DUST DRIFTED BEHIND US AS THE TRUCK puttered down a dirt road and stopped in front of an exposed adobe home, flanked by a large barn and corral. An older woman came flying out of the house dressed in a polyester pantsuit with her hair rolled up in pink curlers like Mrs. Schneider's. On each side, she clasped the hand of a young child.

A three-legged mutt barked wildly at us.

Eduardo leaped from the back of the pickup with Brooklyn and Zorro on leashes.

The three-legged dog growled, showing serious teeth.

"Shush, Concha," Eduardo said to the Labrador mix, who immediately settled down. He handed me the animals' leashes and gave the woman a huge hug.

"*Mi hijo! Finalmente, estás en nuestras casa.* Son, you are finally home."

"For good this time, Mama."

As I stepped from the cab, the dog growled again.

"Stop that, Concha," Ramon shouted.

The dog retreated behind Eduardo's mother.

The two children ran up to Eduardo.

He placed the little girl on his shoulders and high-fived the boy.

I smiled at his mother.

She glared at me then turned to Eduardo. "*Quien es esa chica?* Who is this girl?"

Eduardo wrapped his arm around my shoulders. "Mama, I want you to meet Laila."

"Hello, Mrs. Quintana." I held out my hand, which she ignored.

"Laila's come to live here and study." Eduardo said.

"*Quien es esta Lailee?* Who is this Lailee?"

"It's Laila, not *Lailee*, Mama," Eduardo said. "She's my girlfriend."

His mother's amber eyes flickered. "*Su amiga?*"

"Mama, please speak English," Eduardo said.

She tossed me a frosty look. "You're not from around here?"

"I'm from New York." Had Eduardo even mentioned me to her?

"New York? I hear you eat big salamis there."

"I'm a vegetarian," I said.

"You don't eat meat?"

"That's right," said Eduardo.

"I made beef stew for dinner. Eduardo's favorite. Full of hot green chiles too."

Eduardo took a deep breath and grabbed my hand. "Let's go inside. I'll find you something to eat."

Concha growled and barked again.

I held the animals' leashes as we moved toward the house.

I placed Zorro back in her carrier but Brooklyn whined and squirmed in my arms. "Can I bring her inside with us?"

"Mama doesn't allow animals in the house," said Eduardo.

Tears prickled my eyelids. "But she's freaked out."

Eduardo squeezed his mother's hand. "Can we bring the dog inside for just a little while?"

Her thin, nervous face screwed up. "Does *el perro* pee-pee in the *casa*?"

"She's totally housebroken," I said. "We lived in an apartment in Manhattan."

His mother shrugged and turned to Eduardo. "Just this once for you, *mi hijo.*"

"Thank you, Mrs. Quintana. I'll walk the animals before I bring the dog inside."

"You want me to go with you?" Eduardo asked.

"Your mama hasn't seen you in a long time. Go in the house and relax. I'll be there soon."

He kissed my cheek and followed his parents into the house.

I spent the next twenty minutes parading around the yard with my girls. They sniffed everything in sight enjoying their newfound freedom and the unfamiliar smells of hay, chickens, horses and cows.

When I was sure they'd done their business, I placed Zorro back in her crate with fresh water and cat chow, and entered the house with Brooklyn. The large entry had exposed adobe walls and wide-planked pine floors. We ambled into the enormous kitchen filled with spicy aromas. Every burner had a pot or pan on top. Mrs. Quintana was busy placing platters of food on the table. The small children scampered about.

Ramon pointed to the long oak table in the middle of the

room set with cobalt-blue china and beautiful old silverware. There were even two candlesticks ready to be lit. "Make yourself at home, Laila."

Eduardo winked at me, then looked up at his mother. "Where's Angie and Kiki?"

"They went into Española to hang out with their friends." She shook her head. "Your sisters don't care about our traditions anymore. Kiki leaves me Little Sylvia and Errol, and her and Angie do whatever they please."

Eduardo introduced me to the children. Little Sylvia climbed on his lap. "Everything is *perfecto*, Mama." He smiled at me. "Our *familia* always starts the weekend with a special candlelit dinner."

"My mother does too, but it's because of *Shabbos,* that's Yiddish for Sabbath."

Mrs. Quintana glared at me. "When I was growing up, someone told me Jews had green horns. Can you imagine?"

Eduardo rolled his eyes. "Mama!"

Ramon shook his head. "I don't think Laila finds that funny."

I endured the onslaught of insults with admirable stoicism. His mother was a cruel creature with tentacles ready to choke me.

Sylvia ignored her husband and turned to Eduardo. "You'll never guess who's back home, *mi hijo.*"

"Never mind," Ramon said.

"Violet, that's who. She's come home for good. Virgie says she's done with that airline hostess job."

Ramon shot her a hard look.

"She'll be at the *matanza* we're having a week from Sunday."

"Oh, that potluck thing," I said.

Sylvia crinkled her eyes. "Uncle Rupert is bringing his prize pig."

My eyebrows drew together. "Oh my God, is it live?"

"Of course," Sylvia said.

"It's time for us to get settled in the trailer," Eduardo said.

"What trailer?"

"We're just going to stay there until I get the house built."

What house was he talking about? There was so much that Eduardo had not shared with me. Brooklyn sniffed around the room and suddenly squatted on an old Navajo rug. "Oh my God, I'm so sorry!" I picked the dog up in my arms. Urine dripped down her legs to my skirt.

Sylvia stood there with her mouth open.

Eduardo rushed to get paper towels and quickly blotted the area where Brooklyn had peed.

I said something stupid like, "I'll pay for the dry cleaning,"

Eduardo said, "*Buenos noches*, everyone."

As we bolted from the house, I felt a dull rumbling in the hollow of my guts. All I could think about was what a disastrous first impression I'd made with Eduardo's mother. That, and the bone-chilling reception I'd received from her.

CHAPTER TWENTY
Sabinal

Violet

Violet sat on the porch painting her long nails carmine-red when she heard Jimmy Buffet's "Margaritaville" blasting from a car stereo.

Seconds later, Ira peeled into the driveway in his big-boat Caddy. He killed the engine, stepped out of the car dressed in cutoff jeans, a stained Lakers T-shirt, and a pair of rubber thongs that squeaked when he walked. His eyes were small and pouched, his nose flat, and his chin ran into the bulge of his neck. Had she never noticed his resemblance to a bullfrog before? He was also in dire need of a shower and shave. "Hey, baby, you sure are a sight for sore eyes. How about a kiss?"

Violet gave him a perfunctory peck on the mouth. His black whiskers scratched her upper lip. "So where the hell have you been, Ira?" She thought he might have forgotten about her.

He looked at her sheepishly. "I made a few ah, pitstops in Reno and Las Vegas."

She suspected he'd gambled away what little money he had left. *What had she ever seen in him? More importantly, what did he have to offer her now that they were out of Los Angeles?*

Mama ambled outside and stood with her arms crossed, a sour expression on her face.

"This is my agent Ira, Mama."

Ira grinned. "And her boyfriend." He gave Mama a big hug.

Her eyes bulged and her body stiffened.

Ira didn't seem to notice. "So great to meet ya, *Señora* Sanchez. I've been looking forward to this *momento* for a very long time." He winked at Violet. "See, honey, I've been working on my Spanish."

Mama nodded. "*Se vey y huele como los marranos en el corral.*"

Ira scratched the bald spot on top of his head. "What did she say?"

Loosely translated Mama had said, 'He looks and smells as raunchy as the pigs in the corral.' Violet interpreted it this way. "She said it's nice to finally meet your handsome boyfriend."

Ira grinned at Mama like she'd just invited him for Christmas dinner. He took her hand and kissed it. "It's my pleasure, Mrs. Sanchez."

Mama wiped her hand on her apron then led Ira over to a metal storage shed where Papa used to put up the occasional illegal Mexican that crossed the border looking for work. Inside the musty shed was an army cot made up neatly with an old wool blanket and a pillow with feathers poking out of it.

Ira's eyebrows snapped together. "What is this?"

"It's where you will sleep."

He scratched the stubble on his chin. "Didn't Violet tell you we're practically engaged? I mean it is 1977."

As far as Violet was concerned, it was just as well. Ira was a ticket to nowhere. The sooner she could figure out a way to rid herself of him, the better.

"*No importa,*" said Mama. "*Donde está el equipage?*"

Ira shrugged. "No *understando.*"

"She doesn't care about our relationship," Violet said. "She wants to know where your luggage is."

Ira's chin jutted out like a chimpanzee. "I don't got no luggage."

Violet rolled her eyes then glared at him.

"Ah, what I mean, Mrs. Sanchez, is my suitcases are being shipped."

Mama shook her head and hightailed it out of the shed.

"Your mama don't like me."

Such an idiot. "When are we going back to L.A.?"

"Like never, honey. We need to make a fresh start somewhere. New York, Chicago. We'll figure it out."

"But what about my career?"

"Be real, honey. Your career is done."

She slapped his face.

Beneath all the black stubble, his cheek burned bright red. "After I dropped you at the airport, I went back to the apartment. Diesel's fat thug was there to make sure I didn't take nothing with me. So basically, I hit the road with *nada* and didn't look back."

"You left all your clothes and shit? And you lost your money in Vegas didn't you?"

"Actually, I made a shitload of money in Las Vegas. I lost it in Reno."

"What use are you to me now?"

He smiled. "I have something better than money." He opened the Caddy's passenger door, then the glove compartment, and returned with a small vial of powder and a tiny silver spoon. "There's at least a couple of ounces stashed in the trunk."

They each snorted a few lines.

Violet wiped her nose with her pinky. "Good shit." The one thing that Ira still had to offer made his presence bearable. Life in general felt better after a few more hits.

The slap of the screen door interrupted her new euphoria. "Mama's coming!" She wiped her nose with the back of her hand.

Ira quickly stashed the vial in his shorts' pocket.

Mama arrived with a big plastic box, which she dropped on the ground and tore off the cover. Inside were neatly folded Western shirts with pearl buttons, Wranglers, socks, jockey shorts and various other clothes. Although her daddy had been dead more than ten years, Mama had kept his old clothing.

"You can wear these," Mama said. "Until your *shit* shows up."

It was rare and never a good sign if her mother cursed. But to Violet's surprise, Mama smiled and clasped her hands together. "Guess who just called?"

"I don't know." Violet could care less who called Mama.

"Sylvia is who. Eduardo's just got back home from New York and they're having a big *matanza* on Sunday. You need to help me make *sopapillas*."

Eduardo? Suddenly Sabinal didn't feel so desperately dismal. "Sure thing, Mama."

CHAPTER TWENTY-ONE

The Chicken Coop

Laila

The stars, like silver sequins, sparkled in the full New Mexican sky as Eduardo and I walked hand-and-hand down the road to a rundown mobile home surrounded by a white picket fence. Zorro and Brooklyn trailed behind us zigzagging off to chase jackrabbits and field mice. I felt a huge sense of relief to get away from Eduardo's mother. On the other hand, a knot in my stomach was telling me I had just made a terrible mistake.

We passed by a small adobe structure with meshed wire surrounding it. "What's that?"

"It's a chicken coop. Wait until you see my plans for it though."

"Plans?"

"The architectural plans I've had drawn up. It's gonna make a terrific house. You won't believe the view from the second story."

"Let me get this straight. You're making a house from a chicken coop?"

He smiled. "You'll see."

I pointed at some type of machine covered with red, blue, and yellow fabric. "What's that?"

"That's my hang glider. I haven't flown since medical school."

"There's obviously a lot I don't know about you."

Eduardo pulled the trailer's gate, which groaned and then

fell off the hinges. The address on the metal mailbox was 102 Eduardo Drive.

I smacked his shoulder. "You named the street after yourself?"

"Papa did. There's also Kiki Street, Angie Court and Carla Avenue. Papa officially registered them with the township of Sabinal." He opened the front door.

I gasped at the sight before us. Dirty dishes filled the sink. Flies buzzed around food left on the kitchen table and countertops. Garbage was strewn everywhere. Age-old layers of dust whirled frantically to life.

Eduardo shook his head. "Shit!"

"This is where you expected us to stay?"

"Damn, my cousin. I let him live here for free and this is what I get?"

The stench made me gag. The knot in my stomach grew larger. "*Really*, Eduardo?"

"Yes, I know, princess. We'll stay at my folks' house tonight."

"Princess?"

"That's what you're acting like."

"Sorry I'm not some Mexican Earth Mama."

"Nice stereotype."

"Call me a JAP if you will, but no way could I ever live here."

"It's supposed to be temporary."

I felt overwhelmed and terribly sad. "It's not just this place. Española is nothing but an Exxon and a Dairy Queen. And your mother . . . she hates me."

"Granted she could have been more welcoming."

"I noticed your father, not *you*, told her the 'green horn' comment was out of line."

"Give Mama a chance. She'll come around."

I pleaded with him. "Please don't make me go back there tonight. Can't we get a hotel somewhere?"

"I've got an idea."

AN HOUR LATER, I LAY WITH EDUARDO UNDER A THICK quilt on a mattress on the roof of the chicken coop. We stared at a full moon in a star-studded sky.

"Have you ever seen anything so beautiful?"

I had to admit it was spectacular.

After the most passionate lovemaking ever, we lay there holding hands.

Eduardo said, "Have faith in me, baby."

"Here I am on top of a chicken coop in the middle of the boonies. We'll see how I feel if it rains."

"We'll work things out. You'll see."

"By the way, who's Violet?"

"She was my girlfriend in high school. You know, the one I told you about."

"The one who dumped you?"

"She wanted to see the world. I don't blame her for that."

"And now she's back in Sabinal to pick up where she left off."

"Don't be ridiculous."

What I didn't say was how "ridiculous" this whole scenario was. Following Eduardo out to Nowhere, New Mexico, receiving nothing but hostile vibes from his Mama, and now sleeping on top of a chicken coop. If you'd told me a few months ago that my life would have followed this path, I'd have laughed it off as a big joke. However, one thing I knew for sure. If our relationship was going to work, I'd need to keep my sense of humor.

Just then, a sprinkle of rain tickled my nose.

Eduardo, blessed with a Ben Franklin knack for practical ingenuity, retrieved the hang glider and hung it up above us.

CHAPTER TWENTY-TWO
The Quintana Sisters

Laila

W hen I awoke the next morning, Eduardo was gone. Still groggy from sleep, wrapped in a blanket, I climbed down the makeshift ladder of the chicken coop and stumbled a few yards away to the trailer.

A battered pickup truck and an old Studebaker were parked on the road. Mops, buckets of water, and miscellaneous cleaning supplies sat on the wood porch of the trailer. The sound of laughter emanated from inside.

"Eduardo?"

"In here, honey."

The aroma of fresh lemons and bleach greeted me. To my surprise, the trailer looked completely different from the pigsty of the night before. The bed was made with a beautiful patchwork quilt; the dishes, counters and floors had been scrubbed until they sparkled. "Holy, shit!"

Eduardo stood at the stove cooking eggs, potatoes and chili. Two young Latina women stood next to him chatting and laughing. Both had big, teased hair and were dressed in tight T-shirts and jeans. One was chubby around the middle, while the other was tall with sticklike legs.

Eduardo kissed my cheek. "What do you think now?"

"Quite a difference."

Skinny legs touched my arm. "Eduardo did most of the work. We helped out a little."

I wrapped the blanket tighter around me. Who were these gals?

"You must be Laila," the plump one said. "Eduardo's been telling us all about you."

"All good things, of course," Skinny Legs added with a giggle.

The heavy one wrapped her arms around me for an awkward hug. To my horror, as I tried to hug her back, I let go of the quilt which slid down to the floor leaving me standing in my birthday suit. A rush of heat scaled my cheeks and neck as I quickly wrapped the blanket back around me.

"No worries. We're all girls here, well, except Eduardo, but I'm sure he's seen you already."

"Jesus, Kiki." Eduardo said then turned to me. "Everyone speaks their mind in my *familia*."

"Your family?"

He smiled. "These are my *hermanas,* my sisters. The tall one is Angie, and the more, ah, petite *chica* is Kiki, the *bebita* of our *familia*."

"You mean *la gordita*," Kiki said.

Eduardo smiled. "No, I mean the lovely, adorable one who's a bit short in stature."

She grinned at me. "I bet you thought I was Violet."

Sylvia had mentioned Violet was back in town. Now his sister had mentioned her too. Evidently, Violet was not as inconsequential as Eduardo had made her sound.

After we all ate breakfast, Eduardo's sisters left. He refused my help and cleaned the dishes himself. "My *hermanas* are something else."

"I like them. They're forthcoming like New Yorkers."

"Really?"

"Yeah, they're also sweet. They made me feel quite welcome." I wanted to say, "Unlike your mother," but restrained myself.

CHAPTER TWENTY-THREE
The Rattler

Eduardo

A few days later, Eduardo awoke to the sound of terrified dog yelps followed by Laila's screams. She was pointing at Brooklyn who stood inches away from a snake.

He leaped up, grabbed a pistol he'd tucked away in a small closet, and carefully aimed at the snake's head.

BANG! With one shot the snake slithered around as if it were still alive.

Eduardo kicked the body to assure Laila it was dead. "Dang."

She smacked his arm. "That's all you have to say . . . 'dang?' That rattlesnake nearly killed Brooklyn."

"Calm down, honey. It was just a garden snake, and this isn't something that happens very often."

Laila's eyebrows shot up to her hairline. "There's no such thing as an acceptable incidence of snakes."

Eduardo placed his arm around her shoulders. "Of course not. I'll fix the hole in the floor tonight. Would you like to come into work with me today? I want you to see your new office."

Her face lit up. "My office?"

"I figured you needed your own space for interviewing the girls."

"I've never had my own office before. When I worked at

Bronx Community College, I shared one with four other teaching assistants. But it will have to be tomorrow."

"Why is that?"

"Your mother's coming for a visit this afternoon."

"Really?" He was thrilled to hear the news. For the last few days—whenever they'd gone over to his parents' house, Eduardo had felt an escalating tension between Mama and Laila. This could be the perfect opportunity for the two most important women in his life to bond. While he was doubtful they would ever become best friends, he was hopeful they'd learn to get along.

Laila kissed him. Then before he knew it, they were back in bed.

"I'll be late my first day of work," he said.

She slipped her white cotton nightgown off. "Call it a medical emergency."

Eduardo gazed at Laila, smiling and poised naked before him, and no longer cared what time he arrived at the office. "You betcha." He stripped off his T-shirt and boxers.

She smiled. "You and that dumb hick expression."

As the sun splashed through the broken slats of the venetian blinds, they made love with a fiery passion that never seemed to diminish. He always felt like he couldn't get enough of her.

After they were done, he stood in the shower enjoying the spray of water running on his body. He couldn't think of a time when he'd been happier. His life's work and new love had all come together with his *familia* in the land of his ancestors.

CHAPTER TWENTY-FOUR
Annie Hall

Laila

After Eduardo left, I clicked on the tape recorder and popped in a cassette with my Spanish language tape. "Lesson three: Days of the week. *Lunes, martes, miercoles.*"

I repeated what the voice on the recorder said as I washed the breakfast dishes, scrubbed the kitchen stove, sink, and countertops. It was important for the house to be spotless when Eduardo's mother came over later. As Eve always said, "Cleanliness is next to godliness."

When I was done with the Spanish lesson, I switched off the recorder and turned on the small portable television and adjusted the rabbit ears. Jane Pauley sat talking with Tom Brokaw on *The Today Show* about the recent release of Woody Allen's new movie, *Annie Hall.* Everyone was raving about it. While I never used to watch daytime television, I was comforted by the show filmed in Manhattan and the jokes about the movie also laden with insider New York jokes. Who could I talk to about those things here in Sabinal?

I called my sister, Rachel, a connoisseur of theater and film. She'd been to *Annie Hall's* premiere in Manhattan. "Best movie I've seen in years," she said. "I'd love to talk more but I have to pick Will up from school. What's your address by the way? I need to forward your mail." She laughed when I told her that my address was literally 102 Eduardo Drive, and she promised to call me back later.

After I hung up the phone, I became obsessed with going to see *Annie Hall*. Somehow the movie represented all that I missed about living in New York. I decided to check the local newspapers to see if it was playing in Santa Fe or Albuquerque. Perhaps Eduardo and I could go see it over the weekend.

Grabbing a mop from the porch, I washed the linoleum floors that Eduardo had just cleaned a few days ago. I glanced back at the television. Jane Pauley's hair was swept up into a chignon. After I showered and washed my hair, I'd try and pull mine up like that. As I stood mopping the floor in an old pair of sweats and one of Eduardo's white T-shirts, I thought about what I'd wear for Sylvia's visit. A nice pair of jeans and a blouse. Nothing too sophisticated, but nothing shabby either.

My thoughts were interrupted by the sound of tires on gravel. I peeked out the window and freaked out at the sight of Sylvia stepping out of her car with Eduardo's niece and nephew. They were three hours early! Should I rush and try to comb my hair a tangled mess of frizz and curls pulled up in a barrette, put on lipstick, or quickly change my clothes? Worst of all, I still smelled like early morning sex.

Seconds later, there was a pounding on the front door. I pulled out the barrette, ran my fingers through my hair then attempted to push open the door. But it was stuck. After a few tries, I kicked the door hard, breaking it off the hinges and pushing it out.

"Ow! *Qué has hecho?* What have you done?" The door had hit Sylvia square in the nose.

"I-I'm so sorry! The door was stuck."

"Do you got some ice?"

"Of course."

She sat down at the kitchen table and the kids ran around

the trailer chasing Brooklyn and Zorro. Fortunately, the animals were used to my niece and nephew and were great around children.

I wrestled ice trays from the frozen section of the old refrigerator, wrapped some ice cubes in a clean dishtowel, and handed it to Sylvia.

She placed the towel with ice on her nose. With her other hand, she pulled out a bag of tortillas from her purse and handed them to me. They were still warm.

"Thank you. This is so nice of you."

"I just made them. Eduardo says I make the best. Are you good in the kitchen, Lailee?"

"My name is Laila with an A." She knew damn well by now. "Not really. Just good in the bedroom, I guess."

Her eyes, brown slits behind her gold-rimmed glasses, suddenly bulged to life. She didn't find my joke the least bit funny.

"Ah, just kidding. Perhaps you can teach me how to bake them."

She sniffed. "You don't bake tortillas; you cook them in a cast iron pan on the stove."

"Of course."

Just then I heard a familiar voice coming from the television that was not Jane Pauley's.

"Oh my God!" I shouted.

"What's the matter?" Sylvia asked.

There was a commercial with Eve sitting in a chair. A burly man was shaving her head with an electric razor. "K-Mart stores are shaving prices to the bone!" said my mother as he shaved off every inch of her hair!

"Tell me you're not doing this," I shouted at the TV.

Sylvia and the children glanced at the television.

"Look at that crazy lady," said the little boy.

"That crazy lady is my mother," I said.

Sylvia eyes twitched. "That's your mama?"

"She's an actress. Well, an aspiring one. She swore she wasn't going to do this commercial."

"Your mama's *muy loca*."

"Yep. My mother's *muy loca* with a touch of *facocta*."

She pointed at the kids. "Don't use such language in front of my grandchildren."

"There's nothing wrong with that word. It's Yiddish for—"

"*Suficiente*. Enough."

"Jeez—" Best not to say that word. Would I need to censor everything before I spoke?

The little boy pulled out a metal top from his pocket and began twirling it on the floor. It stopped spinning near me.

I picked it up surprised to see it was engraved with Hebrew letters. "Where did you get this?" He looked up at me. "Tatti gave it to me."

"Who's Tatti?"

"That's what they call Ramon," Sylvia said. "He's had that dumb toy around ever since I can remember."

I handed the top back to the little boy. "I used to play with one just like that. We called it a dreidel."

Sylvia shook her head. "We don't have no dreidels here."

"It appears you do."

"It's a toy is all." She shook her head. "So, what are your plans?"

"What do you mean by plans?"

"Do you want a job? Ramon knows the owner of the Exxon in Española. He could use *a muchacha* in the office."

"I have a grant to do research on teen pregnancies."

"Hmmm. We don't need some New Yorker telling us what to do with our *bambinos*."

"Eduardo and I will be working together. Perhaps he forgot to tell you?"

"Did he tell you about Violet?"

"As a matter of fact, he told me she left him years ago."

"Her mama says she wants to settle down now and have *niños*. She wants—"

"Eduardo back?"

"*Si*, why not?"

"Well, for one," I sputtered. "He's in love with me."

"We have a saying here, Lailee. *No cuentes tus pollos antes de que salgan del huevo.*"

"I have no idea what that means."

She smiled coyly. "Don't count your chickens before they hatch."

"We have a saying in Yiddish where I come from too. *Bobbemyseh.*"

"What does that mean?"

"It means, 'that's nonsense.' *Capiche*? That's Italian for, 'You get it?'"

Sylvia puckered up her lips, and then shouted to the kids. "*Vamonos*," She grabbed their little hands and flew out the open door.

What would I tell Eduardo? His mother hated everything about me. I saw no way to turn that around. And what if she was right about his old high school sweetheart? I was beginning to believe the odds of Eduardo's and my relationship working out were about as good as Sylvia and I going to see *Annie Hall* together.

CHAPTER TWENTY-FIVE
The Matanza

Laila

During the week, all the Quintanas kept talking about that *matanza* / potluck thing they were holding on Sunday. Eduardo helped his father clean out the barn. Sylvia asked Kiki and Angie to each prepare a salad or vegetable dish. When I asked her what I could bring, she wrinkled her nose and said she had plenty of food already.

A pattern of insulting remarks became the norm whenever Eduardo and I came to visit, which, unfortunately, was often. Of course, she generally delivered them when her son was out of earshot.

At dinner one night while Eduardo was helping his father clean the barn, she said, "Can you believe those New Yorkers are taking over Albuquerque and Santa Fe?"

"I'm from New York," I reminded her.

"Tee-hee," Sylvia cackled. "I wasn't talking about you."

"It was still a mean thing to say, Mama," Kiki said. "You—"

"Shush your mouth," Sylvia said. "What do you know anyway?"

Later that same night, her eyes bulged in my direction as I ate a bowl of rice and beans. "You should start eating meat, Lailee. I heard that skinny girls not only have *mas problemas* getting pregnant but they have trouble delivering their babies."

This time Angie came to my defense. "Where did you hear such a ridiculous thing?"

Sylvia's face burned the color of the red chili cooking on the stove. "A real doctor is who said it. On that *Phil Donahue* show. They all got to have Caesarean sections."

Angie glared at her mother. "Remember we watched that show together, Mama. The girls weren't just skinny like Laila. They had a serious disease called anorexia."

I learned not to tango with Sylvia and was eternally grateful to Eduardo's sisters for their support.

On Sunday morning, Eduardo arose at sunrise to help his father get ready for the *matanza*. I opened one eye and squinted at the patterns of early sunlight filtering through the venetian blinds. "Isn't it a bit early for a party?"

"There are a lot of preparations for a *matanza*. Go back to sleep and walk over later when you're rested."

I remained in bed for another hour tossing and turning. A continuous parade of vehicles clacking and sputtering down the dirt road made falling back to sleep impossible. Finally, I stepped out of bed, showered, and stood by the closet trying to decide what to wear to this thing. A sundress? Jeans and a T-shirt? Khaki shorts and a red sleeveless silk blouse? I'd forgotten to ask Eduardo what the dress protocol was for a *matanza*.

After changing my clothes a half-dozen times, I settled on a pair of Levis and a long-sleeved blue-plaid shirt (going for a cow-girlish look). Then I braided my hair and put on lip gloss and mascara. It was unusually hot, as I ambled down the road to the Quintanas' house. Perspiration pooled under the arms of my Western shirt. Halfway there, I turned around and raced back to the trailer, washed my underarms, and changed into an NYU T-shirt. Then, I started down the road all over again.

At least twenty old cars, vans and trucks were parked around the barn a few-hundred feet from the Quintanas' adobe house. Ramon and Eduardo had built a makeshift stage and dance floor where five men with guitars, trumpets, violins, and various other instruments were setting up music stands. They wore full mariachi outfits, black suits with gold embroidery on the jackets, red ties and matching sashes, and the traditional, wide-rimmed Mexican hats. I had no idea this potluck was such a big deal.

Ramon and a group of his compadres stood around an enormous table chatting in Spanish and drinking beer. Most were dressed in fancy Western shirts with pearl buttons, Stetsons, and well-shined cowboy boots. One of the men wore a white jacket stained with blood and gravy as he sliced meat with an enormous butcher knife.

A couple of older women emerged from the house and handed the men a plate of thick tortillas. Some were decked out in bright-colored broomstick skirts, concho belts and cowgirl boots. Others wore polyester pants suits and wedge sandals. I gulped at the realization I was clearly underdressed.

To my horror, what appeared to be a pig head hung on a pole next to a large vat of boiling fat. Could it possibly be real? No, it must be papier-mâché or something. Who would display a real pig's head on a pole?

One of the men stirred the pot with a big stick. He removed globs of fat and placed them on a plate. "*Chicharrones* are ready."

The men each rolled a tortilla around pieces of the fat smothered in red chile.

Eduardo strolled out from the house with a huge iron pot full of beans and placed it on the table. He stood joking with the men in Spanish, oblivious of my presence.

I cleared my throat. "Eduardo."

He narrowed his eyes at me. "Sorry, honey, I didn't see you. Let's go inside. I'd like you to meet my sister, Carla."

"I want to say hello to your father first."

"You can say hello to him later."

I pointed at the pig's head. "Is that real?"

"Of course not."

"You're lying aren't you?"

"Yes."

"Oh my God!" The reality of a real decapitated pig head made me nauseated. I clasped my hand over my mouth and raced behind the barn where I threw up.

Eduardo arrived a few seconds later and handed me his handkerchief. "Are you okay?"

I shook my head and swallowed hard.

"I'm sorry, honey. You'll get used to it."

"I don't think so."

"Then you don't have to attend these things. We only have them a couple times a year."

"That poor pig. You cut off his head."

"No, the butcher did that. He was already dead. We kill them quite humanely."

I placed my hands on my ears. "Enough. I don't want to know more."

Eduardo walked me back to the trailer where I brushed my teeth and changed my clothes again. This time I put on the red silk sleeveless blouse and a pair of black linen slacks. We walked back to the *matanza* holding hands. Eduardo waved at the men but guided me directly into the house filled with delicious aromas. The kitchen was packed with women chatting in Spanish as they rolled tortillas, and prepared a variety of vegetable and fruit salads, potatoes, beans and chili.

When we entered the room, everyone simultaneously stopped the chopping, rolling, and stirring, and stared at me with smiles plastered on their faces. Sylvia nodded but immediately went back to slicing tomatoes and green peppers. Everyone else followed her example and returned to preparing food.

An attractive young woman wearing black jeans and a white tailored shirt stepped forward and hugged me. "I'm so glad to finally meet you."

"Laila, this is my sister, Carla," Eduardo said.

She smiled at him. "Go out with the men. I'll introduce her to everyone."

"I'll see you in a bit," Eduardo said, and then rushed off.

"This is Grandma Rosa," said Carla pointing at an old woman rolling tortillas. She grinned at me, revealing a lack of front teeth.

"And my favorite aunts, Marie and Juanita."

They each stopped chopping and dicing vegetables and hugged me.

A large woman with big black hair and thin painted eyebrows glared at me from the stove where she stood with Sylvia. "Violet will be here any minute," she shouted loud enough for everyone in the room to hear.

"That's Aunt Virgie," Carla said. "She's Mama's best friend."

The woman ignored me and said, "Wait until you see *mi hija*. She still looks like a movie star."

Violet. It was clear to me she was more than Eduardo's old high school fling. I felt like I'd stepped into a nineteenth-century Mexican *fiesta*. Everyone around me was speaking Spanish and there was a distinct separation of the sexes. The men all huddled around a fire outside, while the women sliced and diced food inside the house. While Eduardo had warned me the *matanza* might be a bit of culture shock, I had no idea it would be this alien.

Carla took my hand. "Why don't we go get some fresh air?"

I followed her outside to Eduardo who was speaking to a thin man decked out in a spiffy cowboy shirt and snakeskin boots. He had a buxom cowgirl on each arm.

Eduardo clasped my hand. "Laila, meet my cousin Billy Quintana. Billy's third in the world of bronc riding."

I smiled at him. "Wow, that's impressive." I had no idea what bronc riding was, but figured if he was third in the world at anything he deserved respect.

Billy gave me a once over but spoke directly to Eduardo. "Looks like you roped yourself one of them fancy New York chicks. A little skinny for my taste but *muy bonita*."

"Nice to meet you too." I glanced at the two cowgirls. "I'm happy to make your acquaintances."

Billy slapped both their behinds. "Go get yourselves a beer. I'll catch up with you later."

The girls smiled, and then wandered off.

Billy whispered in my ear and then ambled back over to where they stood.

I burst out laughing.

Eduardo smiled. "What did he say to you?"

"He asked me to meet him in the back of the barn in half an hour!"

Eduardo's smile widened. "Are you going?"

I smacked his arm. Before he could say anything else, a man with stringy carrot-red hair and a face full of freckles appeared in front of us.

"Who is that?"

"My cousin Rojo."

"He doesn't look like part of your family."

"Shhh. Aunt Juanita's a bit touchy on that subject."

I bit my lip. "Are you saying . . .?"

LATER THAT AFTERNOON, EDUARDO AND I STOOD listening to the mariachi music as couples shuffled around the makeshift dance floor. Ramon and Sylvia danced with Little Sylvie between them. After a few beers, I started to relax and enjoy the festivities. Everyone seemed so happy. I no longer felt alienated.

The distinctive roar of motorcycles captured my attention. Their owners, rough-looking hombres—complete with headbands, leather vests and multiple tattoos—joined the party. One of them toppled off the back of a Harley and into a wheelchair a woman brought over for him. His right arm and left leg were in casts.

I whispered to Eduardo, "Who are they?"

"That's the Sandoval side of the family. They live up north."

The guy in the wheelchair rolled up to us. "Hey cuz, long time no see."

Eduardo shook his head. "You okay, man?"

"I am now that you're here. It'll come in handy to have a doc in the *familia*." He smiled at me.

"Laila, this is my big cuz Tito. We go way back."

Tito grinned, revealing a gold front tooth. "Remember our lizard collection?"

"We must have had over a hundred different species." Eduardo said. "It's what got me interested in biology."

Tito slapped Eduardo on the back with his cast. "See, man, if it wasn't for your cuz, you wouldn't be a big-shot doctor now."

Before Eduardo responded, a young champagne-blonde stepped out of a car in a skintight leather skirt, and a thin white halter-top that displayed ample cleavage. *Was that Violet?*

Every man at the *matanza* gaped at her.

"Gotta go, that's my honey," said Tito. "She's teaching me all about genealogy, man. Amazing shit." He wheeled the chair around in the direction of the woman.

I looked at Eduardo. "What happened to him?"

"Well, he was having an affair with my cousin Nober's wife, Blanca. When Nober found out, he broke Tito's arm."

"And the leg?"

"He broke the leg when Blanca threw him down the stairs."

I squinted. "Why did she do that if they were having an affair?"

"After Nober found out about the affair, he threw Blanca out of the house. She went to live with Tito but he didn't want her anymore. So she got mad and—"

I held up my hand. "Got the picture."

Just then, an old black Cadillac clamored down the road to the barn and jerked to a stop. Seconds later, a beautiful woman with jet-black hair to her waist stepped out of the passenger door and theatrically perused the party.

Ah! Enter Violet.

A balding man, dressed in a Western shirt and jeans that looked too big for him, emerged from the driver's side.

Virgie and a few of the other women rushed up to the car. Each in turn gave the beautiful woman a hug while her friend leaned on the Cadillac wiping his sweaty face with his sleeve.

After hugging everyone, the woman walked down the path with her entourage in tow.

As she got closer, her eyes penetrated Eduardo's.

Sunlight sparkled in the gorgeous woman's hair as she floated in our direction. Her eyes remained focused on Eduardo while her friend trailed a few steps behind her. When she reached us, Eduardo locked eyes with her.

Then with a grand gesture known to all divas, she embraced him. Tears streamed down her face. "It's been too long."

He cleared his throat. "Seventeen years, no?"

"I didn't think you could get more handsome, but you are."

"Ah, I want you to meet someone. Violet, this is my girlfriend, Laila."

Violet produced a charming smile. "Nice to meet you."

"Eduardo has told me all about you." I said.

"Good. I hope we can be friends."

Friends? Who was she kidding?

"So you're here to stay then?" Eduardo asked.

"I think so. I've had it with flying. And my acting career . . ." She pointed to the guy with whom she'd arrived. Perspiration poured down his face as he jerked at the stiff collar of his shirt. "Ira, over there, is my agent, and well, not much has happened recently."

As if on cue, Ira trotted up to us and shook Eduardo's hand.

Violet ignored both Ira and me, and chatted on with Eduardo about people they knew in high school.

Ira smiled at me. "You don't look like you're from these parts."

"New York."

"I knew it." He pointed his thumbs at his chest. "Los Angeles."

"So you're just visiting?"

"A few more days. Beautiful country." He touched Violet's elbow. "Honey, where's all that great food you told me about?"

I figured if he was calling her honey, he must be more than just her agent.

Violet continued her eye lock with Eduardo like he was the only one in the universe. "I hear you bought old Doc Lopez's practice."

"Yes, we just got home last week."

"Such a coincidence. I've just been back a short while too. It feels real . . ."

Her words slurred and then she fell to the ground.

Eduardo tried to catch her but it was too late. He took off his shirt, and rolled it up as a makeshift pillow for her head.

She awoke slowly and stared at him.

"Someone run get my medical bag. It's in the trailer up the road."

One of the *hombres* hopped on his motorcycle and zoomed off.

Eduardo lifted Violet and carried her to the house with all

the women in tow.

Ira and I stood awkwardly alone together. He shook his head. "Not the first time she's done that."

"Are you and she—?"

"It's a complicated relationship."

"Aren't they all?" I said.

"Hey, I've got some toot in the car if you wanna party."

"College is over." I frowned at him, and then jogged off toward the house.

"Hey, don't leave me alone out here." He trailed behind me huffing and puffing to keep up.

Sylvia was surrounded by a number of the women in the kitchen. I walked up to Violet's mother who stood off to the side of the crowd. "How's your daughter?"

"In good hands," she said. "Eduardo's taking care of her."

"Where are they?"

"*En Sylvia's dormitorio.*"

"Ah, in Sylvia's bedroom." I turned and headed down the hall toward the master bedroom.

"You can't go in there!" shouted Virgie.

"Why not?"

Sylvia stepped forward. "They don't want to be disturbed."

"What?" It took me a moment for her words to register. Then I did an about-face and tore out of the house.

Behind me Ira said, "Is there anything to eat around here?" He clearly was in culture shock too.

But mine was so much more than culture shock. A blind rage swept over me. Had my life really come to this? I'd been so careful protecting myself after Julian. And here I was, two thousand miles away from everything and everyone I knew. Betrayed once again.

CHAPTER TWENTY-SIX
The Misunderstanding

Laila

As a burnt-orange sun set over the mountains, I raced full-throttle down the road to the trailer. What was I thinking following a man to Nowhere, New Mexico, where I was isolated from the most basic city amenities, and subjected to crude traditions like cutting off a pig's head? Worst of all, I had to endure snide remarks and stony-faced hostility from his mother.

I stripped out of my clothes, showered, and changed into my comfort clothes: an oversized Yankees T-shirt and shaggy slippers with puppy-dog heads. Then I padded into the kitchen and fed the animals.

After pouring myself a healthy glass of Chardonnay, I sat musing over my options. A sane woman would admit she'd made a big mistake and hightail it back to New York. But would a sane woman ever have come out here in the first place? Had I become so desperate for love after Julian, that I'd lost all semblance of rational thought?

I turned on the TV and watched episodes of *Rhoda* and *All in the Family*, comforted by their New York locales. But they only exacerbated my feelings of homesickness. By the time *Kojak* ended and the local news came on, I was so furious I could barely breathe. Eduardo had been gone for five hours. Where the hell was he? I grabbed the phone from the cradle and dialed my old apartment.

Rachel picked up on the fourth ring. Her voice was barely a whisper. "Hello."

It suddenly dawned on me that it was midnight on the East Coast. "I'm sorry, Rachel. I just remembered the time difference. I'm so sorry."

"It's okay, Sista. *Como estás?*"

"Please skip the Spanish. I've had enough of it for a lifetime."

"What's the matter?"

I confided everything that had transpired in the last few weeks ending with the Violet scenario.

"It sounds challenging," she said.

"Ya think I should come home?"

"I wouldn't leave so quickly."

"But I'm miserable."

"Bottom line, do you think Eduardo would cheat on you?"

"Things are still so hot between us. But he's been gone for hours."

"Does he have feelings for this Violet chick?"

The squeal of tires out front would soon answer my sister's question. "He's opening the front door. I'll call you back tomorrow."

Eduardo's face was pale and his eyelids drooped.

Brooklyn nuzzled up to him and then Zorro nudged her away.

He smiled and petted each animal in turn. "Don't fight over me, girls,"

"Admit it. You just love all of us 'girls' fighting over the big country doctor."

"What are you talking about?"

"If you expect me to hang around and 'fight for my man,' you're kidding yourself."

His posture stiffened. "Jesus, Laila, she passed out."

"I'm well aware of that."

"I'm a doctor. What did you want me to do, call 911?"

I gave him the finger.

He shook his head. "I've never seen you like this."

"This place brings out the worst in me."

"What are you so mad about?"

"Did you have to hang out in your mama's bedroom with the door closed? And why are you so late?"

"I didn't close the door. You could have come inside anytime you wanted."

"That's not what Virgie and Mama said."

He tried to hug me, but I yanked him away. "Okay," he began. "I admit . . . Mama and Virgie would like to see Violet and me back together."

"Big of you to admit that. What about the fact your mother is downright horrible to me. Can you acknowledge that?"

"I grant you her behavior has been less than stellar."

"Less than stellar? That's the understatement of the century."

He stroked my hand with his fingers. "I honestly didn't realize how unhappy you've been."

I snatched my hand away. "What took you so long to get home?"

"I checked Violet into the hospital in Española for some tests. For the record, it's been over with us for a long, long time."

"You could have fooled me."

"I care about her as a friend, that's all. Why would I want hamburger when I have steak at home?"

"You and those crazy cowboy expressions." Yet, they were oddly charming to me.

"Come here." He held out his arms. "You know, this is our first real fight."

"If you don't count the one we had over me helping out Rachel."

"How about some makeup sex?"

I half-smiled, almost ready to give in. Was I a fool to believe him? Or a bigger fool to doubt him?

CHAPTER TWENTY-SEVEN
Cecil's Motor Cars

Eduardo

Eduardo lay snuggled in bed with Laila. Violet's arrival at the *matanza* had clearly unnerved her. He hoped he'd convinced her that his romantic feelings for his high school sweetheart no longer existed.

Sleep eluded him. After staring at the popcorn ceiling for over an hour he slipped out of bed and made himself some of Laila's Constant Comment herbal tea. Seeing Violet today had brought him the closure that had evaded him for all these years. While she was still very beautiful, he was shocked and seriously worried about her emotional and physical state.

They had spent a long time talking at Presbyterian-Española Hospital. Eduardo sat with her chart in a plastic chair next to the bed. Violet's eyes were unfocused as she rattled on about her life in semi-incoherent sentences. "I hate Ira," she said. "Hate, hate, hate him! He's one big pain in the ass." She sounded delirious.

"Then why did you bring him to Sabinal?"

She sighed. "There's so very much you don't know about me, Eduardo."

"Of course," he said. "I haven't seen you in years."

"But we've always had a connection." Her hands were shaking and her skin looked as frail as tissue.

"Yes, of course." He thought about the years he'd pined for her. "Are you on some type of drugs, Violet?"

"How dare you ask me that, asshole!"

His eyebrows shot up. No doubt she was on drugs. He had ordered blood work and would know soon enough. "I'm sorry."

She put her hand over his. Her eyes watered. "Forgive me. You're the one person in the world I trust. In fact, I think I'm still in—"

"Don't go there, Violet. At this point we're practically strangers."

"I know you, Eduardo. Better than some skinny girl from New York. We both know Laila will never survive life in Sabinal." She smiled slyly, aware she'd hit a nerve.

Eduardo changed the topic. "Tell me about your life in L.A."

She chewed her lip before speaking. "Cecil McDougal, do you remember that bastard?" Her voice grew deep and raspy.

"The name sounds familiar."

"Cecil's Motor Cars in Española. Does it ring a bell?"

"Of course. He still has a billboard on I-25," Eduardo said.

"The bastard died last year of a heart attack. His sons-in-law run the car lot now."

"So what about Cecil?"

"When I was a girl, Mama used to take me there every Monday night while Daddy was at work. "Uncle Cecil" had a trailer behind the car lot. He always gave me a Tootsie Roll lollipop and I'd watch a little portable TV while he and Mama hung out in the back bedroom."

Eduardo shook his head. "This is none of my business."

"But I want you to know. Do you recall how my Papa died?"

"He had a heart attack, no?"

"I told him about Mama and Cecil. Mama was pregnant.

It never occurred to me that Cecil might be the father." Tears spilled down her cheeks. "After school the next afternoon, I found Papa hunched over in his La-Z-Boy. It was all my fault."

"It wasn't your fault, Violet."

"Juanita was born six months after Papa died. Daddy's name is on her birth certificate. But she's no Sanchez."

"You should get counseling."

"No way. It's all in the past, as are all the men in L.A. who—"

"Who what?"

"Never mind."

What a terrible burden for Violet to carry around all these years. But Eduardo was more worried about her current behavior. No doubt in his mind, she was on drugs. He just needed to find out which ones so he could help her recover.

WHEN EDUARDO RETURNED TO BED, HE GLANCED OVER at Laila. "Are you asleep?"

"Now I'm not," she said in a groggy voice.

He pointed to the dog and cat cuddled together on their pillow bed. "If they can work things out, I don't see why we can't."

"You get an A minus for the analogy, but I'll never fit in here."

"That's not true. You need to get started on your research. Why don't you come to work with me tomorrow? I've arranged for you to interview some pregnant teens."

"Wow, that's great."

"And then I'll take the afternoon off and we'll go to Santa Fe."

"Really? I've been wanting to see *Annie Hall.*"

"What's that?"

She rolled her eyes at him. "It's only the hottest new movie out right now. I should have known you wouldn't know about it."

He didn't miss the snootiness in her tone. "Geez, forgive me for not hearing about a new movie." He honestly had no idea why she found this to be such a big deal.

CHAPTER TWENTY-EIGHT
Violet's Disappointment

Violet

At 7:15 a.m. Violet had already embellished herself with a dewy face of Estée Lauder foundation, rosy powder blush, lip-gloss, and a touch of mascara, attempting to look like she hadn't put makeup on at all. Dressed in a slinky black negligee that Ira had brought over last night, along with her toiletries, she hoped that Eduardo would stop by on his morning rounds. She was still groggy from the Valium drip she'd begged off a naive young nurse with buzzed red hair and a face of freckles. The girl had told Violet it was her first night on the job. Easy, peasy.

Two hours passed as Violet waited for Eduardo, but so far there was no sign of him. The new shift nurse, an old bitch whose arms jiggled like loose Jell-O, entered the room. "You've been discharged, Miss Sanchez. Call someone to pick you up." She licked her finger, turned the page of Violet's chart, and slid her reading glasses up her stub nose. "Who authorized the Valium drip?"

Violet ignored her as she applied another coat of gloss.

Miss High-and-Mighty sniffed, "I'll get to the bottom of this," and waddled from the room. *Poor little freckle girl will probably get fired before she receives her first paycheck.*

Violet refused to leave the hospital until she had a chance to speak with Eduardo. Last night had been a total disaster. She could not remember specifically what she'd said to him, but she knew in her drug-induced state it hadn't been a pretty picture. Damn. She had blown a perfect chance to woo him away from the clutches of the chick from New York.

Hushed voices outside the room interrupted her thoughts. *Thank you, God for listening to me. I won't forget this.* Violet propped herself up and primped her hair.

Mama entered the room with a breakfast burrito and a giant Styrofoam cup of coffee. "Why aren't you ready to go home?"

Violet sank back into the pillows at the sight of her mother. "Because, dear Mama, I was waiting for Eduardo. Come back later."

"No way. Your sister is coming home from detective school this afternoon."

"You mean half-sister."

"*Cállate la Boca.* Shut your mouth."

"We both know who her daddy was. Too bad Cecil never divorced his wife and married you."

"If you ever say that again I'll—"

"You'll what? Kill me? Like you did Daddy."

Mama's eyes brimmed with tears. "Why are you bringing this up now?"

Violet was furious at herself for screwing up a chance to win back Eduardo. There was no reason to take it out on Mama. For years Violet had been blaming everything wrong in her sorry life on her mother. She wasn't sure why. "Forgive me Mama, I'm not myself these days."

"Of course you're not, *hija.* You're sick, and Eduardo will help make you better."

"I hope so."

"Get dressed. It will cheer you up to have lunch with

Juanita. It's been so long since you've seen her. She's grown up to be a beauty just like you."

About the last thing Violet wanted right now was to see a younger version of herself. Juanita was eight years her junior. Violet had resented her from the day she was born. "I'm not going home until Eduardo stops by."

"I can't afford to pay for you to stay another day. The lady at the desk—"

"Okay." Violet stepped out of bed and stood on the cold tile floor. But she felt so shaky she had to grasp onto the bed rail to keep from falling down.

"What's wrong with you?"

"I-I don't know." But she did. She and Ira had done a shitload of coke before they'd gone to the *matanza* yesterday. Between the hot New Mexico sun, all that blow, beer and the Valium, she felt wretched. As she steadied herself, Eduardo sailed into the room holding a clipboard.

Violet smiled, positively thrilled that he'd seen her standing in the black lace negligee that showed off her cleavage and clung to her curves. She took a few deep breaths and hoisted herself back on the bed.

"Eduardo!" Mama held out her arms for a hug. "Should I be calling you Dr. Quintana?"

"Of course not, Aunt Virgie." He turned to Violet. "I thought you'd be gone by now. When I saw you didn't have insurance, I released you this morning. How are you feeling?"

She swept a lock of hair from her forehead. "Better, now that you're here."

Mama headed to the door. "I'll leave you two."

"You can stay." Eduardo said. "I'm just going to—"

Before he could finish his sentence, Mama had flown out the door.

Violet took his hand. "There's so much I want to say."

"There's no need."

"There is. I know this whole business with our mamas is making you uncomfortable."

"I don't want Laila to feel—"

"Like she's not wanted here," Violet said.

"I hope I haven't given you or your mama the wrong impression somehow."

"Of course not. And I want you to forget anything I said last night. I was sick and . . . I-I just want you to be happy, Eduardo. If Laila's the one, I will leave you alone. I had my chance, and I blew it many years ago."

He squeezed her hand. "I only want the best for you too, Violet."

"Then we can be friends?" she said in a chirpy voice.

"Of course. But we need to find out what's going on with you. I'll have the test results in a couple of days."

"Sounds good." That meant he would have to see her again. And this time she had a plan.

CHAPTER TWENTY-NINE
Peaches, Brenda and Mandy

Laila

I had never been to Eduardo's office before. We drove through Española, past the Dairy Queen, some old motels, three bars, and two gas stations. B-O-R-I-N-G.

As if Eduardo could read my mind he said, "You know the Spanish founded Española over twenty years before the Pilgrims landed at Plymouth Rock. It was known as the Jewel of Northern New Mexico."

I looked around at the dismal landscape where trailers sat squarely beside stucco homes. Low riders jammed up traffic on Main Street as they rumbled alongside old pickups stacked with firewood. "Where are they hiding the jewels?"

He chuckled. "You'll get used to it, honey."

Eduardo parked the Studebaker in front of a small tin-roofed adobe house located in the Plaza de Española. Stenciled on the front window was the following:

DR. EDUARDO QUINTANA - FAMILY PRACTICE

Eduardo introduced me to his receptionist, Yolanda, an older Hispanic woman sporting a tight perm and coke-bottle glasses. She sat typing on an IBM Selectric. To my surprise and delight, she stood up, walked over, and gave me a hug. "Eduardo's told me you were *muy bonita*. So nice to finally meet you."

"Pleased to meet you too." If only Sylvia were half as nice to me.

Three teenage girls with protruding round bellies sat in the waiting area chatting and giggling.

An old man in a wheelchair, accompanied by his wife whose hands were gnarled with arthritis, sat on the other side of the room.

Eduardo walked over to the old couple. *"Buenos dias, Señor y Señora Ortiz."*

Yolanda escorted them to an examining room.

Eduardo turned to the girls. "Peaches, Brenda and Mandy, please follow me. Dr. Levin, you come too."

We walked through a hallway that led to examining rooms and offices.

A small sign that read DR. LAILA LEVIN was posted on the door of the room we entered. A beautiful old Navajo rug hung over an antique rolltop desk with a plush leather chair. Four vinyl seats sat across from the desk. Thanks to Eduardo, my very first office was beyond my dreams. For the first time since I'd arrived in New Mexico, I felt like I had a purpose for being there. "This is amazing."

Eduardo grinned. "I hoped you'd like it." He turned to the pregnant girls and pointed at the chair. "Have a seat, ladies. You're going to spend some time with Dr. Levin before I examine you." He asked each girl to state their name, age, and where they'd grown up.

Peaches, a petite Hispanic girl with big teased hair, spoke first. "I grew up in Sabinal just down the road from Dr. Quintana's *familia.*"

I leaned back in my plush new leather chair. "And how old are you?"

"I just had my *quinceañera*."

"What's that?"

"It's like a coming-out party for girls when they turn fifteen," Eduardo said.

"Ahh. Like a sweet-sixteen party a year early," I said.

"Something like that," he muttered.

Brenda, a bleached blonde with exposed black roots, was also fifteen and grew up in Española.

The third girl, Mandy, a rail-thin Anglo girl with coppery hair and stooped posture, refused to speak. She looked down at her red cowboy boots.

"Mandy don't like to talk much," Peaches said. "She grew up in Santa Fe. But she's staying with me right now."

I rubbed the back of my neck. "Why is that?"

"She don't want her Mama to know she's pregnant," Peaches said.

Eduardo stood in the doorway. "I'm going to leave you girls now. Please cooperate with Dr. Levin."

Peaches flapped her hands. "Why should we talk to *her*?"

"Dr. Quintana has offered to waive his fees if you participate in some research I'm conducting," I said.

Brenda tugged at her collar. "Are you a real doctor?"

"I have a doctorate in sociology."

"Dr. Levin's degree is every bit as real as mine," said Eduardo. "She's doing research on teen pregnancies."

"Okay with me," said Peaches. "I didn't know how I was gonna pay."

"Shoot, free exams. I'm in," said Brenda.

Mandy remained quiet chewing on her finger.

I turned my attention to her. "How about you?"

She shrugged but said nothing.

"I'll see you girls later then," Eduardo said, closing the door behind him.

I removed my cassette player from my purse. "Does anyone mind if we tape these sessions?"

The girls looked at each other. "As long as my *vato* don't hear it," said Peaches.

"I'm going to use parts of your stories in my book. But your names will be changed. And your identities will remain private."

"Cool," said Peaches, who clearly was the leader of the pack. The other two girls nodded.

"Okee-dokey, then." I switched on the tape recorder. "The first thing I need to ask you—"

"Okee-dokey?" mimicked Peaches. All three girls burst out laughing.

I joined in, chuckling along with them.

The girls continued giggling, quite literally howling out of control.

After a few minutes, I said, "Enough! We need to get started now."

Brenda belched.

Peaches poked her swollen stomach.

Mandy took a cigarette from her large macramé purse, noticed me glaring at her, and then stashed it back in her bag.

I cleared my throat. "Have any of you heard of condoms?"

Peaches wrinkled her nose. "*Mi vato* says he don't feel nothing with one of them things."

Mandy toyed with a lock of hair.

"How about the pill or IUDs?"

Once again, Peaches spoke. "I was an A student, never made no trouble at home. My mama would have killed me if she found birth control pills."

I leaned forward. "But how'd she react when she found out you were pregnant?"

"Mama cried a very long time," Peaches said.

Brenda spoke up. "Mine smacked me across the face and called me a fucking *puta*."

I gulped. "What's a *puta?*"

Peaches smirked. "You don't know what a *puta* is?"

"It means a whore," said Mandy, speaking up in a husky voice for the first time.

"Oh." A lump formed in my throat as I tried not to appear judgmental or even surprised. "Did your mama throw you out of the house?"

"Nah," said Brenda. "After a couple of days, she started shopping garage sales for cribs and shit."

I drew in my breath, and then slowly exhaled. "So your mothers plan to help you raise your babies?"

"Why not?" asked Peaches. "Mama helps my sister Virgina raise her *niño.*"

I shook my head. "What about the fathers?"

"*Mi vato* don't have a job," Brenda said.

"Mine don't want nothing to do with the baby," Peaches said.

I leaned forward in the chair. "Are you sure about that, Peaches?"

"He dumped me just like he did to my sister when he knocked her up."

Brenda's brows snapped together. "Marcus knocked you both up?"

"He's a motherfucker, all right," Peaches said.

I tried not to wince as a lump formed in my throat. It took me a moment to compose myself. Then I turned to Mandy. "What about you?"

Patches of red bloomed on her cheeks and neck.

I restrained the temptation to hug her. "What's the matter, honey?"

She stayed silent. Tears rained down her cheeks and pooled in dark spots on her collar.

Peaches clasped her hand. "She's just embarrassed 'cause she don't know who the daddy is."

My jaw dropped.

Peaches glared at me. "You can stop looking down your nose at her."

"I-I'm not. Just surprised is all." Their stories were heartbreaking. "Do any of you plan on finishing high school?"

"Nah," said Peaches. "As soon as I'm old enough, my sister Virginia is gonna get me a job at El Rio."

Brenda touched Peaches arm. "Can she get me in there too? I hear the waitresses make great tips."

"She does pretty good. But she says the *viejos* pinch her butt all the time."

"If you finish school, you could become a teacher, or doctor, or maybe an engineer. That's a lot better than a job where *viejos* pinch your butt," I said.

"Or hey, we could end up a sociologist living in an old trailer like you." Peaches nodded her head and manufactured a self-satisfied smile.

I was surprised she knew about my living arrangements. But then I remembered she just lived down the road in Sabinal. I laughed. "Yes, that is a possibility." My laughter was all I could do to keep from crying. "That's enough for today. We'll see you girls again next Tuesday."

Eduardo appeared in my office after the girls left. "How did the interviews go?"

"They were very emotional. But their irresponsible behavior is beyond my comprehension. They don't appear to regret their situations. And for the most part, their mothers are enabling them."

The muscles in Eduardo's jaw tightened. "In the Latino culture, the *familia* is everything. We take care of our own."

"How is it good to encourage little girls to have infants they can't take care of?"

"Look," he said, "I know firsthand about the merry-go-round of problems those girls face."

"If they'd consider abortion—"

"Abortion is not an option for these girls. Do you understand?"

"I understand more than you think. Rachel got pregnant right after high school. She agonized over what to do before marrying Bob. That's how I first became interested in teen pregnancies."

"We'll talk later," he said. "I need to see a few more patients before we leave for Santa Fe."

I felt like I'd landed on an alien planet. While I'd studied all the statistics, I was unprepared for the reality of an impoverished culture that so enabled teen pregnancy. My research would be much more complex than I'd ever imagined. Even worse, I had serious doubts that teaching girls about birth control would improve the scenario. No amount of education could change the deep cultural mores of a population that didn't want change. Nor would they trust the advice of an outsider. Between the personal rejection of Eduardo's mother, and now the professional rejection of these young women, I feared my move to New Mexico was probably a huge mistake.

CHAPTER THIRTY
Santa Fe

Laila

After clinic, Eduardo and I drove down to Santa Fe to meet Carla and her husband. I had never spent any time in Santa Fe during my years as a student at UNM. From the minute we arrived, I was enthralled by the culture and diversity. Tourists with cameras, men in cowboy hats, city dwellers in chic outfits, and a couple of old hippies promenaded past upscale galleries and shops in Santa Fe's sienna-and-pastel adobe buildings. Low riders with mirror-like paint jobs were joined by minivans and Mercedes, Lincolns and Cadillacs . . . all parading down Canyon Road.

We followed a vintage Chevy into a parking lot. I stepped out of the Studebaker with a wide grin. Why hadn't Eduardo brought me here before?

He locked the car and took my hand as we sauntered through Cathedral Park to the Romanesque St. Francis Cathedral. We passed by spiffy shops, and galleries full of contemporary art, Indian paintings, turquoise jewelry, pottery and pricey rugs. On the plaza, Indians from various pueblos sat next to their wares displayed on blankets.

I bent down to look closer at a ten-inch ceramic Indian woman with babies crawling all over her.

"This called a Storyteller," said the old Indian woman wrapped in a colorful shawl. "Pick up if you like." The woman handed it to me and pointed at the signature on the back. "My sister make this. She very famous."

"Look at the babies," I said to Eduardo. "They're so cute."

"Storyteller symbolic gift to those who want to have baby."

I counted the little ceramic babies on the Indian mother and smiled. "Nine is a bit much . . . don't you think, honey?"

Eduardo leaned down to have a closer look at the Storyteller. "I've always wanted a big family."

My eyebrows twitched.

He smiled. "Okay, maybe seven."

"You're not serious?"

"I'd compromise at five."

The Indian woman squinted. "You want to buy Storyteller?"

I handed it back to her. "I don't think so."

As we continued walking down the row of vendors, Eduardo looked me square in the eye. "You do want children?"

"Children, yes. A tribe, no."

"Mama wanted a big *familia*. If it wasn't for Papa having a vasectomy, they probably would have had a dozen or so."

"Wow! Isn't a vasectomy, like . . . anti-Catholic?"

"Very unusual, to say the least for a Hispanic-Catholic man of his generation. But Mama refused to use any birth control. She took the Pope at his word."

"Your father was more practical, and ahead of his time."

"Mama had terrible pregnancies. He knew she couldn't take much more."

"He's a real special guy, isn't he?"

Eduardo nodded. "My best friend in the world."

"My ex-husband hated his father."

"Your ex-husband?"

I sighed. "Didn't I tell you about Julian?"

"I would have remembered that."

"You never mentioned I would be competing with the lovely Violet. Besides, we were only married for—"

"Laila!" said a familiar voice. "Is that you?"

I glanced over at an earthy, overweight woman dressed in sweatpants and a large T-shirt. As we drew closer, her blonde hair and face of freckles looked very familiar.

She smiled. "Laila?"

"Allison? Allison Patrick?"

"One and the same. But my last name is Harvey now." I'd met her in my dorm at UNM and, like my roommate Katie Birnbaum, she'd been a transplant from New York. That fact had bonded her to me. I was beginning to realize how much I now craved to be around people from New York.

"This is my boyfriend, Eduardo."

"Nice to meet you." She extended her hand.

Eduardo shook it and charmed her with his perfect smile. "The pleasure's mine."

Allison turned to me. "I thought you had gone back East."

"I did for a while. But as you can see I am back here in the Land of Enchantment. And yourself?"

"Never left. I live here in Santa Fe." She suddenly laughed. "Remember that Shakespeare Tragedies class we took together?"

I giggled. "How could I forget? We pulled how many all-nighters and I squeaked out a C."

"And those sangrias at Okie Joes." She looked at Eduardo. "You two should visit us sometime. My husband Leo and I live just outside of town." She fished out a piece of paper from her purse, wrote down her phone number, and handed it to me. "I've got to rush off, or I'll be late for my doctor appointment.

Call me." She gave me a warm hug and hurried down the road.

Eduardo pointed across the street at a thin woman with long brown hair and a tall Hispanic man. "There's Carla and her husband Rando. We need to talk later."

I stuck Allison's information in my purse. "Talk about what?"

"Your omission."

"My what?"

"Your marriage."

Carla greeted us with warm hugs. "It's so good to see you again, Laila."

We spent the day checking out his sister's favorite art galleries and the Georgia O'Keeffe Museum. As Eduardo predicted, his sister and I hit it off well. We all sat chatting and drinking the infamous margaritas at the Pink Adobe restaurant. While Eduardo and Rando talked about sports and politics, Carla asked lots of questions about my family and my research. She winked at Eduardo and joked how their mother had been "razzing" me.

I winced as she made light of the serious pain her mother had inflicted. But I didn't share how deeply Sylvia had hurt me. "Who told you?"

Carla laughed. "There are no secrets in the Quintana family. Give Mama some time. She'll get used to you," Carla said.

"That's what Eduardo says, but I'm not so sure."

She clasped my hand. "Please don't give up on our *familia*. Eduardo is so smitten with you."

On the way home, I got right to the point. "Your sister has

persuaded me to give my life with you in Sabinal a little more time."

Eduardo's clenched his jaw. "You were thinking about leaving?"

It troubled me how oblivious he was about how unhappy I'd been . . . the backward world in Sabinal, living in a trailer, and most of all, the disdain of his mother. Everything was on his terms. Did he not know I was homesick for my family and life in New York? How unwelcome his mother continued to make me feel? No, he appeared clueless to it all.

CHAPTER THIRTY-ONE
The Fight

Eduardo

Eduardo didn't mention anything further about Laila's former marriage on the drive back to Sabinal, but he was fuming just the same. He wasn't angry about her being married before, but was incensed that she had omitted telling him about such an important life event. On the other hand, Laila appeared happier than she'd been since her arrival in New Mexico. He debated if he should even bring it up, ruin what had otherwise been a perfect day. It probably was best to wait until Laila was more acclimated to her life in Sabinal. But he couldn't deny that her omission made his Latino blood boil. Years ago, he had been devastated by an important omission of Violet's.

Later in bed, he and Laila made love with such intensity that Eduardo felt literally drunk, despite the fact he'd had nothing to drink for hours. She smiled up at him so lovingly he felt she'd touched his soul through the prism of physical pleasure.

Afterwards, they lay wordlessly holding hands, staring at the cluster of stars shimmering in the New Mexican sky through a skylight above the bed. "Can I get you anything?" he finally asked, after fifteen minutes of silence.

"Some water would be great."

He stood up, slid on his boxers, and walked to the kitchen. "I had such a great time today," Laila said, when he returned with two tall glasses of ice water. "We should go to Santa Fe more often."

Intellectually, he knew it best to keep his mouth shut about her omission, but his emotions won out. He could hold it in no longer. "I'd like to talk about Julian."

Laila's body stiffened. "You make passionate love to me and *now* you want to discuss my former marriage?"

She had a point. "I didn't plan it that way."

"What do you want to know?"

Brooklyn nudged Zorro to make room in the bed.

Zorro hissed and raised a threatening paw at the dog. Brooklyn growled back at her.

"Stop it, you two," Laila said.

Eduardo sat on the edge of the bed. "When we began dating, you claimed you'd been celibate for two years."

Laila's cheeks burned. "What do you mean 'claimed'? I *was* celibate for two years."

"I just want to make sure you weren't omitting anything else."

"What is that supposed to mean?"

"I can't believe you never told me you were married before."

"Would that have made a difference?" She looked at the dog. "Come here, honey." Brooklyn jumped on her lap.

The cat leaped onto Eduardo. She purred as he petted her behind the ears. "You should have mentioned it."

"It's so insignificant."

"Marriage is insignificant?"

"If you'd let me finish."

"What's there to say?"

"A lot." She told him about the duration of her marriage and the cause of the annulment.

Eduardo was stunned. He tried to imagine her humiliation. "I'm sorry. I had no idea."

"One of the worst days of my life, for sure."

"What could be worse than that?"

She paused for a minute. Was there something else she wasn't telling him? "Not much."

"You still should have told me about it."

"It would have been nice if you'd mentioned you had some hot Latina and her big fat mama waiting for you here like vultures in the tumbleweeds."

"I didn't know Violet would be here."

"And let me be clear with you on another thing. This gal ain't having ten *bambinos,* either."

"What's wrong with a big *familia?*"

"Nothing, if you like being barefoot and pregnant," she sniffed.

His smile widened. "I'll let you keep your Birkenstocks."

"Yuk, yuk. How the hell could we afford to get the tribe through college?"

"If they don't go to some fancy school like NYU?"

"I went to UNM for most of undergraduate school. But when I got to NYU for my doctorate program, I discovered there's a big difference between a top-rated private school and a mediocre state university."

"Not everyone can afford private school. Some of us had to pay our own way."

"I paid my way with loans and scholarships."

"And a little help from Mommy and Daddy, no?"

"F you!"

"I don't like omissions, Laila."

"I thought we were done with that topic."

"Just checking if you've forgotten to mention anything else."

She threw his pillow at him. "Why don't you sleep out on the couch?"

"Fine." Eduardo lunged from the bed and left the room. The cat crept behind and snuggled next to him on the lumpy couch in the living room.

Damn, this was exactly what he hadn't wanted to happen. Now Laila would feel even more alienated than before and might seriously consider returning to New York. From the beginning, Eduardo had known that living out in Sabinal would be difficult for Laila, but he naively assumed that their love would overcome the obstacles of parking a city girl in the country. As he lay on the couch with Zorro cuddled next to him, he came to a serious realization. If he wanted Laila to make a life with him, he'd better start paying more attention to what was going on in her life.

CHAPTER THIRTY-TWO
The Studie

Laila

The next morning, I awoke with a jolt, following a nightmare that involved my college boyfriend, his best friend and my roommate. It was a recurring dream that never made sense when I woke up.

The aroma of fresh coffee filled the trailer. After washing up in the tiny trailer bathroom, I headed to the living room still dressed in my extra-large UNM T-shirt and fuzzy slippers. I found Zorro perched on the couch. "Eduardo."

No answer.

"Are you here?"

I stumbled into the kitchen where I discovered car keys and a note scribbled in Eduardo's handwriting on the table.

"I caught a ride into Española with Kiki. Feel free to drive the Studie. Let's talk more tonight. Love, Eduardo"

I poured myself a cup of coffee and sat down at the table. It had been stupid of me not to tell Eduardo about Julian. For two years I'd done my best to bury the memory . . . pretend it never happened. Everyone except Eve made a point not to bring up the topic. I had misjudged what a big deal it would be to Eduardo.

All at once it dawned on me that he was madder at me for keeping a secret than the secret itself. When he returned later, I'd share that epiphany and hope he'd forgive me. But I still wrestled with the concept of whether an omission was a secret.

Did I need to share everything about my former life? Had he shared everything about his with me?

I decided to surprise Eduardo with a romantic candlelit dinner. I'd make my signature dish, spinach lasagna, a foolproof recipe that would take me most of the day to prepare. But first, I would practice my Spanish. If Sylvia was ever going to accept me, I needed to learn her language. Could I turn things around with her? Perhaps we could start over. I would stop off at his parents' house to get directions to a grocery store. As I got dressed, I popped in a conversational Spanish tape in the cassette player in my bedroom:

VOICE ON TAPE: Lesson Four: At the Airport

Where is the bathroom please? *Donde está el baño, por favor?* Repeat.

ME: *Donde está el baño, por favor?*

The Spanish tape continued.

VOICE ON TAPE: Where can I find a doctor? *Donde está un medico?* Repeat.

ME: *Donde está a medico?*

VOICE ON TAPE: I need a surgeon, please. *Necesito un cirjuano, por favor.*

ME: *Necesito un cirjuano, por favor.*

VOICE ON TAPE: Lesson Five: Parts of the Body

Head. *Cabeza.* Repeat.

ME: *Cabeza*

Brain. *Cerebro.* Repeat.

ME: *Cerebro.* Who cares? I'd had enough!

A short time later, I sat in the driver's seat of the Studebaker. Springs popped out through the torn upholstery and pinched my tush. When I tried to adjust the side mirror, it broke off and fell into the dirt. I left it there, turned on the ignition, slipped the gearshift into neutral, and stepped on the gas. The engine sputtered and then stalled out. Putt-putt-putt, then nothing. Finally, after numerous tries, it purred to life.

The Studie peeled out of the driveway and motored down the road toward the Quintana house. The jury was still out on whether I would be happy here in Sabinal. Yesterday's visit to Eduardo's practice and the tour of Santa Fe had put a few more plusses on the list to give my life here more time. The office Eduardo had set up for me was the perfect place for my research. And the city of Santa Fe made me feel like I was back in real civilization. If we made a point to meet Carla and Rando for dinner, catch an occasional movie (first on the list, *Annie Hall*), check out the galleries and museums on a regular basis, my life here *might* work. There was even a world-renowned opera house right outside the city of Santa Fe. The cultural significance of having a universally respected venue resonated with me. I also planned to follow up on my friend Allison's invitation.

The Studie, which had been puttering along fine, suddenly stalled. A few minutes later, I managed to get it running again, but it made jerky movements forward like a drunken frog hopping down the dirt road.

Halfway to the Quintanas' house, two of Eduardo's cousins, dressed in cowboy attire, sat on horses, pointed at the Studie and smiled. One wiggled his eyebrows.

The Studie continued to lurch through the plumes of dust. It finally jerked to a stop in front of the Quintanas' barn.

Ramon's pickup was parked next to an old black Cadillac which as I came to remember, belonged to Violet's boyfriend. What were they doing here?

Ramon stood loading bags of feed onto his truck. He looked up, smiled, and waved.

I waved back, turned off the engine, and stepped outside.

"Having trouble with Eduardo's old jalopy?"

"I've never driven a stick shift before."

"Why didn't he teach you?"

I shrugged. "Can you give me directions to a supermarket?"

"Of course. But first, do me a favor and go inside and say hello to the wife. Then, come get me at the corral and I'll give you directions. Also, if you want, I'll teach you how to drive that old jalopy."

"You must have better things to do."

"Nothing is more important than making sure you are comfortable here in Sabinal. *Mi familia* has been in the ranching business for three-hundred years. If there's one thing I've learned, you need new bloodlines to keep a healthy herd."

One thing was certain about Ramon. He didn't mince his words or sugarcoat his intentions.

When I hesitated entering the house, he dusted off his jeans with his hands, wiped his boots on the front doormat, and told me to follow him. The now-familiar aroma of spicy Mexican food filled my senses as we walked into the kitchen.

Violet sat at the large oak table with Little Sylvie on her lap. She was speaking with the toddler in Spanish. There was no sign of her boyfriend.

Sylvia stood at the stove stirring a pot of beans. When she saw us, she shot me a hard look, and an even nastier one at Ramon.

He leaned forward and kissed her forehead. "I'll leave you ladies now."

I cleared my throat. "Hello Sylvia."

She forced a tense smile but said nothing.

"Laila, right?" Violet said.

"Yes. It's nice to see you again, Violet."

She smiled at Sylvia. "*Y conoce mi nombre.* She knows my name."

"*Y ella sabe mi nombre,* and she knows my name," Sylvia said with a smirk.

Violet grinned. "*A genuine cirujano cerebro.*"

They giggled like two schoolgirls.

I mouthed the words. "*Cirujano cerebro.*" They were so familiar.

"Lailee," Sylvia said. "I thought you went back to *Nueva York.*"

Why would she think that? "Nope, still here. And my name is Laila with an A." The futility of befriending Sylvia was clear enough, but the cruel camaraderie of Violet and her caused my throat to constrict. I could barely swallow. Was there anything left for me to say? Without a word, I tore out of the house and climbed into the Studebaker.

To my surprise, Violet appeared at the passenger door. "Sylvia didn't mean anything."

"Please, I don't need *you*, of all people, to try and make peace between Sylvia and me."

"You'll never fit in here, Laila."

"You think Eduardo would be better off with you?"

"He loved me once. I did some very stupid things back then. Did he tell you about the baby?"

I gulped, "You have a baby?"

She appeared genuinely choked up with emotion. "I-I had a miscarriage. I think Eduardo blamed me somehow. We didn't talk for a very long time. I'd like to make it up to him."

"I'm sure you would. Look, I've got to go. Say hi to your boyfriend for me. Ira, right?"

"Ira's leaving as soon as he gets his act together. He hates Sabinal."

I took a deep breath. "Me, I love it here. Where can you breathe fresh air like this? And the peace and quiet is incredible."

"Surely you miss the big city."

"City, pity. This is a nice change." I had no idea why I was lying to her.

"Aren't you lonely?"

I produced a smug smile. "Lonely? No way. There's Kiki, Angie, and of course *you* to hang out with me."

"Do you really think of me as a friend, Laila?"

"No, Violet. While I'm not a brain surgeon, or as you say, a *'cirujano del cerebro,'* I'm not a birdbrain either." I switched on the ignition, and headed down the road, stalling out periodically.

The same two cousins still sat on their horses at the side of the road. They chuckled as the car sputtered past them. The whole scenario felt surreal. Why had I not seen it before? The passion I shared with Eduardo and the bond to work with pregnant teens was not enough. I could not go on feeling so disrespected and out of my comfort zone. Something needed to change for me to continue to live here. And it certainly did not appear like Eduardo even noticed how unhappy I'd been.

CHAPTER THIRTY-THREE
The Family Secret

Sylvia

After Violet left, Sylvia rolled fresh tortillas for Ramon's lunch. Like always, he returned from the corral at noon, sat at the table, took his Stetson off, and placed their grandson, Errol, on his lap.

Errol took Ramon's hat and put it on his own little head.

Both Sylvia and Ramon laughed at their eldest grandchild. Their daughter, Kiki, had only been sixteen when she'd gotten pregnant from some *vato* she'd met at an Española High School dance. He'd refused to do the right thing and marry her, so here they were raising the little boy like he was their own, while Kiki studied for her LPN. Little Sylvia followed two years later, and although they were furious with Kiki for her *promiscuida*, they ended up raising Sylvia too. It was common among her friends to bring up their grandchildren. She never understood how young *gringas* who found themselves pregnant either went to a clinic that legally killed their babies, or gave them up for adoption. After all, what was more important than *familia*?

Sylvia fried up the tortillas and placed them with beans and chile on a plate, which she served to Ramon.

He mumbled a *gracias* then touched her arm. "We need to talk about Laila."

"What's to talk about?"

"You've got to be nicer to her. It's obvious she's the one."

Sylvia shook her head. "But Violet is back. Who knows what will happen?"

"It's Laila he's in love with."

"She'll never be a part of us. And remember that the Jews killed Jesus—"

"Then we're guilty of that too."

"You promised never to bring those old *familia* rumors up. We don't even know for sure."

"Things happen for a reason, *mi querida esposa,* my dear wife. This is not just a coincidence."

How could her husband not see the obvious? "In the end, I don't believe she'll make him happy."

"Eduardo has chosen her. You must accept his decision."

But she couldn't. She refused to give up so easily. It infuriated her that Ramon stuck up for the *gringa*. She would call Virgie and tell her they were running out of time to reunite their offspring. They needed to do something *más drástico*.

CHAPTER THIRTY-FOUR
Zorro

Laila

I drove to the local grocery store to buy the ingredients for the spinach lasagna. I was not ready to give up on Eduardo. If anything, Violet joining forces with Sylvia made me more determined to make our relationship work. When I returned to the trailer, Brooklyn was barking frantically. I killed the engine, stepped out of the car, and opened the gate to the small front yard where she hung out when I was gone. "What's the matter, girl?"

The dog kept jumping up on me. "It's okay. I'm back." This was not normal behavior for the mellow animal I nicknamed Buddha Dog. "Get down." I pushed her off of me. "Knock it off."

Instead of leaving me alone, she tugged on my Levis and then nudged me with her nose toward the gate. I followed her. "Okay, girl." The gate groaned as I pushed it open.

Brooklyn prodded me toward a mesquite bush behind an old abandoned storage building where a ball of fur lay lifeless. Zorro! I picked her stiff body up and cradled her in my arms. When I looked down at her, I noticed bite marks on her neck.

It couldn't be true. How had she gotten out of the house? Still holding her in my arms, I rushed inside the trailer and looked around for clues to how she'd escaped.

Inside the bathroom, the window was half-open. Zorro's death had been a result of my carelessness leaving it open. I stumbled back outside and collapsed with her next to me.

I don't remember much after that other than crying until my throat burned, and my head aching something fierce. Brooklyn lay next to Zorro whimpering.

I had no idea how much time passed before Ramon pulled up in his truck, hopped out, and shook his head. "I'm sorry, Laila. It looks like your cat was bitten by a diamondback rattlesnake." He fetched out a handkerchief from his pocket and handed it to me.

I wiped my tears on the soft white cloth. "Thank you."

He rummaged around the back of his pickup where he found an old cardboard box. I handed him Zorro and he gently placed her inside the box. Then he grabbed a shovel from the truck, dug a hole, and placed the box with my beloved cat in the ground. While he was burying her, I picked wildflowers, putting them together with small rocks to mark the spot.

The setting sun washed yellow-orange over everything while Brooklyn circled the makeshift grave.

Ramon's eyes were wet as he sat down next to me and said, "My first Appaloosa escaped from the corral, ran out in the road and got hit by a car. Bandit was his name."

"That must have been tough."

"I was just a little boy. *Mi padre* said I was carrying on like a *bebé*."

"He didn't understand how much you loved your horse, I guess."

"He didn't have time for a son grieving a horse. With thirteen kids and a ranch to run, he wanted me to get back to my chores. Fifty years later, I still think of that damn horse."

I brushed a tear from my cheek with my thumb. "I'll never forget Zorro. She really loved Eduardo."

"Most animals and *niños* do."

"I've noticed that."

"I hope you learn to be happy here, Laila."

The sound of rubber on gravel interrupted our conversation. A shiny red Mustang convertible appeared on the horizon. Surprisingly, Eduardo was at the wheel. He parked next to Ramon's truck and stepped out of the car with a wide grin on his face. "Hi, Papa." He turned to me and dangled a set of keys in front of my face. "What do you think of your new car? It's an old one, but in great shape." He looked at Ramon. "I bought it from Nester for a thousand bucks."

Neither Ramon nor I said a word.

"Why are you both so quiet? I can take the car back if you don't like it." He reached inside his pocket, pulled out a dog biscuit, and dropped it next to Brooklyn.

She ignored it.

"What's going on?"

Ramon shook his head.

I could barely say the words. "Zorro's been killed."

"Oh, Jesus!" His eyes watered as I explained what had happened to her.

The three of us sat there quietly with Brooklyn as a spectacular blood-red-orange sunset filled the expanse of the New Mexican sky. I held Eduardo's hand and wept unabashedly.

CHAPTER THIRTY-FIVE
The Weirdo

Laila

I spent a good part of the night in a dejected state of shock. Eduardo heated up some leftover zucchini casserole but I couldn't eat a bite. We watched the CBS news with Walter Cronkite and then the local New Mexico news. Later, we played a game of chess and Eduardo let me win. He held me for a long time in his arms before we both finally fell asleep.

I awoke an hour later and slipped outside where I sat on an old lawn chair. Brooklyn hopped onto my lap. At twenty-eight years old, I'd never really dealt with the finality of death before. Yes, Grandma Levin had died at the ripe old age of ninety-three, but I was only seven years old and had not been all that close to her since she'd lived a thousand miles away in Miami Beach.

The next morning, Eduardo woke up early and cooked a stack of cornbread pancakes with fresh cherries inside. He put a plate in front of me and I took a small bite. "Yum! An old family recipe?"

"Grandma Ramona used to make them every Sunday after church."

I had no appetite but picked at the pancakes with a fork, making a token attempt to eat a few bites.

After cleaning the dishes, Eduardo kissed my forehead. "Do you want me to stay home with you today?"

"Please don't." I saw no reason for him to cancel a full

schedule of patients. It's not like he could bring Zorro back and a lot of sick people would suffer from his absence.

"You're sure."

"I'll be okay."

After Eduardo left, I refilled my mug with coffee and reflected on what had happened. A vision of the open bathroom window haunted me. Zorro's death was my fault. If I'd never come out West, she would still be safe in my Village apartment. And now, not only was I devastated from her loss, but I had no one to talk to about it. Yes, I could have called Kiki or Angie, but the thought of them coming over held little appeal.

Just then, the phone rang.

"Hey, Lai," said my sister Rachel. "What's happening?"

I flopped down on the couch comforted by the sound of her voice. "Your timing is impeccable, Sista." I filled Rachel in on what had happened to Zorro.

"I'm so sorry. Didn't you find her in college?"

"Yes. I heard some mewing and found this tiny kitten curled up in an arroyo behind my house. Part of her ear had been gnawed off, presumably by a rodent, and she had the worst case of mange the veterinarian had ever seen. I bottle-fed her with the help of my roommate Katie, and nursed her back to a healthy cat."

"Maya and Will sure loved her," Rachel said.

"She was more like a dog than a cat." I reflected on the irony that in death she had returned to the place she'd been born.

I grabbed a tissue and blew my nose. "What's going on with you?"

"You had to ask? Bob's declared bankruptcy and

permanently moved to Florida with his bimbo. Not one word to the kids. He's totally forgotten he's a father."

"I'm so sorry."

"The job at Sesame is great, but it's a struggle to make the bills."

"You can always come live with us in the chicken coop."

"Not this month. But I'm keeping my options open. By the way, some weird guy stopped by the apartment looking for you the other day."

"What weird guy?"

"He said he knew you from high school but then he didn't even know you'd gone to West Meadow. He wanted me to tell him where you'd moved."

"Did you?"

"Of course not."

"How did he get in the building?"

"Tailgated someone, I presume. Don't worry. You're two-thousand miles away from this crazy city."

"I'm more worried about you and the kids."

"We're safe in West Meadow."

"What did he look like?"

"Short for a dude. Muscular, with hazel eyes. Wore a black leather jacket."

I scratched my head. "He sounds like a guy I saw loitering around before I moved. For a minute, I thought he might be the Son of Sam."

"Thank God they have *him* behind bars."

"Tell me exactly what you told him."

"I said I had no idea where the previous tenant had gone. His face turned a blustering red and he accused me of lying. It made me rather nervous. Oh, and he had a stutter."

"That's definitely weird." I searched my brain but couldn't recall anyone I knew who stuttered.

"I told the children to run and then Maya dropped Mr. Boonie. I was so scared, I pushed the kids inside. Maya started screaming for Mr. Boonie. After we were all safely in the apartment, Maya had a major tantrum. I grabbed a butcher knife from the kitchen and headed back downstairs to see if I could retrieve Mr. Boonie."

"What happened?"

"The guy was gone and so was the stuffed bunny. The kids and I drove out to Long Island and spent the night with Mom and Dad."

"Maybe he's a Son of Sam copycat. You should call the NYPD."

"I'm sure they'll come right over and set me up with 24/7 bodyguards."

"I see your point."

"Do you have any idea who he could be? An old boyfriend or admirer?"

I shrugged. "No one comes to mind, but you're not gonna like what I'm about to say, Rachel."

"You think I should stay with Mom and Pop for a while."

"Exactly. This guy sounds dangerous."

"But he hasn't done anything."

"Yet." I said. "Think about the kids."

"Okay, okay, I'll stay in Long Island for a while. Eve will be in seventh heaven."

"You bet."

"Lai—"

"Yes."

"The weirdo spoke to Mrs. Schneider and she told him you've moved to New Mexico."

I sucked in my breath. Who was this man? I honestly had no idea. When I hung up the phone, I grabbed a pencil an old black notebook and created a list of old boyfriends. There was Julian, Ben and Chris from college, and a couple of others. But none of them was very short in stature. Certainly not as small as Mrs. Schneider. I reminded myself that New Mexico was a big state, and the chances of him finding me were ridiculously low. Even so, I latched the deadbolt on the front door before heading into the bedroom for a nap.

CHAPTER THIRTY-SIX
Children Having Children

Laila

I buried myself in research the next few weeks, trying my best to make a go of life with Eduardo. On Tuesdays and Thursdays I met with Peaches, Brenda and Mandy in my office in Española. Peaches had given birth to Little Markie, a healthy baby boy in September, yet she continued attending our little pregnancy group. She'd bring Markie along and share how tough her life was now that she was a mother.

I spoke to the girls about the need for birth control in the future. Eduardo provided them with pamphlets on the pill and IUD, and answered their questions about the pros and cons of each of the options.

As the aspens and cottonwoods of the Sangre de Cristo Mountains became a palette of glorious fall colors—bright yellows to glimmering golds, reds and splashes of purple—I settled into my life in New Mexico. The days were now sunny and cool. Locals referred to fall as the "magical season." I did not share with Eduardo the never-ending distress that I felt around Sylvia. She persisted to utter endless barbs with a calculated sneakiness. The majority of her hurtful comments occurred when Eduardo or Ramon were out of earshot.

On the bright side, Eduardo was making an extra effort to be romantic. Often, he'd come home with a single rose or a special bottle of Chardonnay and cook special candlelit dinners. Grilled trout *almondine*, poached salmon, or cheese *relleños*. He initiated outings with Carla and Rando in Santa

Fe. I'd come back to the trailer feeling more positive about my decision to move there.

As Sylvia's caustic comments continued, I managed to bury my slow-burning indignation. By immersing myself in research, there was little time to dwell on hurt feelings. I wrote up a case study on each of the girls identifying their behavior, family background, and cultural mores, as well as their reaction to our educational sessions. My research focused on the value of teaching girls about birth control options and alternative lifestyles.

Mandy and Brenda gave birth in October. Our meetings continued with all three babies attending with their mothers. I had discovered a wonderful program for them and hoped that they'd consider going to it. "Did you girls receive the information I sent you about that school in Albuquerque?"

"Can't do," said Brenda. "Mama's sick and I gotta take care of her and Rosie."

"Who's supporting you?" I asked.

"We're living with my grandma. She's got Section Eight, and food stamps, and shit."

"What about you, Peaches?"

"I've registered for the program."

Brenda's eyebrows flew up at the news. "You didn't say nothin' to me about it."

"Well, I'm telling you now," Peaches said. "My Uncle Juan lives in Querque and me and Markie can stay with him while I go to school. His wife said she'd watch the baby when I'm in class."

I smiled. "Perfect."

Peaches glanced at her baby. "I want more for him.

College, graduate school . . . who knows? Maybe he'll be a doctor or something."

"Wonderful. Now, I need to ask you more questions for my research." I cleared my throat. "Are you girls having sex with anyone now?"

"*Mi vato* started coming round again," Brenda said.

"Are you using protection?"

"Dr. Quintana gave me the pill."

"And you take one every day?"

"I take it most of the time."

I shook my head. "You can't forget, not even one pill." I looked at Peaches. "How about you?"

"Dr. Quintana gave me a prescription, but . . . I-I think it's too late."

"What?"

"Marcus came by a few weeks ago and, well one thing led to the other. We wasn't s'posed to, but—"

"Hopefully, you're not pregnant," I said.

"The thing is—I think I am."

"What about the program in Albuquerque?"

"Does it matter if I'm pregnant?"

This couldn't be happening. I naively thought I had gotten through to these girls. A cycle of children having children and a recipe for generations of poverty to come. I believed after all these sessions, I'd made a difference in these girls' lives. But it appeared that I had failed miserably.

CHAPTER THIRTY-SEVEN
The Invitation

Sylvia

Gray clouds blanketed the sky as Sylvia stood in the doorway of Eduardo's trailer with her favorite silk scarf wrapped around her head. She paused before knocking on the door. The New Mexico summer was gone and the New York *chica* had not left. Ramon had insisted that she drive over and make peace with her. "This can't go on," he'd said. "You're going to have to accept her."

"What if I can't?" Sylvia didn't think it was possible.

His eyes bulged to life behind his reading glasses. "Do you want to lose our son?"

The thought of losing Eduardo had never occurred to Sylvia since she hadn't given up on Virgie's plan to get their children back together. However, she had to admit *que las cosas no se dirigían en esa dirección*. Things were not heading in that direction. For one thing, Violet appeared to have health problems, and her stupid Los Angeles boyfriend remained in Sabinal. Virgie couldn't understand what Violet saw in Ira any more than Sylvia could about Eduardo and the Lailee girl.

Sylvia arched her shoulders, made a fist, and pounded on the door.

Lailee appeared in a terry robe with her hair wrapped in a towel. Surprisingly, her skin was flawless without makeup. Her pale-green eyes widened. "Sylvia, ah, what a nice surprise. Would you like to come inside?"

"If it's not a bad time."

"No, no, it's fine. I just stepped out of the shower. I'll put up a pot of coffee."

Sylvia sat at the kitchen table, took off the scarf, and carefully folded it. "Thank you."

"That's a lovely scarf."

"Eduardo bought it for me from New York City. It was *muy caro.*"

"Yes, it looks like something from Lord & Taylor."

"He bought it at a church?"

"Lord & Taylor is a store."

"Never heard of it."

"Of course . . . never mind. Is there a reason for your visit?"

Sylvia eyed the girl warily. "*Sí.* I came to tell you there's a big storm rolling in. We may lose *telephono* service and electricity."

Laila ground coffee beans in a device that whirred to life when she pressed the button. Then she placed the ground coffee in a filter on top of a glass coffee pot. "Excuse me. While the coffee's brewing I'll get dressed. It should just take a minute."

Sylvia sat at the chipped Formica table scrutinizing the coffee as it dripped down into the glass pot. Such a fancy deal. She used an old electric pot, a wedding gift from Ramon's sister, with whatever ground coffee was on sale at Safeway. The girl looked thin, prim and rigid. Why would *mi hijo* want such a skinny girl? She half-chuckled as she recalled that she herself had been *muy flaca,* very skinny, when she was younger. Now she had a nice *pansa,* tummy. Stretch marks crisscrossed her stomach like a map with roads and highways . . . a living remembrance of birthing her *quatro niños,* four children.

Laila returned to the kitchen dressed in a sensible pair of jeans and a white blouse and then poured a mug of coffee for each of them. Her bolt of chestnut hair streamed wildly around her shoulders. "Would you like cream and sugar?"

"Black is fine." Sylvia took a sip and grimaced.

Laila's lips twitched. "Oh dear. We like our coffee strong in New York. Let me water that down for you."

"I don't want to be a bother." She took another sip and involuntarily spit it back into the cup. "I-I didn't mean to do that."

"No problem." Laila heated up water in a teakettle and then poured some into Sylvia's cup.

Sylvia picked up the cup again and sipped the watered down coffee.

Laila arched an eyebrow. "Better?"

It was still bitter but Sylvia turned the corners of her lips up. "Much better, *gracias*."

Laila flopped into a chair at the table. "When's the storm supposed to get here?"

"Soon. Ramon asked me, *we* would like to invite you to come to our *casa*."

"I appreciate your concern."

"I don't have nothing against you. Lailee . . . Laila." Sylvia needed to remember *la chica's* name.

"Well, I don't have anything against you either, Sylvia."

"Is there a chance you might become a Catholic? Our family priest—"

"Did you know there's over a billion Catholics in this world and only fifteen-million Jews? It makes more sense for Eduardo to convert to Judaism."

"You-you, want my son to become a Jew? *Estás loca?*"

"I'm not *loca,* I just—"

At that moment, Lailee's dog jumped up on Sylvia's lap. "Shoo!" She pushed the animal but instead of jumping down, the dog licked her face. "Disgusting to have dogs in the house." She shoved the dog harder and it landed on the floor.

But then that dumb *perro* jumped right back on her lap.

"Get down, Brooklyn!" Laila shouted. "What's wrong with you?" She turned to Sylvia with a strained smile. "She must really like you."

Brooklyn refused to move.

Sylvia said, "Dogs belong outside."

"Sorry, I respectfully disagree."

¿Que no esta chica que ella era desafiar a sus major? Who did this girl think she is to challenge her elders?

As Laila removed the dog from Sylvia's lap, the stupid thing bit down on Sylvia's scarf.

Laila attempted to pry the scarf from her, but the animal's jaw was clenched tight and the scarf ripped. The girl looked up at Sylvia. "I'm so sorry." She seized the dog and hauled her to the bedroom.

Thunder rumbled outside, followed by flashes of lightning through the windows.

Laila returned to the kitchen with a bright red face. "Again, my sincere apologies. I'll replace the scarf."

Sylvia stood up and clutched her vinyl purse. It took every inch of moral fiber to keep from screaming. She was not a woman who was known to restrain from an emotional outburst, but Sylvia did it for Eduardo. She eyeballed Lailee and let out her breath. "I better get home before the downpour. Are you coming or not?"

"I'll, ah, wait it out here. Thanks so much for the invite."

Sylvia saw no reason to insist Laila come home with her. As she rushed to her car, she imagined that the trailer was struck by lightning. That would take care of her problem. "I don't mean that, God," she said out loud. All she wanted was for Eduardo to be happy. But for the life of her, she couldn't understand why he and Ramon could not see the obvious. This girl would never fit in.

As the sky roared with thunder, Sylvia crouched inside the car and the truth became evident. From the moment this girl had arrived, she'd never given her a chance. What if Ramon was right and they lost Eduardo forever? What if he decided to go back to New York with *la chica*? By driving this Lailee girl away, she was chasing her son along with her. But she couldn't help herself. *Una madre sabe major.* A mother knows best.

CHAPTER THIRTY-EIGHT
The Storm

Laila

I felt an enormous sense of relief as Sylvia drove off. The sky was dark and bruised with angry streaks of gray. After a few claps of thunder, everything was still for a short while. Then the winds kicked up and the rain beat down on the roof. I rushed to the bedroom where Brooklyn was whining, opened the door, and hugged her. No point in punishing the dog.

"What's wrong with you, girl?" She'd jumped on people's laps before but never so defiantly. Yet, most people encouraged her. She didn't understand Sylvia's blatant rejection.

Bullets of raindrops continued to pound on the roof. Puddles formed where water leaked through the ceiling. I placed pots and bowls strategically throughout the trailer, clicked on the television, and adjusted the rabbit ears until I had reception.

"A much needed rainstorm is currently hovering over central and most of northern New Mexico," said a local weatherman. "Expect up to three inches in the next hour. A safety advisory has been issued for the Santa Fe area and vicinity. Unless it's an emergency you should stay in your homes. The arroyos are quickly filling up and it's dangerous driving out there."

"Great." I switched channels to an old Spencer Tracy movie and fell asleep on the couch. Hours later, I awoke to the sound of rain still pelting down on the roof. The trailer was dark. I stumbled to the kitchen and picked up the phone, but there was no dial tone. For a brief moment, I considered driving to Ramon and Sylvia's but thought better of the idea. Eduardo was most likely holed up in his office. At least I hoped he was there, and not stuck in some arroyo.

I walked into the bedroom. The carpet below my feet was soaked. I got into bed and Brooklyn cuddled up next to me. I felt comforted by the sound of her even breaths. Despite the clanking of rain into metal pots, I soon fell asleep.

Hours later, I awoke to the sound of a rooster crowing and a rosy dawn splashing through the window. Still no sign of Eduardo.

I staggered to the kitchen and picked up the phone, but there was no dial tone. It was time for me to take action. I rushed into the bathroom, splashed water on my face, brushed my teeth, and tied my hair back in a rubber band.

The engine of the Mustang purred to life immediately. I was grateful for the car's automatic transmission. Twenty minutes later, I pulled up to Eduardo's office, stepped out of the car, and glanced through the big front window. As I feared, it was dark inside.

I jumped back in the Mustang and drove down the street to the hospital. The lobby was empty except for an older Hispanic woman sitting at the information desk crocheting a blanket. "Excuse me, ma'am. I'm looking for Doctor Quintana."

She pointed down the hall. "Room 12."

I pushed open the door to the room.

Violet lay sleeping in a hospital bed with an I.V. attached to her arm. Her face looked pasty and her lips were chapped and bruised. Eduardo sat slumped in a plastic chair close to the bed. From the disheveled look of his clothes and hair, it appeared he'd been sitting there all night.

I stood silently in the doorway.

Violet slowly opened her eyes and smiled at Eduardo. "Thank you for staying with me. I was so frightened."

I bet she was.

"You certainly gave me a scare. We need to run more tests."

She sat up and leaned forward. "I still love you Eduardo. Don't you have any feelings left for me?"

"I loved you once but—"

Violet craned her head toward his and smothered his mouth with a kiss.

Did Eduardo try to push her away? I wasn't sure. Unable to restrain myself any longer, I burst into the room. "Why go out for hamburger when you have steak at home!"

He tore away from Violet. "This isn't what it looks like."

"It doesn't matter." I bolted from the room and heard the sound of his boots clacking on the tile floor behind me.

When he caught up to me, he grabbed my arm. "Let me at least explain."

"It's not necessary."

"Nothing's going on with Violet. She's got a serious drug problem."

"Don't you get it? Even if what you're saying about you and Violet is true, I hate it here. This just gives me an excuse to get the hell out of Dodge."

"You hate it here?"

"Hello? You've been so busy with your family and your practice, you haven't noticed how miserable I am."

"I-I thought things were better."

"You can tell your mama and Virgie they've won the battle and the war."

"Why do you always bring Mama into everything?"

"Oh for crissakes, Eduardo. When are you going to cut the apron strings?"

"What? You're crazy."

"You're right about one thing. I'm crazy to be here. I'll be gone by this afternoon." I flew out the door of the hospital resolved never to see Eduardo or his *famila* again.

I DROVE BACK TO THE TRAILER AND TOSSED MY CLOTHES into the suitcases I'd brought from New York. Then I wrote a check to Eduardo for one-thousand dollars. Along with the check, I left him a note on the kitchen counter.

> *I really don't know what to say to you, Eduardo, except goodbye. I tried my very best to make this work. Perhaps Violet will make you happy. But know this. She is NOT the reason I am leaving. You and I are just too different. I will never be happy in Sabinal. Please take care of Brooklyn until I get settled somewhere. Right now, I have no idea where that will be. I wish you all good things. Do not try to get in touch with me. Our relationship is terminado.*
>
> *P.S. The check is for the Mustang.*

Brooklyn trailed behind me as I opened the trunk of the Mustang and threw the suitcases inside. Was this really happening? While Eduardo and I had amazing chemistry, the relationship would never work out in the long run. Right? I was miserable in Sabinal. His mother would never give me a chance, and Violet would always be lingering in the shadows. And yet I felt such a deep sadness leaving him.

The hardest thing was leaving my beloved Brooklyn. Since I had no idea where I was going, I couldn't take her with me. A hotel? A plane back to New York?

She barked as I opened the driver door of the car.

"I'll come get you soon, girl." Grabbing her collar, I forced her into the front yard and tossed out a handful of pepperoni dog treats. I rushed out and closed the gate behind me. By the time I left the driveway, the barking turned to howls.

I rolled down the window and shouted, "I love you."

Her howls became fainter as I barreled down the road but they continued to ring in my ears long after I was out of earshot. When I got into Española, I stopped at a pay phone in front of the Exxon station and called the only person outside of Eduardo's family that I knew in New Mexico.

My friend Allison answered on the second ring.

I tearfully filled her in on what had happened with Eduardo. It made everything seem more real to say it out loud. Eduardo and I were finished.

"Come stay with Leo and me," she said.

It was the response I was hoping for. At least I'd have a place to perch while I figured out the rest of my life. An hour later, I arrived in Santa Fe in a neighborhood where yuccas, cactus, and cornflowers embellished the yards of large southwestern-style homes. The street was lined with big cottonwood and willow trees. Their leaves displayed fall colors of butter yellow and orange with a smudge of red. What had happened to summer?

I drove down a long driveway and parked the Mustang in

front of a pink stucco house. The name HARVEY was spelled out in cobalt blue and white ceramic tiles.

Allison opened the front door before I even knocked. Her freckled face broke out in a smile. "Come inside."

Sunlight flooded through the many windows on the south side of the house. Allison explained their home was a passive-solar adobe. "We have like no heating bills. Leo read a how-to book on building houses off the grid and we did most of the work ourselves. A labor of love."

"It's beautiful," I said. "Eduardo, my, boy, ah, ex-boyfriend, was planning on building something just like this."

Leo joined us in the living room a short while later. A tall man with a fro of blonde curly hair, he smiled at me and then placed his hand on Allison's protruding belly. "How's our little goddess?"

"She's quite active today."

Leo grinned, disappeared momentarily and then returned with three goblets. He handed me one, then passed one to Allison. "Welch's grape juice for you, my love."

Allison held up her glass in a toast. "To our little goddess."

Leo and I clinked glasses with her. "May she be healthy, wealthy and wise," I said.

"And to new friends," added Leo.

After the toast, Leo left the room. Soon the aroma of fish sizzling on the grill in the courtyard wafted through the open French doors. "Hope you like salmon," he shouted.

"Love it. I don't eat meat."

"Neither do Leo and I," said Allison.

I was thrilled to be with people who shared my culinary lifestyle. "Can I help? Make a salad or something?"

"I've already made one," Leo shouted from the deck. "Just

relax and talk to Allison. She hasn't been around anyone from New York in a long time."

Allison grinned. "You can take the girl out of New York, but you can't take New York out of the girl."

"My thoughts exactly." So I wasn't the only one who missed the place of my origin. I told her about *Beatlemania* and a revival of *Romeo and Juliet* I'd caught on Broadway before Eduardo had entered my life. "My favorite films so far this year are *The Goodbye Girl* and *Saturday Night Fever.*"

"We do get most movies here in Santa Fe. I just loved John Travolta."

"Is *Annie Hall* playing here?"

"Yes, and I'm dying to see it. But I can't go to the movies right now."

"Why is that?"

"I've had two miscarriages. The doctor thinks it best I stay home for the rest of the pregnancy."

"That's tough."

"We've tried to adopt, but the waiting list is insane. Leo's almost forty, so we want children soon."

"Eduardo wants . . . wanted kids. I'd consider two, maybe three. He'd like a tribe."

"It appears you had differences," Allison said.

"Too many, I'm afraid."

Allison winked. "He was rather good looking."

I playfully slapped her hand. "No need to remind me of that."

Leo reappeared from the courtyard with a platter of appetizing fish. "Let's eat."

We all moved to the round oak table in the kitchen and Leo served us each a plate of salmon and salad. Over dinner, I gave them a synopsis of my research and how I ended back out in New Mexico. "I'm not sure what I'm going to do now. I can't stay in Sabinal and frankly, I don't really want to go back to New York."

"Have you ever thought about moving to Santa Fe?" Leo asked. "All the things you love about New York without all the things you hate about New York."

"It never crossed my mind," I said.

Leo touched my hand. "You're more than welcome to stay with us. We have a nice guest room, if I do say so myself."

"I could use the company," Allison added.

After dinner, I insisted on doing the dishes and Leo brought my suitcases into the guest room. It was a small room with thick exposed adobe walls and a double bed made up with a colorful Indian blanket. That night, I slept better than I had in weeks, despite the fact that leaving Eduardo left me with mixed emotions. Was it possible he was telling me the truth about Violet? That he wasn't another Julian? But even so, I saw no solution to our cultural differences. He'd never go back to New York, and I was done with Sabinal for good.

CHAPTER THIRTY-NINE
The Split

Eduardo

When Eduardo arrived home that night, the Mustang was gone. Had Laila moved out? The sound of Brooklyn barking comforted him as he stepped out of the Studie. She raced up to him in a frenzy.

He entered the trailer and looked around. Most everything looked normal. But when he opened the bedroom closet, he discovered her clothes and suitcases were gone. Suddenly, all the air got sucked out of him. Her toothbrush and toiletries bag were missing from the tiny bathroom. His only solace was the fact she'd left the dog. No way would she go far without Brooklyn.

He picked up the phone and dialed his parents. Mama answered on the first ring. "Have you seen Laila today?"

"No, mijo. Is she gone?"

"Let me speak to Dad." It wasn't that he didn't trust his mother . . .

His father confirmed he hadn't seen Laila either. When they hung up, he called Rachel numerous times, but no one answered. He thought about calling Laila's parents, but intuitively knew that wouldn't be a good idea. Laila would be furious with him and Eve would probably freak out. Chances were good the Levins knew nothing about their daughter's departure, and he'd be fueling up a fire that would burn him in the end.

Then he noticed the check and note on the kitchen table.

His heart sank as he read it. He spent the night listening to the locusts and crickets, with his ears peeled for the sound of tires on the gravel of the driveway. For some reason, he thought she'd change her mind. At 3:22 a.m. he slipped out of bed and sat on the porch in his boxers, reflecting on all the mistakes he'd made. Why hadn't he found a nice house for her in Española? How could he expect a New York girl to live in a broken down trailer?

It's not that he hadn't noticed Laila had issues living in Sabinal. He'd talked to Papa about it and even sat down at the kitchen table and asked Mama to be nicer to Laila. He'd honestly thought things had improved. But perhaps he was wrong. He'd ignored the signs right in front of his nose. Of course, Laila was miserable. Maybe she just needed time alone. Perhaps she'd checked into a hotel in Santa Fe or Albuquerque.

And then there was Violet. He needed to set her straight as soon as possible.

For the next few days, Eduardo barely slept. He stayed really busy at work, arriving early and staying late. Despite her insistence that he shouldn't get in touch with her, Eduardo called Rachel every night. Still no answer. After a few days, he made up his mind to call the Levins after work. He had to speak to Laila. Surely they would find a way to work things out.

That morning, when he arrived at the office, there were already three patients in the waiting room.

Yolanda handed him a clipboard with the patient forms.

He smiled at the eighty-year old woman sitting with her husband José. "*Como estás, Señora Ortiz?*" She showed up at his office weekly in hope Eduardo could fix the numerous ailments that plagued her. As he took her elbow and led her toward the examining rooms, Violet burst into the office dressed in a silk blouse, skintight jeans, and stilettos. Unlike Laila, she walked quite steadily in high heel shoes. She touched his arm. "We need to talk."

"This is not a good time."

"Of course. How about lunch? I can pick you up around noon. My treat."

Eduardo shook his head. "I've got a very busy schedule today. I wasn't planning on taking a lunch break."

"Dinner, perhaps? It's really important."

Could she possibly know that Laila had left him? He hadn't told anyone except Papa. But he did need to get things straight with Violet. He smiled at Mrs. Ortiz. "Please step into examination room one." Then he turned to Violet. "Go into my office. I'll be there after I'm done examining *la Señora*."

Mrs. Ortiz had pain in her abdomen. She had trouble going to the bathroom, so she'd taken a bunch of Ex-Lax. Now she couldn't stop going to the bathroom. Her dentures hurt so much she couldn't bare the pain when she put them in. She was having trouble swallowing.

Eduardo felt her glands, took her pulse, and listened to her heart. He had her stick out her tongue and examined her mouth with a small flashlight. Her gums were red and inflamed. He sent her home with a bottle of Pepto-Bismol and told her to leave her dentures out for a while. Then he called an old dentist friend in Santa Fe and asked if he'd see her pro bono.

As usual, Eduardo had become so absorbed in his patient he'd forgotten his other woes. After he finished the examination, he remembered that Violet was waiting for him in his office. When he opened the door, her face lit up like a five year old about to blow out candles on her birthday cake.

Eduardo cleared his throat trying to find the right words to use with Violet about the cocaine and other drugs that had been discovered in her blood work. He didn't want to alienate her. "We received the results—"

His words were interrupted by the sound of the phone. Normally, Yolanda took his calls, but if she had forwarded one to him, it must be important. Could it be Laila? He picked up the receiver, listened to the voice on the other end and looked across the desk at Violet. "I need a favor."

"*Por supuesto,* Of course."

"Brooklyn, Laila's dog, got out of the front yard. Can you go to the trailer and put her back inside? I have a room full of patients and—"

"Where's Laila?" Her face was smug.

"She, ah, went away for a few days. I can ask Yolanda to go."

"*Voy a ir immediatamente,* I will go right away. But I want to have lunch with you when I get back."

He slipped the trailer door key off his key ring and handed it to her. "It's a deal. We need to discuss your lab results." He also needed to make sure she understood there was nothing but friendship between them anymore. And there never would be.

CHAPTER FORTY
Laila's Niche

Laila

The first two weeks in Santa Fe had gone quite well for me despite the sadness I felt about ending my relationship with Eduardo. Leo and Allison went out of their way to make me feel welcome. I'd secured a couple of speaking engagements at local high school PTA meetings, which led to private counseling sessions. Parents often ignored the signs their teenagers were sexually active, and they felt even more uncomfortable initiating a dialog about pregnancy prevention. Many followed the Catholic church's stand against contraception and premarital sex. I helped them find the words and consider all options. After a few counseling sessions, they began to share their innermost fears and feelings.

Everything about my life in Santa Fe was falling into place. I'd finally found a niche where I felt respected and valued, a place where I made a difference. If only I could get Eduardo off my mind. No matter how I tried, his image haunted me. I wondered what he'd think of Allison and Leo and if he'd appreciate my new approach of working directly with families. At night I dreamed of him holding me in his arms. Often, I'd be disappointed when I awoke to the reality of our separation. But I couldn't go back to our life in Sabinal. We were just not meant to be together.

Now that I finally felt settled in Santa Fe, I drove back to Sabinal to retrieve Brooklyn. I purposely chose to go on a weekday confident Eduardo would be at work. A part of me knew that one shared meeting of our eyes might tempt me to give up the new life I was building in Santa Fe. There was no point in that.

As I approached the trailer, I noticed an old black Cadillac was parked next to it. At first I had no idea who it belonged to, then I recalled seeing it at the *mantanza.* It was Violet's boyfriend's car. What were they doing at Eduardo's?

Determined not to lose my cool, I killed the motor of the Mustang. My goal was to pick up Brooklyn and immediately drive back to Santa Fe. I placed my key in the lock of the trailer and opened the door.

"Laila!" said Violet. "Where have you been?" She was wearing tight jeans, a low cut black Danskin, and three inch heels. There was no sign of Ira.

Brooklyn rushed right past her and jumped up on me barking.

I bent over, scratched her ears, and let her kiss my face. "I've missed you too, girl." I glanced up at Violet. "Didn't take you long."

"It's, ah, not what you think."

"It doesn't matter anymore. I'm curious about your boyfriend though. Isn't that his car?"

"Ira? He's leaving Sabinal, ah, today."

"That's handy." My voice sounded bitter. Was it possible she and Eduardo were already shacking up?

"So where are you living? Eduardo has been worried about you," Violet said with a smirk.

"Tell him I've moved to Santa Fe."

"It's the least I can do."

I was not foolish enough to believe Violet would relay the message. But it didn't matter. Since I was done with Eduardo, it was best to make a clean break. "The least you can do for what? *Me* leaving Eduardo so you could have him?"

"*You* didn't leave him. I'd already won the game."

It wasn't a "game" to me, but she could think whatever she wanted. I looked her in the eye. "Maybe so. But there was a good reason you left here seventeen years ago. You may think you want Eduardo and Sabinal, but my guess is you really want Hollywood or Broadway and will be happy with nothing less."

Violet pressed her lips together. Had I struck a chord?

She shrugged. "I needed to experience the world before settling down. Now I'm ready to spend my life here with Eduardo."

"Well, you have him now. Good luck."

She smiled. "Looks like yours ran out."

As I drove away with Brooklyn cuddled next to me, I realized I had never really known Eduardo. The man I knew had sworn he had no feelings for Violet anymore. I'd seen them together at the hospital, and now she'd taken up residence in the trailer. What more proof did I need? He'd turned out to be just like Julian. And my college boyfriend, Chris. I flashed on my recurring nightmare in which I found Chris with my roommate clad only in a bra and underwear. Were all men like that? Or did I just have a streak of bad luck? Yet even though all the evidence lay in front of me, a tiny part of me still had faith in Eduardo.

CHAPTER FORTY-ONE
Violet's Web

Violet

What an amazing *golpe de suerte,* stroke of luck. Things couldn't have gone better for Violet if she'd planned the encounter herself. After Laila left the trailer with her dog, Violet found a bottle of Chardonnay in the fridge and poured herself a celebratory glass. She sat on the porch, gloating as she sipped the wine. Then she recalled what Laila said about why she, Violet, had left Sabinal in the first place. Did she really want Eduardo, Sabinal . . . the whole enchilada she'd escaped from seventeen years ago? Or had her mother succeeded in making her feel guilty for leaving?

After a second and third glass of the Chardonnay, she felt better. Laila was gone for good. Now all she had to do was rid herself of Ira. She had no use for him anymore. The coke was almost gone. He had no money or job prospects.

She felt downright glorious on the drive back to Mama's. When she entered the house, Ira was sitting in the kitchen talking on the phone. A cigarette dangled from his lips. Was it possible he'd gotten her new work in Hollywood? Who else would he be talking to?

After a few minutes, he hung up the phone and kissed her cheek. "We're back in business, sweetheart."

"We're going back to California?"

"L.A. is done for us. But my daddy's retiring and wants me

to go into the family business in Wisconsin with my brother, Billy."

"What type of business?" He'd never told her about a family business. Come to think of it, he had never mentioned he'd grown up in Wisconsin. She'd assumed he was from California.

"Big O Tires. It's a swell opportunity."

"Swell?" He was already talking like a country boy.

"I want you to come with me, honey. You'll love Oshkosh."

"Are you joking?" She could picture him coming home to her every night with grease in his fingernails.

"It's not as bad as it sounds. We'll get a new doublewide like my brother Billy, and his wife, Edna."

"A far cry from the home you promised me in Beverly Hills."

"Ah, c'mon, that life is over for the both of us."

"Maybe for you."

"Get real, honey. You'll be the prettiest girl in Oshkosh, but at thirty-four, you're a hag by Hollywood standards." He got down on one knee. "Will you marry me, Violet?"

So her life had now come to this. She stood still and proud as the Sandia Mountains, but inside she felt empty and lost.

"Whaddaya say?"

"No friggin' way. I'd rather eat mothballs than go to Oshkosh b'Gosh with you."

He screwed up his eyes. "You'll regret this."

"I don't think so." There had to be something better than living in a doublewide with Ira Krazinski.

He shook his balding head, split from the house, and sped off in his Caddie.

The Caddie's dust hadn't settled before Violet dialed Eduardo's office. His secretary Yolanda answered on the first ring.

"Please relay this message to Dr. Quintana," Violet said. "Laila came and got her dog. She's on her way back to New York."

Good riddance. She and Eduardo were both back in Sabinal for the first time in seventeen years, and now they were both free. Surely it must be divine intervention. Mama and Aunt Sylvia thought so. She looked heavenward. "*Gracias a Dios por darme otra oportunidad.* Thank you, God, for giving me another chance."

Yet Laila's words echoed in her ears and ruined her moment of triumph. Violet had left this dustbowl years ago, and she stayed away for a reason. But she put that out of her mind. When Mama got home, she would borrow her Chevy, head into Española, and make a spare key to Eduardo's trailer at the Ace Hardware Store. If only she could unlock the key to his heart. Hopefully, her time had finally come.

CHAPTER FORTY-TWO
The Kidnapping

Laila

I returned to Leo and Allison's Santa Fe home with a dull thudding in my chest. As we stood on the porch, Brooklyn stuck to my leg like she'd been super-glued there.

Allison answered the door with a face so pale it looked like she'd coated it with flour. She bent down and petted Brooklyn's head. "Hello, girl. Welcome."

Brooklyn responded with a series of tail wags, all the while keeping her eyes peeled on me.

"How did things go?" The tendons in Allison's neck stood out. She looked so fragile I didn't want to burden her with my deep disappointment.

"Okay. Eduardo wasn't home. More importantly, what's wrong with you?"

"I-I had some breakthrough bleeding. Leo's on his way home to take me to the doctor."

"Oh, geez. I'm sure you'll be fine."

"You're probably right. But . . . this is how it started the last two times."

I put my arms around her. "Sit down, and I'll get you a glass of water."

I'd barely returned from the kitchen when Leo charged into the house out of breath. "Let's go, honey." He helped her out of the chair and shook his head at me.

"Is there anything I can do?"

"Say a prayer," Leo said, as he and Allison rushed out the door to the van.

While they were gone, I cleaned the sink full of breakfast dishes, washed the Saltillo tile floors in the whole house, and made a pan of eggplant parmesan—the least I could do to help them out.

Three hours later, the kitchen smelled of fresh garlic, oregano and spicy tomato sauce. Leo and Allison entered the house, but before I even said hello, Leo escorted Allison straight into their bedroom and closed the door. I took that as a bad sign.

Minutes later, Leo lumbered into the kitchen where I anxiously awaited the news. "Everything's okay. The bleeding's stopped but the doctor wants complete bed rest for the next few weeks."

"Let me know how I can help."

He looked around at the clean house. "You've done a lot already. Thank you." Then he checked out the eggplant parmesan that I had just taken out of the oven. Mozzarella cheese bubbled down the side of the pan. "Yum, this looks delicious."

After cutting three slices and placing them on glass plates, Leo took one for Allison and one for himself and walked back to their bedroom.

I looked out the kitchen window as I picked at my plate of food. The pale yellow sun had just begun its descent, casting a golden light over the Sangre de Christo Mountains.

THAT NIGHT, I CALLED RACHEL AT MY PARENTS' HOUSE. I hadn't had time to share the news that I'd left Eduardo.

Eve answered on the first ring. No "hello how are you," just, "Has the doctor proposed yet?"

"I'm fine, Ma. How are you?" For a second I considered confiding in *her* about my split with Eduardo. But I quickly came to my senses. Instead, I chatted about the endless sunny weather and the enchanted mountains of New Mexico.

Eve bragged about the pricey ballet and tap lessons she'd found for Maya. "We didn't have the money for such things when you girls were growing up."

"It's terrific you're helping her out."

"When you have children, I'll help them out too, darling. Of course, there's probably not much ballet or theater out there in the West."

"There's just a lot of cowboys and Indians, square dancing, and weekend campfires where everyone sings "Kumbaya," I said. I should have mentioned the *matanzas,* but she'd think I was joking if I told her I'd eyeballed a pig's head.

"Really?"

I stifled my giggles. "Is Raach around?"

A few minutes later, my sister picked up a phone.

"Is there any way Ma's listening to this conversation?"

"I don't think so," Rachel said. "She was already late for her mahjong game when you called. And I heard the garage door open."

"There's something I need to share with you but—" The phone made a clicking sound. I didn't need an FBI certification to know that Eve had snuck back inside and picked up the extension phone in the den. "Hello, Mother."

No answer, but more clicking.

"Hold on," Rachel said. She returned a few minutes later.

"T'was her. But she's gone now. I watched her car drive down the street. See why I can't live here?"

"I get it, Sista."

"So what did you want to tell me?"

"Nothing." I was now afraid to share anything on the phone. Eve was capable of returning any time. She had no boundaries and no shame.

"Call me at work tomorrow if you prefer. I'm taking the kids and moving back to the apartment."

"You should give it more time."

"I can't stay here. Besides Ma being Ma, the commute to work and the kids' school is killing me."

"What about the weirdo?"

"I spoke to Mrs. Schneider. She says she hasn't seen him in days."

"Do you think he's on his way to New Mexico?"

"Who knows? You need to be careful, Laila. I believe he's dangerous."

I had enough on my plate without worrying about some weirdo driving two thousand miles from New York to track me down. "It's a big state. The chances he'd find me are slim to none." Who was this guy? I searched my memory once again for a clue.

The next morning I called Rachel at *Sesame Street* but she was busy working on an emergency costume repair for Big Bird. I gave the receptionist Allison and Leo's phone number and told her to have my sister call me back the minute she was available.

When she hadn't returned my call by 11 a.m. (1 p.m. in New York), I called the apartment.

Rachel answered on the first ring, but she was crying so hard I couldn't understand a word she was saying.

"Slow down. What's wrong?"

"Maya's gone!"

"What are you talking about?"

"I went to pick her up at school, and they said she'd already gone home with her father."

"Bob? Isn't he in Florida?"

"I've called him a gazillion times but he's not answering his phone. It's not like him to do something this crazy."

CHAPTER FORTY-THREE
Uncle Dave

Dave

Her eyes glowed like two green emeralds. Just like Miss Levin's.

She clutched the stuffed bunny he'd found on the street by her apartment. It had been so easy. For the past few days he'd been following her mother all over Manhattan. He'd watched her drop the little girl at the Peanut Butter & Jelly preschool every morning at nine, and pick her up at noon. Dave had shown up at 11:30 a.m., when the kids were on the playground wearing a blonde Beatle-style wig and fake mustache. He walked up to her and held out the bunny.

She ran right over to him and held out her dimpled hands. "Mr. Boonie!"

He handed her the bunny. "Would you like ice cream?"

She shrugged. "Sure."

"Wait here, little girl." He strolled up to the teacher aid on duty. "I'm M-maya's father. I'm p-picking her up a little early today."

The woman squinted at him. "Does Mrs. Morris know?"

"Of course she does. Call her if you like."

Just then, a small boy ran up to the woman crying. His face was flaming red. "Billy punched me!"

Dave padded back to the little girl, clasped her hand, and led her from the playground. *Thank you, Billy.*

The girl looked up at him as they walked down the street. "Who are you?"

"I'm your Uncle Dave."

"I don't have an Uncle Dave."

What the hell was he doing? Kidnapping? No, he was just borrowing the little girl for a few hours. He would die before he hurt one hair on her head. Who would believe that? But the wheels in his head were in motion and he couldn't halt the train.

"I'm your daddy's brother."

"Daddy doesn't have a brother."

The kid was no dummy. "Your name's Maya, right?" He'd heard her mother call her that.

"Yes."

"Ready to get some yummy ice cream, Maya?"

"Okay."

They took the subway to Mother Bucka's Ice Cream Parlor on West Eighth Street. Little Maya held onto the bunny, and he held onto his dream of finding Miss Levin . . . Laila. He'd been studying maps of New Mexico that he had scotch-taped up on the wall in his studio apartment. He'd never find her without a specific address. It was a hell of a big place.

When they arrived at the ice cream shop, he bought the little girl a double-scoop chocolate cone with extra sprinkles. "Wait here. I'll be right back." While she was busy slurping the ice cream cone in a red vinyl booth, he headed over to the pay phone in the corner of the store.

She began to cry, "I want my mommy."

The Puerto Rican clerk at the counter glared at Dave with beady eyes.

Dave dashed back over to Maya, grabbed her hand all sticky from the ice cream, and skeddadled out of there.

"If you're a good girl, you'll see Mommy soon."

"I want Mommy now!"

"You must be quiet if you want to see Mommy. Okay?"

She looked down at her pink sneakers. "Okay."

He continued walking briskly, practically dragging her by her little hand.

"My tummy hurts."

"You ate the ice cream too fast." Jesus. What was he gonna do with a little girl? Should he take her home with him? But if he called her mother from his apartment, the police might trace the phone call there. He spotted a phone booth on the corner, pushed open the accordion door, and retrieved some coins and the piece of paper Barney had given to him about Miss Levin from his jacket pocket. "I'm calling Mommy now." He dialed the number.

Maya tugged at this pants leg. "I wanna talk to her."

"Shhh. In a minute."

"Hello," said a woman on the other end in a teary voice.

"I h-have your daughter."

"Oh thank God! Is she okay? Please don't hurt her."

"I-I'd never do that." Dave said. "Have you called the p-police?"

"N-no, I didn't."

"Your daughter is fine. But do *not* call the c-cops or else—"

"I won't. Can I talk to her? Make sure she's okay?"

Dave put the receiver to Maya's mouth. "Say hello to Mommy."

"Mommy!"

"Are you all right, sweetheart? Has he hurt you?"

"I have a tummy ache."

"Where are you?"

Dave grabbed the phone. "That's enough."

"What's wrong with her stomach?"

"Your d-daughter just gobbled down two scoops of chocolate ice cream."

"She's four years old. That's way too much ice cream for her."

"Sorry, I didn't know. All I want—"

"How much money? I'll get whatever—"

Dave hadn't thought about money. He had just wanted Miss Levin's address in New Mexico. His chance at happiness with the woman of his dreams. But money would help. "Ten thousand dollars."

"I'll get it. But promise me you won't touch my daughter."

"Look, lady. I'm not some kinda pervert. But there's something else I need from you."

She was sniffling. "What?"

"The previous tenant, Miss Levin . . . I want her address in New Mexico. And if it turns out to be the wrong one, I'll be back and—"

"I'll get it for you."

"G-g-ive it to me now."

"Ah, okay." She swallowed, and there was a brief silence.

"I said now, lady."

"Two Eduardo Drive, Sabinal, New Mexico."

"You're not b-bullshitting me are you?" He'd been memorizing the cities in New Mexico. Alamogordo, Albuquerque, Deming, Las Cruces, Santa Fe. He did not recognize the name. "What part of the state is Sabinal in?"

"How should I know?"

"Never mind." He realized it was an unreasonable request. He was lucky she had the address.

To his surprise, she said, "Ah, someplace like Espanoola. Does that sound familiar?"

All his hard work studying the New Mexico maps had paid off. Española was north of Santa Fe. "When can you g-get the cash?"

"I'll have to talk to my parents."

"No later than t-tonight."

She was sobbing. "I'll do my best. Where should I drop it off?"

Dave needed time to figure out the logistics. "I'll call you b-back in an hour. Remember no c-cops, or else I won't be so nice."

"I promise. No police."

He hung up the phone hopeful she'd pony up the cash so he could begin his adventure to New Mexico. But what was he gonna do with the little girl? No way could he bring her home or to Barney's. Who else could help him out? For the first time in his life, it dawned on him that other than his cousin, he had no real friends.

Then miraculously he had the answer. He reached in his jacket pocket and pulled out the crumpled cocktail napkin where Cherry had written down her home address. She'd told him she had kids. Twin girls if he remembered correctly. For the right price, she'd take care of Maya for him. If everything worked out, he would have the money and be long gone by the time Maya's mother picked her up there.

The plan was risky, but if things went well, he'd have it all. A new life in New Mexico with Miss Levin, and money to get them started. He knew Cherry's shift at Déjà Vu started at seven p.m. If the plan was to work, he needed to get the little girl to Cherry's house before she left for work.

First stop, 149th Street - Grand Concourse Post Office. After taking the MTA subway and walking up a flight of stairs to the post office, Maya cried out. "I can't walk no more."

"Uncle Dave will carry you." He picked her up and threw her gently over his shoulder. In a matter of minutes, she was asleep tucking her little head over his shoulder. He liked the feeling it gave him and looked forward to a day when he and Miss Levin had children of their own.

Dave waved at the postal workers at the counter and carried Maya to the small office of his boss.

Mrs. Rodman sat in a swivel chair typing on an IBM Selectric. She looked up at him with squinty brown eyes that had grainy circles of black under them. "Mr. Burke, how can I help you?"

"I need some time off."

"Okay." She flipped through a drawer in a file cabinet and pulled out a manila folder with Dave's name printed on it. "Looks like you've been here close to thirteen years and never taken a day of vacation."

"I'd like a few weeks, Ma'am. Also, my paycheck."

She smiled at Maya. "You never mentioned you had a little girl."

"She's, ah, my niece."

Mrs. Rodman was friendlier than he ever remembered. "The little cutie looks exhausted. Is she the reason you're taking time off?"

"Yes, I-I'm going to ah, find a new place to live with her."

"What happened to her parents?"

He had to think fast. "Sadly, her folks were killed in a car accident. I'm all she has now."

"Poor little thing. You certainly can have the time off you've requested." She pulled out a big checkbook, wrote him a check, and handed it to him.

"Thank you, Ma'am."

"Good luck to you, Dave."

Still carrying a sleeping Maya, with a check for 304 dollars and change tucked in his pocket, he hopped a subway to Port Authority on Eighth Avenue.

Between the stench of urine, B.O. and garbage, and the constant crush of commuters jousting with dimwitted tourists, he got a migraine headache within minutes of stepping inside the building.

Dave scanned through the hundreds of destinations posted on the giant data board. While there was a bus to Albuquerque, he decided to purchase a ticket somewhere else. That way, if Maya's mother called the police and they put the dots together, they'd be searching the wrong bus. Once he was out west, he could transfer to another bus, or rent a car. "One ticket on the 6:15 bus to Oklahoma City," he told the clerk, a thin man with a Colonel Sanders white mustache and goatee. That was three quarters of the way to New Mexico.

He pointed at Maya. "Kids are half price."

Dave told the truth. "Oh, ah, she's staying here with her mother."

Next, he looked around for a locker. There was a long row of them on the west wall. He chose locker number 2324 and conceived the rest of his plan. He would tell Maya's mother to place the money in the locker. He would need to find a place to stash the key. It had to be a place that he could easily identify. Under a chair in the waiting area? Wrapped in a newspaper under a vent? Then he remembered the Capizzi's behind the Port Authority building on Ninth Avenue. It was his favorite pizza joint in the city. A bit of an oddball location made it the perfect place for a drop off.

Still carrying a sleeping Maya, he left the building and scurried down the grimy street to Capizzi's. In front of the restaurant stood a large, metal rubbish can. Perfect.

He called Maya's mother from a phone booth across the street from the restaurant. "Did you get my money?"

"I have it. But I want to talk to my daughter."

He shook the sleepy girl awake and held the phone to her mouth. "Mommy?"

"Where are you, honey?"

Dave grabbed the phone from Maya's hand. She began to cry.

"Please don't hurt her," said the mother in a frantic voice.

"D-don't ask her about her whereabouts."

"I'm sorry."

He placed the phone to Maya's head again. "Tell Mommy nobody's hurt you."

"Come get me now, Mommy."

"Very soon, sweetheart."

Dave gave her the specific instructions about buying the locker, placing the money inside, and where to leave the key. "Once I have the c-cash, I'll phone you and reveal where you can pick up Maya."

"How do I know she'll be there?"

He shook his head. "Trust me. I have no use for your daughter."

"What time?"

He checked out his watch. "It's almost four o'clock. C-can you be there in an hour?"

She gulped. "Yes."

"Wrap up the dough like it's a Christmas present."

Twenty minutes later, he was knocking on Cherry's door in Brooklyn. She looked unrecognizable without makeup and her hair all done up. The only reason he knew it was her was at six feet, she towered over Dave. She was only too happy to watch his "niece" until her mother picked her up. Didn't even ask him for any money although he handed her a twenty.

Then he remembered why she'd given him her number in the first place. "Want me to check out the toilet?"

"My brother fixed it." Cherry said.

"Sorry I didn't make it over sooner." He turned to Maya. "You be a good girl. Mommy will be here very soon."

"I wanna hug," she said as he turned to leave.

Had he heard her right? He moved toward the front door.

Her green eyes sparkled. "Please, Uncle Dave."

Blinking back a tear, he bent down, and the little girl wrapped her arms around his neck. He couldn't remember the last time anyone wanted a hug from him.

LATER THAT NIGHT, AS HE STOOD IN FRONT OF CAPIZZI'S Pizza behind the Port Authority building, Dave felt this surreal sense of heightened sounds. People shouting, dogs barking, cars honking. Was the old man eating a calzone and glaring at him from a table an undercover cop? Maybe the lady chatting in the phone booth with a nose the size of Rhode Island was FBI. He'd read somewhere they were hiring women now. Or was that the CIA?

A painful tightness gripped his chest and his mouth was dry as a hobo's elbows. Sweat oozed from every pore in his body. He had never done anything illegal before. Never even had a speeding ticket. Of course he never owned a car.

This whole thing had gone too far. Maybe he should forget about the ransom money. He already had Miss Levin's address and could head to New Mexico without increasing his risk of getting caught. The kid was safe at Cherry's, and the stripper didn't know nothin' about Dave, other than his first name and the fact he patronized Déjà Vu.

No, he couldn't risk going to prison where schmoes like him were targets for the all the hardened criminals. Where some horny dude would fuck him in the ass. No way. Time to go to his apartment, pack his things, and hop the bus out West. That made sense. But the money in locker 2324 was calling his name.

Just then, a toothless dude held up a tin cup to Dave's face.

Suddenly, he had an idea. He wagged a crisp ten-dollar bill in front of the old man. "What's your name, buddy?"

"Martino." The guy reached for the money.

"Not so fast." Dave explained what needed to be done and when Martino agreed, he placed the money inside his cup. "There's another one where this came from when you hand over the package."

Dave slipped on his aviator sunglasses and sat at on a bench, pretending to read a newspaper. He surveyed the area to make sure no one was checking out Martino, as he reached below the trash bin and picked up the key. So far, so good.

Dave shadowed the old man inside the Port Authority standing about ten feet behind him.

Martino placed the key into locker 2324 and pulled out a gift-wrapped box with a big green bow.

Blood pulsated in Dave's ears as he scrutinized the area for possible FBI or undercover cops. Then he tailed Martino as he strolled casually out the door of the Port Authority building onto 42nd Street.

After he was certain Martino was not being followed by anyone but himself, he crept up behind him and tapped his shoulder. Martino handed Dave the gift box, and Dave tucked a twenty-dollar bill in the old man's outstretched hand. That was ten bucks more than he'd promised.

Martino's face lit up and he gave Dave a gummy smile. "That's most kind of ya."

Dave felt good about himself as he headed off with the package, hoping the extra good karma would help him get safely to New Mexico and into Miss Levin's arms. He took the subway to his apartment in the Bronx, opened the box, and counted the money. It totaled exactly ten grand. Shit, he should have asked for twenty. He packed a large brown valise, walked to the corner phone booth, dialed Maya's mother, and gave her Cherry's address.

CHAPTER FORTY-FOUR
The Cat's Outta the Bag

Laila

I had just booked a flight to New York when the phone rang.

"Laila?" said Rachel.

As I gripped the receiver, I was drenched in sweat. "Please tell me Maya's okay."

My sister let out her breath. "She's fine."

"Thank God." I had never felt so relieved in my life.

"Maya," said Rachel, "Say hello to Auntie Lala."

A few seconds later my niece said, "Mommy bought me a new Barbie."

"Cool. Are you okay, sweetheart?"

"Mommy said I can't go anywhere with Uncle Dave again."

"Mommy's right. Never, go anywhere with strangers."

"But Mr. Boonie's not a stranger," she said defiantly.

"Put Mommy back on, okay?"

Rachel explained how she'd dropped off ten grand in a locker at Port Authority, and then returned to the apartment where she received a call with an address in Brooklyn. "When I got there, Maya was playing with some twins about her own age. The girls' mother was a tall redhead who works as a dancer at a strip club on 44th Street."

"Did she know the kidnapper?"

"Only that his first name is Dave and he was a regular at

the club. She'd given him her address one night because he said he'd fix some plumbing for her."

"But she didn't know his last name or address?"

"No. Now that we have Maya back I'm not sure what to do," said Rachel.

"Call the police," yelled Eve in the background. "Don't forget he's got my ten grand."

"We've got Maya. Who cares about the money?" Pop shouted.

"Let me speak with your sista," Ma said.

"Laila," she said breathlessly, "tell Rachel to call the cops. My heart can't take much more of this."

"I agree with you, Ma. If he kidnapped Maya, who's to say he won't do it to another child?"

"And Rachel gave him your address in New Mexico."

"But I don't live there anymore," I said without thinking first.

"Really! Did you and the doctor break up?"

The cat was now out of the bag and there was no stuffing it back inside. "Kinda."

"I knew this whole thing was a mistake," Ma shouted. "If I—"

The sound of screaming pierced my ears. Then I heard a cry for help. "I gotta go, Ma. Tell Rachel I said to call the police."

I raced into Allison's bedroom and helped her stand up. The sheets were soaked in blood.

I could barely see through the flood of tears, as I dialed 911. My voice was so choked up that the operator asked me to repeat the address three times. Then I called Leo. When I told him the news, he yelped like a wounded animal.

CHAPTER FORTY-FIVE
The Escape

Dave

Dave hailed a cab back to Port Authority where he caught the bus to Oklahoma City. He sat down in the last seat of the bus and let out a big sigh. He'd done it. In his pocket was the address of Miss Levin, and in his suitcase was 10,000 dollars. He thought about Maya's hug and slept like a baby until they stopped in Louisville, Kentucky.

A dumpy woman boarded the bus and sat in the empty seat next to him. She had a beehive of hair, shellacked with a thick coat of hairspray that made Dave gag. First, she yacked on and on about her no good husband leaving her penniless, and then she fell asleep and snored like a wild boar.

When they arrived at the Oklahoma City bus station, an exhausted Dave stepped into a Yellow Cab and instructed the driver to take him to the closest used car lot.

"Just so happens my cousin Joe is selling his old Lincoln. It's a helluva good car if you don't mind the loud muffler. Probably needs a new one."

Perfect. Two hours later, after treating himself to an onion burger and chili-cheese fries at the Hungry Frog Restaurant, Dave was driving the old white Lincoln on I-40 toward Miss Levin. He had a full belly and 9,654 dollars in his suitcase. Crystal Gayle's "Don't It Make My Brown Eyes Blue" blasted on the radio.

God, life was good!

CHAPTER FORTY-SIX
The Hospital

Eduardo

Eduardo walked inside the surgical waiting room of Santa Fe Hospital where Mama and his three sisters waited with swollen, tear-stained faces. He handed his mother a Styrofoam cup of coffee. "He's going to be all right, Mama."

Her hand trembled as she reached out for the cup. "He was riding his horse just yesterday."

Carla put her arm around Mama. "Remember, Eduardo says Dr. Peterson is the top heart surgeon in New Mexico."

"Yes, we have the best," Eduardo said, trying to reassure himself as well as the rest of the *familia*. A few hours earlier, Mama had found Papa lying on the ground in the barn. He complained of chest pains. She had called Eduardo right away.

After stabilizing his father at Española hospital, Eduardo contacted Dr. Christian Peterson, a professor of his from Columbia Medical School and a renowned New York heart surgeon. A few years ago, on Eduardo's recommendation, Dr. Peterson had vacationed in New Mexico and his wife had fallen in love with the Land of Enchantment. Shortly after, he'd accepted a position at St. Vincent's Hospital in Santa Fe.

Christian arranged for an ambulance to bring Ramon down to St. Vincent's where they had more sophisticated facilities. After examining Ramon, he recommended an immediate heart valve replacement. Eduardo agreed and he advised his father to sign the necessary papers. Then he wheeled Papa down to the operating room.

When they arrived, Papa squeezed Eduardo's hand. "If something happens to me—"

"You're gonna be fine," Eduardo said reassuringly.

"If something happens, *hijo,* promise me you will follow your heart. Go fight for that girl."

Eduardo's eyes misted up. Even in the possible face of death, his father was thinking about Eduardo's happiness. He hoped that someday he had the opportunity to be as good a father as Ramon. "I love you, Papa. See you after the surgery."

"I love you too, *hijo.*"

These were words they rarely exchanged. But he'd never doubted his father's love for him. Papa had always been there for him. He'd never missed a baseball game or a teacher's conference. He always made time for Eduardo. And he had kept Violet's secret.

"I'll be here throughout the surgery," Eduardo said.

"No, go sit with your mother. She needs you more than me."

Christian had just entered the room in his scrubs. "It may be best for you not to watch, Eduardo."

Eduardo nodded, and then looked at his father. "I'll see you in recovery."

He found Mama and his sisters fluttering around the waiting room.

"Cómo es Papá?" Kiki asked.

Everyone looked up at him.

"He's doing fine," Eduardo said. "He may not be able to ride a horse for a few weeks though."

As everyone smiled, Aunt Virgie and Violet arrived with a huge vase of flowers. "We just heard. *Cómo es, Ramon?*"

Carla explained that he was in surgery.

"I'm here for you," Violet whispered in Eduardo's ear.

He half-smiled, aware that he could not continue this charade. But this was not the time or place to tell her what was on his mind.

A few hours later, Dr. Peterson appeared in his scrubs. He walked up to Mama and smiled. "Your husband got through surgery with flying colors. With some rest, he's going to be good as new."

"That ain't going to be easy for my dad," said Angie.

"Don't you worry, Doctor," Mama said. "I won't let him out of my sight."

Carla smiled. "Uh oh, poor Dad."

Everyone hugged, and tears of joy replaced those of sadness.

Violet embraced Eduardo, and then snuck a quick kiss on his lips.

Eduardo stiffened. "Let's get some coffee."

They walked together in silence to the hospital's cafeteria where Eduardo purchased two Styrofoam cups of coffee, then sat across from Violet in a booth at the back of the room. He loosened his necktie. Now that Papa had come through surgery, he could breathe again.

As he sipped the coffee, he tried to find the right words to say to Violet. He didn't want to hurt her. It was ironic that the last time his father had suffered a heart attack, Eduardo had been at the senior prom with her. Now, seventeen years later, Papa had another close call with death as he sat across the table from Violet again. But years ago, she had ended their relationship. Now he had to make her understand that he had no intentions of having one with her now. Even without Laila in his life, he no longer had feelings for his high school sweetheart. Life had changed the girl he once had adored. Or maybe he had never really known her. They had just been a couple of teenagers. "You've been lying to me about your fainting spells."

"What are you talking about?"

"I tested your urine and blood for drugs. You have a lot of cocaine, in your system."

"So I party occasionally." Violet pulled out a cigarette started to light it, looked up at him scowling at her, then returned it to her purse.

"The point is . . . you lied to me when I asked you if you were taking recreational drugs. You also had oxycodone, Valium, and traces of amphetamines. Who prescribed those drugs to you?"

"Doctors in L.A., and now there's ah . . . one in Santa Fe. What is the big deal?"

"No big deal, if you want to slowly kill yourself."

"You're overreacting, Eduardo. But I'm willing to get clean if that's what it takes to win your affection again."

"You lost that a long time ago. Dr. Lopez told me the truth about the miscarriage. You lied to me back then."

"What did he tell you?"

"You had an illegal abortion in Juarez. I found out a year ago, when he and I started discussing the terms of me taking over his practice."

"Oh, Mr. Righteous, big city doctor. Tell me you don't believe in a woman's right to choose!"

"That's not the issue, Violet." His eyes teared up, despite

his best effort to keep that from happening. The wound felt fresh even though he'd tried to forget it ever happened. "You told me nothing. Don't you think I had a right to know before you ended the pregnancy?"

She looked into his eyes. "If I had to do it over again, I'd do it differently."

Did she think that would make things better?

Just then a red-faced Carla appeared. "Dad's in trouble."

CHAPTER FORTY-SEVEN
The Miscarriage

Laila

Allison moaned as she sat on towels on the ride to Santa Fe hospital. She and I rushed past the Information Desk into the Emergency Room, while Leo parked the car.

"Stop," shouted a nurse who dropped her knitting on the desk. "You need to check in."

As I filled out the paperwork for Allison, I thought I saw Eduardo's mother and sisters leaving through the revolving door. Or was it my imagination? But I was too busy comforting Allison to check it out.

Leo and I sat in the waiting area while Allison was being examined. An hour or so later, the doctor appeared. His eyelids fluttered as he said in a deep voice, "I'm sorry Mr. Harvey, your wife lost the baby."

Leo's shoulders drooped, and he squeezed his eyes shut.

I slumped in the chair and couldn't help but think about how Peaches and the other girls became pregnant so easily. If there was a God, he or she certainly worked in mysterious ways.

I composed myself before entering Allison's hospital room.

Unfortunately, she was inconsolable. "It feels like I'm cursed. What have I done that is so terrible?" she cried.

"Nothing, honey," Leo said. "Life isn't always fair."

She dabbed at her eyes with a tissue. "I-I can't take this, Leo. I want to die."

"Don't say that," Leo said. "We'll figure something out."

I felt helpless sitting there. There were no words to comfort her. Finally, out of desperation, I asked if I could get them coffee.

Leo nodded.

I turned to Allison. "You want anything?"

"I want my baby," she cried.

"Allison, I'm so sorry. What can I do to help?"

"You've been a good friend, Laila. But I need to be alone right now. Leo please leave the room too."

As Leo stood alone in the hall, he too began to cry. He'd been holding his tears, trying to be brave for Allison. Now the dam had burst and he sobbed out loud. I moved close to him and he cried on my shoulder. "I just don't know if we'll ever have a child," he said through sobs.

"Sure you will." I truly believed it. These two wonderful people so deserved a child of their own.

I decided to go home so that Allison and Leo had time to themselves. On my way out, I passed the Information Desk where the same clerk was still knitting. "Excuse me, is there a Quintana checked in as a patient here?"

The clerk shuffled some files. "We have three Quintana's admitted: Victoria, Gene, Ramon."

"Ramon?" I swallowed.

She pulled out the one with RAMON QUINTANA printed on the label, and read the contents.

"What does it say?"

She pursed her lips. "Are you related?"

"Ah, yes. I'm his, ah, niece." I was a terrible liar.

"I'm sorry; he's deceased."

"Oh my God, no!" The next thing I remembered was the

cold tile floor, the strong scent of smelling salts, and a dark-skinned nurse twitching her thinly plucked eyebrows as she looked down at me. "Are you okay, Miss?" When I didn't answer she tried again. "*Estás bien, señorita?*"

"*No hablo español,*" I said.

The nurse smiled. "Well, I guess you're all right." She handed me a paper cup of water, which I sipped slowly.

Then I recalled what she'd said about Ramon, and I felt like I'd been sucker-punched. With deep sadness, gummy eyelids and a scratchy throat, I left the hospital and walked out to the parking lot. I could barely drag myself through the rows of cars. Life made no sense to me. Why were these terrible things happening? "God, please give me an answer. This is so unfair."

Suddenly, a patch of blue mist floated by on the horizon. I could swear I saw a vision of Ramon riding an Appaloosa, together with a chubby baby, and my beloved Zorro cuddled next to him on the saddle.

A dream or hallucination? Perhaps. But it was real for me. So real that for the first time in my life, I believed in something much greater than ourselves. A force? A higher being? God? I don't know. Yet in that moment, I felt a sense of tranquility and warmth.

TWO DAYS LATER, I ARRIVED AT THE GRAVEYARD BEHIND the small adobe church, and snaked my way through pampas grass, interspersed with cottonwood trees, tumbleweed, wood crosses, and gravestones. I had seen the obituary in the newspaper.

The Quintanas were gathered around Ramon's casket. At

least a hundred family members and friends had also come to pay their respects.

I crept shyly up to the outside of the crowd.

A few Harleys were parked among the pickups and old sedans. A priest stood with his arm around a tiny woman dressed in a flowing black dress. A veil covered her face, but I was certain it was Grandma Rosa. Sylvia and Eduardo's sisters stood next to her. I recognized many of the relatives, Rojo and Billy, Aunt Marie and Aunt Juanita, whom I'd met at the *matanza*. Tito, no longer in a wheelchair, pranced about with a perky blonde on his arm.

I spotted Eduardo knee deep in *familia,* and drifted through the relatives and friends toward him. As I got closer, I saw Sylvia clinging to Eduardo, and then caught a glimpse of Violet standing on his other side. She stood greeting each of Eduardo's relatives like she was already his wife.

Ironically, she was the only one who recognized me. She raised her chin and sneered at me with a clear signal of victory. Or was it all in my imagination that she'd even seen me at all?

CHAPTER FORTY-EIGHT
The Funeral

Violet

Violet stood next to Eduardo at the graveyard, but he'd barely said a word to her. A soft breeze shot through the cottonwoods as Ramon's casket was placed in the ground. Eduardo's eyes looked strangely vacant with no sign of tears. His face was pale as parchment.

After the priest said some prayers, everyone lined up to offer their condolences. Relatives hugged Eduardo, then her in turn, as though she was his *esposa*. Everyone seemed to think they were a couple, except for him. *Was that Laila in the distance pressing her way through the crowd?* Violet curled her lip and nodded at her with an air of superiority. Then she looped her arm through Eduardo's.

The bitch retreated toward the parked vehicles.

Violet barely had a moment to bask in her victory before Eduardo jerked his arm away and glared at her with scornful eyes. *Had she blown her chances with him?*

She walked off, found Mama and walked with her to the car. "Let's go to Sylvia's house," Mama said. "You need to be there for him now, *hija*."

"I'm trying, Mama, but he shows no interest in me."

"Try harder," Mama said. "You are *muy bonita*. Surely, now that the New Yorker is gone, you can win his favor."

The delicious aroma of pinto beans, green chili stew, *carne adovada*, and fresh tortillas filled Violet's senses as she and Mama entered the Quintana house. Violet had even spent hours baking a batch of *biscochitos*, crisp lard-based cookies flavored with cinnamon and anise. They had been Eduardo's favorite when they were children growing up together.

Sylvia greeted them in the large kitchen with warm hugs. She whispered in Violet's ear, "The next time we're all together will be your wedding to Eduardo."

"I can only dream," Violet said, but feared Sylvia's prediction would never come true. Even with the bitch out of the game, Eduardo showed no interest in her charms.

Violet scanned the crowded kitchen in search of him. After checking out the rest of the house, she returned to the kitchen and sidled up to Sylvia. "*Donde está* Eduardo?"

Sylvia shook her head. "Poor *mi hijo* looked exhausted. He probably went home to take a nap."

Perfect! Perhaps in a moment of weakness, he'd allow her to comfort him in the way only a woman can do for a man. The only way Violet knew how. She wrapped up a dozen *biscochitos* in napkins and told Mama she was heading to Eduardo's.

Mama hugged her. "This is your chance, *hija*. Good luck."

CHAPTER FORTY-NINE
Bait and Switch

Violet

Violet's legs pumped like pistons as she careened down the road toward the trailer and her last chance of capturing Eduardo's heart—maybe, her last chance at happiness. Suddenly, one of the heels of her black pumps got caught in a pothole and snapped off. "Damn it!" She stopped running, took both shoes off and began to doubt herself. *Was this really such a good idea?* She couldn't handle any more rejection. *Ya era suficiente para toda la vida.* She'd had enough for a lifetime.

She stood in her bare feet and watched the sun fall behind the horizon, painting the New Mexico sky shades of crimson, gold and pink. The afternoon sun felt warm on her face as she thought about all the pain she had suffered. Getting fired from TWA after she was caught tooting up powder in the bathroom, her failed attempt at an acting career in Los Angeles. She stopped counting all the agents and casting directors who had used her for sexual favors.

Her life so far had been one big fiasco. This was her last chance to turn things around. *I will beg Eduardo for his forgiveness and promise that I am done with drugs forever.* She needed to go cold turkey anyway. Ira had only left her two grams of coke.

She arrived at the trailer out of breath. There was no sign of Eduardo's Studebaker. Violet rapped on the front door numerous times, but no one answered. She turned the doorknob which snapped off into her hands. After tossing it to the ground, she pulled open the front door and walked inside. "Hello, is anyone here?"

No answer. "Hello." Looking around, Violet made note of the cracked linoleum floors and scratched Formica countertops. Cabinet doors hung off their hinges and the pea-green carpet was unraveling. The place was worse than Ira's L.A. apartment. *Do I really want to live here? But what choice do I have? Run to Ira in Oshkosh? No way. Eduardo had loved her once. She would make him love her again.*

Violet sat on the old tweed sofa and switched on the small portable TV. She would wait for Eduardo, no matter how long it took him to get home. As the hours passed, she watched *60 Minutes, Rhoda,* then *All in the Family.* She could give a shit about Archie Bunker. Was this what her life would be like married to Eduardo? Sitting in a rundown mobile home waiting for him to come home from the hospital? No, he would build them a beautiful home and they'd live happily ever after. Sylvia said he'd already had architectural plans drawn up.

When the ten o'clock news came on, she picked up the phone and dialed Sylvia's number.

"*Hola,*" Sylvia said in a tired voice.

"Is Eduardo there?"

"He called from the hospital. Some *emergencia.*"

Violet slammed down the phone. Should she leave? That meant calling Mama to come pick her up. Admitting defeat. Perhaps there was another way. *I'll undress and wait for him in under the covers. What man could resist a beautiful woman in his bed?*

Still barefoot, she padded into the bathroom, washed her dirty feet in the tub, gargled with mouthwash, and doused herself with rose-scented cologne left by the bitch. Minutes later, she unzipped the matronly black dress that Mama had made her wear to the funeral, slid it off, and slipped into the double bed, dressed only in her black lace bra and bikini panties. She adored the luxurious silk sheets on her skin and wondered if Laila had brought them from New York. Of course she did. Eduardo would never buy something that extravagant for himself.

With the help of a Valium, two to be precise, Violet began to relax and soon fell soundly asleep. She dreamed of a beautiful wedding in the Quintanas' barn. Her silk dress hugged her curves and hundreds of pearl beads covered the bodice. Papa was walking her down the aisle with tears in his eyes. The aroma of Lava soap and a trace of cigar smoke filled her nostrils. But Papa . . .

Tires crunched on the gravel outside the trailer window, followed by a loud muffler exploding repeatedly.

Violet's stomach knotted up. Could her plan really work? The slam of a car door was followed by pounding on the front door. Why would Eduardo knock on the door of his own house? Come to think of it, she didn't recall his car having such a noisy muffler. She gulped as she remembered that the doorknob was laying on the ground. An invitation for anyone to come inside.

Who could be at the door? A thief or worse? A rapist or murderer? *Take a deep breath. You're not in L.A. anymore. Crime in Sabinal is practically nonexistent.* But over the years Violet had learned to be prepared for the worst. She dashed into the kitchen and grabbed a butcher knife just as someone pulled the door out and entered the house.

Violet snapped on the light.

A short muscular guy in Wranglers and a hooded sweatshirt stood before her.

She glared at him. "Who the fuck are you?"

CHAPTER FIFTY
Along for the Ride

Dave

A dark-skinned woman pointed a large knife at Dave. She had long shiny hair and wore only a sexy bra and bikini underwear. "You're not M-miss Levin."

Her black eyes smoldered like two embers of charcoal. "What are you doing here?"

Shit, what could he say? That he'd come to find the woman of his dreams? Borrowed her little niece for a few hours and then hopped a bus out West in search of her? "I'm D-dave."

"Are you an old boyfriend of Laila's?"

Best to keep certain things to himself. "S-something like that. Who are you?"

"What business is it of yours?"

He looked into her enormous eyes. "N-none, I guess." Such a beauty. But he had come a long way to see Miss Levin. Had Maya's mother tricked him? "Do you know where I can find Laila?"

The woman shrugged. "I think she went back to New York."

"You're sh-shitting me, right?"

She took a step back. "Why would I do that?"

"D-damn. Now I'll have to go back home to f-find her."

"You've got a place in New York?"

"Yeah, in the B-bronx."

"Is that near Manhattan?"

"Just a subway ride away." He turned toward the door.

"Wait a minute. Don't leave so fast. Let me get dressed and I'll put on some coffee."

Hell, what did he have to lose? "Okay."

She pointed at a vinyl chair. "Have a seat." She scooped coffee into a paper filter and filled a glass decanter with water. "Hope you like it strong."

A few minutes later, the aroma of the drip coffee filled the kitchen as the pretty *señorita* returned to the kitchen wearing a black dress that didn't do her curves justice. She filled two mugs with coffee and handed one to Dave. "Cream or sugar?"

"N-no, I like it black."

"Yeah, me too." She eyeballed him as she sat down and sipped the hot coffee. After an awkward silence, she began to speak. "Your girlfriend hated it here. She was smart to hit the road. Now *I'm* the one stuck in this Podunk town."

"What's keeping you here?"

"That's a good question." She held up the glass coffee pot. "Have time for another cup?"

As sunlight peeked through the slats of the trailer's mini-blinds, Dave learned more than he had bargained for about the chick's sorry life. Hell, it wasn't much better than his own. But it crossed his mind that if he played his cards right, he might get into her underpants. Yes, she wasn't Laila, but why not have a little fun with this drop-dead gorgeous chick now? He would catch up with Miss Levin later. "You're not stuck. Why d-don't you come to New York with me?"

CHAPTER FIFTY-ONE
New York, New York

Violet

She needed time to think. Realistically, she had probably blown her chances with Eduardo. And that damn New York *chica* had been right when she'd reminded Violet that there had been a good reason why she had left this two-horse town years ago. She hated Sabinal.

Had divine intervention come in the form of this idiot? Of course, she would dump the stuttering fool as soon as they got to the Big Apple. If things didn't work out in New York, she could always come back home. With time, maybe Eduardo would change his mind about her. The more Violet thought about it, the jerk's offer sounded appealing. "Okay, I'll ride with you. But only if you promise no monkey business on the road."

His Adam's apple bulged as he struggled to speak. "S-s-cout's honor. When c-can you leave?"

"I need to stop by my mama's house to get my things." Her mother would be serving breakfast at the Española Diner. The less Violet had to explain to Mama, the better.

Ten minutes later, the Dave guy parked the car in the driveway of Mama's small stucco house. Violet opened the passenger door. "Wait here while I pack up my stuff. It will only take a few minutes." She hurried inside and glanced around at the crucifixes and family photos on the walls. Had growing up here been so bad? She stared at a picture of Papa dressed in his U.S. Air Force uniform from WWII. With his high cheekbones and chiseled profile, Papa was as handsome as a Spanish Conquistador and had always been very kind to her. If Mama hadn't cheated on him, maybe he wouldn't have had a massive heart attack. After he died, nothing was ever right for Violet. Blinking back the tears, she removed the framed photo from the wall.

When she entered her childhood bedroom, she broke out sobbing. A giant poster of Elvis still hung on the closet door. When they were in sixth grade, Violet and her friend Maria had taken turns making out with the poster. What happened to that confident young girl who thought she could take the world by storm? Even then, she knew there was more to life than Sabinal. Maria, on the other hand, ended up marrying Reggie Garcia after dropping out of high school to have his baby.

Violet hauled out two plaid suitcases from under her bed, jerked clothes off of hangers in the closet, and emptied her dresser drawers. Expensive lingerie and low-cut silk dresses from her time in L.A. mingled with wool socks, T-shirts, and old jeans from high school. She stuffed the luggage with her belongings, taking the time to carefully tuck Papa's photo between two mohair sweaters.

As Violet headed out the door, the phone rang. She stared at the ringing avocado phone hanging on the wall, trying to decide whether to pick up. *Who would be calling this early in the morning? Could it possibly be Eduardo looking for her?* Finally, after six rings, her curiosity got the best of her and she grabbed the receiver. "Hello."

"Hey, baby, it's me, Ira. You'll never guess where I am."

"Let me see. Oshkosh B'Gosh, if I remember correctly."

"Wrong. But you were right about the place being b-o-r-i-n-g. I've moved to the Big Apple."

Was he shitting her? "New York? Seriously?"

"Of course I'm serious. I'm staying with an old buddy of mine. He's got connections on Broadway."

"Yeah, right. Like your connections in L.A."

"This is different. Swear to God. I showed him your glamour shots and he's quite impressed."

"I thought thirty-four made me an old hag."

"That was LA. It's a different ballgame in New York. I'm, ah, still short on cash, but I'll send you a ticket in a few weeks. Whaddaya say?"

Violet thought for a minute. Was this part of God's plan of divine intervention? His insurance that she would leave this shithole and take a different path? It made so much sense. She belonged in New York. "I'll see you in a few days." She filled him in on the Dave guy.

"What do you know about this dude?"

"Have you forgotten who you're talking to? Violet Sanchez can take care of herself. Besides the guy is an idiot."

"I love you, Violet. Be very careful."

"Love you, too." In truth, Violet didn't know what she felt about Ira . . . or anyone else, for that matter. She wasn't even sure about her feelings for Eduardo. But Ira's call only confirmed that her decision to leave was the right thing to do. She strolled out of the house and got into the car with Jerkface. "I'm ready."

To her surprise, rather than switch on the motor, he opened the console and stuck his hand inside.

She held her breath. *Oh my God! Is he reaching for a gun?*

A few seconds later, Dave held up a vial of white powder. "Wanna hit, b-baby?"

She let out her breath and swallowed. This ride wasn't going to be as bad as she thought. "Sure." Violet was now certain she had made the right decision. *New York City, here I come!*

CHAPTER FIFTY-TWO
The Capture

Dave

He restrained himself and didn't make a pass at Violet throughout the entire cross-country ride. The coke kept them buzzed, so they only stopped one night at a cheap motel in St. Louis. She had insisted on separate rooms. If Dave played his cards right, she would give him some nookie when they got back to the Bronx. After all, there was only one bed in his apartment.

As they drove through Pennsylvania, it dawned on Dave he had no place in the city to leave the Lincoln. Most of the cars parked overnight in his South Bronx neighborhood got vandalized by hoodlums. That's what had happened to the old Valiant that his mother had left him. When they stopped for gas in Pittsburgh, he called his cousin, Barney, from a phone booth at the Shell station.

"Where have you been?" Barney asked. "I've been worried about you."

Dave thought that was strange. He often didn't see Barney for weeks, even months at a time. "I've only been gone a few days."

"Well, yeah. But I've called you the last few nights, and you're never there. I even stopped by the apartment."

Dave told him he'd gone out West and was coming home with a new girlfriend. "And I bought myself a car. I was wondering if I could keep it in your driveway in Long Island. I'll pay you rent, of course."

"No need for that," Barney said. "When will you get here?"

"Late tonight," Dave said. "I really appreciate it."

It was after midnight when they drove up to Barney's small Cape Cod in Massapequa. Suddenly, red-and-white lights flashed on the Lincoln from all directions. Then the screeching sound of sirens as squad cars surrounded them.

Violet jerked back in the seat. "What's going on?"

"I don't know." Dave said. But he did.

Barney appeared at the driver's door dressed in uniform. "Get out of the car, Dave."

Dave did what he was told.

A tall cop handcuffed him and read him his Miranda rights. Was this really happening to him? Suddenly, Dave was drenched in sweat. Surely his cousin would understand this was a big misunderstanding. "All I d-did was buy the k-kid an ice cream c-cone. I'll give back the m-money."

"Sorry buddy," Barney said as two cops forced Dave into a squad car.

Barney got in the back seat next to him. "When I read the APB, they said the little girl had been found with a dancer from Déjà Vu, that place you always brag about. And the dancer described you as having a stutter. That did you in, bud. It didn't take me long to put the puzzle pieces together. If you hadn't come back, you might have gotten away with it."

If it hadn't been for Miss Levin, Dave wouldn't have ever come back. She had ruined his life. Maybe he could have settled somewhere with the Mexican beauty. Too late for that now.

CHAPTER FIFTY-THREE
The Adoption

Laila

One afternoon in late April, I received a surprising phone call from Florence, the Española High School secretary. "Mr. Jaramillo has agreed for you to speak at our next PTA meeting on the condition that your presentation is no longer than fifteen minutes."

Mr. Jaramillo, the principal at Española High School, had flatly turned me down when I had spoken to him a few weeks ago. "What made him change his mind?"

Florence was quiet for a minute, and then blurted out, "You didn't hear this from me, okay?"

"Of course not."

"He just learned his son, Roberto, knocked up his girlfriend. The boy had received a football scholarship to Texas A&M. Now he's gotta turn it down."

"I'm sorry about his son," I said. "But fifteen minutes is not nearly enough time."

"Please, Miss Levin," Florence pleaded. "Mr. Jaramillo had such high hopes for Roberto. And . . . my daughter's only fourteen. She needs guidance now *before* something happens."

"Have you spoken to her about birth control?"

There was a long pause. "*Mi esposo* . . . my husband forbids me."

"When is the meeting?"

"Thursday night at seven. I'll make sure you get on early in the agenda."

I had serious doubts about going to Española but finally acquiesced to Florence despite my better judgment. My presentations at school board and PTA meetings in cities like Santa Fe and Albuquerque had been successful. But rural schools were more resistant to addressing the issue of teen pregnancy and for the most part, had rejected my offer to come.

The night of my presentation, the auditorium filled with parents, teachers, school administrators, and a few teenagers.

Florence, a petite woman, dressed in a broomstick skirt and white blouse, greeted me with a warm hug. "Thank you, so much for coming." She placed her arm around a tiny girl with curly black hair. She looked more like twelve than fourteen. "This is my daughter, Isabel."

Mr. Jaramillo, a large man with a bushy black mustache, wore a starched white shirt and polka dot bow tie. He barely nodded at me when Florence introduced us. So much for a warm welcome.

Florence squeezed my hand as I walked with her to the podium on wobbly legs. "Our first speaker this evening is Dr. Laila Levin. She holds a doctorate from New York University and is going to talk about the epidemic problem of teen pregnancy—*el problema de la epidemia del embarazo en la adolescencia.*"

There was light applause as Florence handed me the microphone. Two girls in the back of the auditorium remained standing.

Rings of perspiration formed under my arms while I attempted to compose myself.

The room was so quiet you could hear grasshoppers on the baseball field. I gave my short presentation, emphasizing the need for sex education classes, in less than the allotted fifteen minutes, leaving time for questions.

As soon as I was done, a number of hands popped up. I pointed at a well-dressed Hispanic woman decked out in turquoise jewelry. "*No te parece que estás animando a nuestros hijos a tener relaciones sexuales, dándoles control de la natalidad?*"

My throat tightened. "Sorry, my Spanish—"

Florence came to the rescue. "Mrs. Santiago asked whether you're encouraging our kids to have sex by giving them birth control."

A woman wearing a red T-shirt with the words "Española Sundevils" in gold lettering, stood up. "*Qué pasa con* abstinence?"

"In sex education classes we encourage abstinence, but in reality many girls still go ahead and have sex," I said. "I'd rather see them armed with protection."

"Ain't that like handing them a loaded gun and telling them not to use it?" yelled a guy in a cowboy hat with broad shoulders and a squared-off beard.

My cheeks burned. "It's an interesting analogy, Sir, but I don't see that it applies. Would you rather have your children have babies—"

"Are you even Catholic?" asked the woman with all the turquoise in the front row.

Another lady said, "Our girls should go to confession and talk to the priest."

My thoughts were scrambled as I tried to diffuse the belligerent scenario. "That's well and good, but statistics have shown—"

"What does a *gringa* from New York know about Española?" said a woman in the back row.

"Do you believe our girls should kill their babies?" shouted the first lady.

I had never spoken to such a hostile crowd before. My gut had told me coming to Española would be a mistake. Why hadn't I listened? Out of the corner of my eye, I saw something headed in my direction. Before I could duck, a spit wad splattered across my nose.

Tears stung my eyelids as I wiped the shame from my face with my hand.

Florence rushed over with a tissue. "I'm so sorry."

The sound of people in the audience whispering filled my ears as I stepped down from the stage.

"Stop!" shouted a young woman who rushed up to me. Either she was pregnant, or she'd swallowed a basketball. Her face looked vaguely familiar. "Please don't leave, Dr. Levin."

"Peaches?" Her face was so swollen I barely recognized her. "Is that you?"

"It's me all right." She looked up at the audience. "I got something to say to *mis amigas*. It ain't no fun staying home with a baby all the time. I missed all the cool stuff like my prom and homecoming. Pay attention to what Dr. Levin is telling you. She knows her shit . . . sorry, stuff."

Mr. Jaramillo walked up to the stage. "I'm ashamed of what's happened here tonight and want to offer Miss Levin my sincere apologies."

I acknowledged his apology with a wave but still felt the sting of the spit wad fresh on my face.

He glared at the two girls in the back of the room. "Angie and Patricia, I'll see you in my office at 8 a.m. tomorrow." Then he gazed down at the audience. "As many of you know, my own *familia* is dealing with the consequences of an unplanned pregnancy. Half of you sitting out there are in the same situation. It's time we all stop hiding this problem under the rug. Please give Miss Levin a big hand for coming here tonight to begin a dialogue."

Florence began to clap followed by her daughter, Isabel. About half of the audience members joined them.

I ducked out the exit to the parking lot. All the research I'd done had not prepared me for such humiliation from this northern New Mexico town. Eduardo's town. I couldn't help but think things would have gone differently if he had been here with me.

As I opened my car door, I had a mixture of emotions. On one hand, that spit wad represented a community that despised people like me who challenged their ingrained cultural mores. On the other hand, perhaps my disastrous presentation had at least brought the issue of teen pregnancy out of the closet.

I had just placed my key in the ignition when there was a knock on the passenger window. I let out my breath fearful of some angry person from the audience was going to give me a piece of their mind. But it turned out to be Peaches.

I stepped out of the car and gave her a hug. She was so huge I could barely wrap my arms around her. "Thank you for standing up for me."

"No problem, Doc. I meant every word I said out there."

"What's going on with you?"

"I didn't get in that program in Querque, and well . . ." Her voice choked up. "Mama's got something called lupus and can't work no more. She can barely take care of Markie when I go to my night job at Denny's."

"I'm so sorry."

Her eyes flooded with tears. "I can't handle *two* babies. Mama's mad as hell and says she ain't gonna help with the new one."

"What are you going to do?"

"Can you help me?"

I took in my breath then let it out slowly. "Have you considered adoption?"

I INVITED PEACHES FOR DINNER THE FOLLOWING NIGHT. Allison worked all day preparing a mushroom quiche. She spent a long time getting dressed and entered the living room wearing a blue silk dress and black pumps. "Do I look okay?"

I thought about Peaches who normally wore torn Levis and T-shirts. "Perhaps a tad overdressed."

Allison bit her lip and folded her hands in front of her.

I hoped my honesty hadn't hurt her feelings. "You look great but—"

"How about your Levis?" Leo said. "And that blouse you bought in Juarez."

"Oh, sure, I get it." A few minutes later, Allison reappeared in denim overalls, an embroidered Mexican shirt, and a pair of old sneakers.

Just then, the doorbell rang. I jumped up and rushed to the entry. When I opened the front door, a young woman stood there dressed in a navy pants suit, dragon-red lipstick, and light blue eye shadow. Her hair was pulled back in a thick braid. If it weren't for the protruding belly, I wouldn't have recognized Peaches once again.

I gave her a once-over. "Wow, you look great."

She shrugged. "Mama bought me this outfit at the Santa Fe mall."

"Let's go inside." We walked into the living room, and I made introductions. "These are the friends I told you about."

Peaches crossed her arms as though appraising Allison. "Where'd you get them overalls?"

Allison smiled. "At the Army-Navy store on the plaza."

During dinner, Peaches adjusted her clothes as if they chafed her. She'd politely answer questions that Leo and Allison asked her like how old she was or where she lived but didn't initiate any conversation herself. I wondered what had happened to the Peaches who belched and said whatever she pleased.

At the end of the evening, I walked her out to her mother's old Chevy. "Are you okay?"

"Mama said I better do good tonight."

"Well, you did great. Next time, feel free to dress and speak like yourself."

"Really? Did they like me?"

"They loved you and they'll take good care of the baby."

"You think I'm doing the right thing?"

I squeezed her hand. "It's got to be a hard decision. You need to go with your gut."

"My gut says yes. But my heart aches."

"I don't want to pressure you. Do what is best for you."

"I already made up my mind," she said. "Those *gringos* will give my baby a better home than I ever could. But it hurts."

"I know it does," I said. Yet in reality, I had no idea how painful this was for Peaches.

When I got back inside the house, Allison sat on the couch rubbing the back of her neck. "What did she say?"

"It's all good."

"Leo and I have had so much disappointment."

"It will be different this time," I said with assurance.

"How do you know?" asked Leo.

"I just believe this is meant to be. Who knows? Maybe the reason I met Eduardo was to be a liaison for you guys to find Peaches' baby."

Allison smiled for the first time in a while. "I think there's more to it than that."

"What do you mean?"

"We'll see what the future brings as far as Eduardo is concerned."

How could she know I still thought about him all the time?

FOR THE NEXT FEW MONTHS, PEACHES CAME TO DINNER at least once a week. She taught Allison to cook Mexican food. They'd spend hours in the kitchen rolling tortillas and preparing cheese enchiladas and beans. Allison taught Peaches about good nutrition. She gave up fast food and even became a vegetarian.

Leo hired an attorney to draw up the legal papers for them to adopt the baby. He and Allison agreed to pay for all of Peaches' medical expenses and they worked out a plan for future visitation rights.

On a cool summer night in early July, a very pregnant Peaches sat with Allison, Leo and me out on the veranda. An alabaster moon brightened the clear New Mexico sky. Suddenly, Peaches eyes lit up. "The baby's kicking." She took Allison's hand and placed it on her stomach.

Allison smiled. "Oh my God, I can feel it."

Leo cleared his throat. "Is it okay for me—"

"Go ahead, dude."

Leo awkwardly placed his hand on Peaches belly.

Peaches moaned.

Leo pulled his hand away. "I-I'm so sorry. Did I hurt you?"

"It's not you. I got a sharp pain. It felt like a contraction."

I waved my hands dismissively. "But you're not due for another three weeks."

Drops of sweat dotted Peaches forehead. "That may be true, but . . .oww . . . I'm pretty sure this is it."

Allison's eyes widened. "Should we call an ambulance?"

Peaches moaned again. "No, just drive me to the hospital in Española."

Leo gulped. "That's at least forty minutes away. What's wrong with Santa Fe?"

"I want Dr. Quintana," Peaches said. "I ain't going to no strange doctor in Santa Fe."

I turned to Leo. "Eduardo only has privileges at Presbyterian-Española. If we move quickly, we can get her there in time." While I knew a lot about teen pregnancies, I knew squat about childbirth. I have no idea why I agreed to her wish to drive an extra forty minutes. Wishful thinking that I'd finally be forced to see Eduardo? As we piled into Leo's Volvo, I prayed we wouldn't be delivering the baby in the car.

CHAPTER FIFTY-FOUR
Peaches' Baby

Eduardo

Eduardo was getting ready to leave Española hospital after an exhausting twelve-hour shift. He thought about grabbing a hamburger at Blake's Lotaburger, and picking up an ice-cold beer at El Rey Liquors, when a voice over the PA system said, "Dr. Quintana wanted in Maternity."

He slumped against the reception desk. Why were they calling him instead of his colleague who had just started the late shift? He was bone tired as he moved into the doorway of Maternity Room One where a pregnant woman lay in bed surrounded by a nurse, a man and two women.

"Are you the father?" the nurse asked the man.

"Well, yes, but not in the way you're presuming."

The nurse shook her head. "I don't presume anything. Just need to know who's staying for the birth."

Eduardo entered the room and smiled. "Peaches? I've wondered what happened to you."

"I was waitressing a lot and didn't have no time for prenatal visits."

Eduardo shook his head. "We could have worked something out."

"Well, she's here now," said a familiar voice.

Eduardo glanced over at the slender woman and did a double take. "Laila! What are you—"

"I came for Peaches."

"I thought you had gone back to New York." Eduardo checked out the other two people in the room.

"These are my friends the Harveys," Laila said. "Peaches has agreed to let them adopt the baby."

Peaches cried out in pain. "For the love of Jesus, Mary and Joseph!"

Eduardo checked his watch. "How often are you having contractions?"

Before Peaches could answer, Laila said, "About thirty minutes apart. I've been timing them since we left Santa Fe."

Eduardo nodded. "Good, I need to examine Peaches now. Why don't you all have a seat outside?" He pulled the curtain around the bed to give Peaches privacy while he performed a pelvic exam. She was 3.5 centimeters dilated. That meant it could be hours before the baby came. Or not. Sometimes labor moved along much quicker.

Peaches hands jammed into her armpits. "Is everything okay, Doc?"

He smiled. "Everything's normal. If I remember correctly, you were in labor about eight hours with Markie?"

"*Seis*, maybe *siete horas*."

"You're almost four centimeters. It will probably be a few more hours." He opened the curtain and waved his hand at Laila and her friends.

Leo introduced himself and shook Eduardo's hand.

"We've heard a lot about you, Eduar—Dr. Quintana," said Allison.

"I live with them in Santa Fe," Laila said. "You briefly met Allison that day we were on the plaza with Carla and Rando."

He vaguely remembered meeting an old college friend of Laila's.

"I'm so sorry about your father," Laila said. "I was at the funeral."

"I didn't see you there." His voice choked as he thought about Papa. Any reminder of his death still evoked pain.

"When I saw you with Violet, I just assumed—"

"There is nothing going on with Violet."

Laila squinted at him. "Right."

He grinned. "Ah, there's hope. You're still jealous."

"Don't flatter yourself, Eduardo."

"I've missed you."

"Please do not go there."

"Why not?"

"Hello," shouted Peaches. "I'm having another contraction!"

Eduardo checked his watch. "Only ten minutes from the last one." At his instruction, the Harveys each held one of Peaches hands. He forced himself to focus on his job, even though there were so many things that he wanted to say to Laila. It was hard to believe she had settled in Santa Fe—only a mere fifty miles away from Sabinal! Violet had told him she'd gone back to New York. He'd been a fool to believe her.

He rubbed ice chips on Peaches chapped lips and massaged her swollen feet with Johnson's Baby Oil, ordering Laila to continue timing the contractions. With each new one, Peaches shouted every cuss word she knew, and then faded away to sleep.

At one point, Peaches body stiffened and her face was as pale as a corpse.

Laila whispered, "Is she okay?"

In truth he had only read about women in labor exhibiting this trance-like state. He glanced up at Laila. "She'll be fine."

He called Peaches' name a few times without any response. Then, he shook her arm. Finally, out of pure frustration, he slapped her face.

Peaches eyes popped open and she spat at him. "Fuck you!"

Wiping her saliva from his white jacket with a tissue, he smiled at Laila and her friends. "Looks like she's okay."

Two hours later, Peaches' eyes had dark circles, and her body was contorted and drenched in sweat. She complained of sharp pains in her back and began crying hysterically. Between sobs, she yelled out for her mother, who no one had thought to call.

Eduardo swished the curtain closed again and performed another pelvic exam. This time she was 7.5 centimeters. He whispered to the nurse to page the anesthesiologist on call then squeezed Peaches hand. "*Excelente.* The baby's coming soon. Take a couple of deep breaths."

"The hell with breathing . . . I want drugs!" Peaches shouted. "Last time they gave me—"

Eduardo wiped the sweat from her brow with a washcloth. "No worries, the drug doctor will be here shortly."

Peaches stopped crying and Eduardo reopened the curtains and turned to Leo. "Can you help me move her from her back to her side?"

On the count of three, they gently pushed Peaches to her left side. Then Eduardo gave her a back a massage with the Johnson's Baby Oil he'd used on her feet.

"Ah, that feels so good, Doc," Peaches said.

CHAPTER FIFTY-FIVE
The Reunion

Laila

I flashed on the first night Eduardo and I spent together. He had surprised me with his talent as a masseuse. As I watched Peaches calm down, I couldn't help but be impressed at how tender and caring he was with her. Despite all the weeks I'd repressed my feelings for him, they all flooded out, as if a dam had burst inside of me.

The color returned to Peaches' cheeks, and her whole body relaxed. Her voice even sounded bubbly when she asked for a glass of water. And then suddenly, another contraction and she was back to screaming and cussing. Fortunately, a six-foot-four man holding her chart entered the room and smiled at Peaches. "I'm Dr. Franklin. I'll be giving you your epidural now."

The miracle of drugs. Minutes later, the color returned to Peaches face and she smiled as the birth process progressed.

"You can start pushing now," said Eduardo.

Peaches' face was purple-red as she groaned and pushed with all she had.

"You're doing *estupendo*, kiddo." Eduardo said. "The baby's head is crowning. Just a few more, and you're done."

Finally, one last grunt, and the baby's head poked out, followed by the rest of its body.

Eduardo examined the tiny thing, still covered in amniotic fluid and blood. "It's a girl!" He handed the baby to the nurse.

After cleaning her up, weighing and measuring her, the nurse placed the baby on Peaches' stomach.

Peaches gestured to Allison. "Come here, and hold your *bebé*."

Both women's eyes filled with tears as Peaches handed over the perfectly formed infant to Allison. Leo stood next to his wife with an ear-to-ear grin on his face.

My own eyes teared up as I felt a sense of euphoria. What a magical moment we all had just shared, bringing a new life into the world. My thoughts were interrupted by Eduardo clasping my hand. "Can we talk?"

I had no idea what I wanted to happen. "Where?"

"I need to sign some paperwork. I'll meet you in the cafeteria in about ten minutes."

Fifteen minutes later, Eduardo sat across from me in a red vinyl booth. My heart was pumping blood into my ears. "How have you been?"

He held my gaze across the table. "Terrible. And you?"

"Well," I began, "I've been okay, but I'd be lying if I said I didn't miss what we had."

"Is there a chance for us? Do you believe that there was nothing going on with Violet and me?"

"I'm not sure that changes anything. I mean I can't live in Sabinal."

"I don't see myself in New York either," Eduardo said.

"I get that. Sometimes love isn't enough."

"Breaking up because of geography is crazy," said a voice from behind us.

I turned around to see Allison standing there. "How's the baby doing?"

"She's great. Leo's watching them perform some tests. We're gonna call her Hannah."

"Beautiful name," I said.

"Thank you," said Allison. "I couldn't help but overhear your discussion." She turned to Eduardo. "Have you ever thought of living in Santa Fe? Or somewhere in between?"

"That's just part of the problem. We'll always be reconciling our differences," I said.

Eduardo grinned. "But the makeup sex will be terrific."

I smacked his arm. Was it possible there was a way we could work this out? Then I had an idea. "Are you available for dinner tonight?"

"Name the time and place, and I'll be there."

CHAPTER FIFTY-SIX
The Abstinence

Laila

Eduardo and I had never had the luxury of time to get to know each other. We made love on our first date. Weeks later, I'd flown out to New Mexico with him. Between living in a funky trailer, his surly mother, and conniving ex-girlfriend, we never had a chance. Plus, the fantastic sex had clouded my judgment of whether we could really thrive in a real relationship.

I suggested we eat at The Shed, a historic restaurant in Santa Fe that Allison and Leo had raved about to me. The plan was for me to meet him there at eight o'clock. I drove around Palace Avenue a number of times in search of a parking spot. Finally, I found one a block away. I was nervous and running ten minutes late.

As I locked up the car and strolled down the street in a tight black dress and strappy sandals, I considered how to approach Eduardo at dinner. If we were going to give our relationship another try, it had to be different this time. Soon, I noticed a colorful, almost psychedelic sign hanging on an old adobe hacienda. People were crammed inside the courtyard talking, laughing and drinking margaritas. I looked around, but there was no sign of Eduardo.

After putting my name on a waiting list, a pretty redhead approached me and asked if I wanted a drink. She recommended the Shed Silver, which turned out to be the most potent margarita I'd ever tasted. It did take the edge off as I waited for Eduardo. I checked my watch. He was already twenty-five minutes late.

A few minutes later, Eduardo charged through the crowd and waved at me. He wore a pair of Wranglers and a white cowboy shirt with the top two snap buttons open revealing a turquoise heishi necklace. He kissed my cheek then gave me a once over. "Wow!"

"Wow what?"

"You look really hot in that dress."

"Order a margarita. They're awesome."

The redheaded waitress zipped over to us with an enormous smile for Eduardo. "Can I get you something, honey?"

He ordered a margarita without taking his eyes off of me. "I mean *really* hot."

"Thank you. Our, ah, table should be ready soon."

He was all apologetic. "After you left the hospital, Mrs. Ortiz—you may remember her from my office—checked into the emergency room with severe stomach pains . . ."

"No further explanation is necessary." If I was going to be with Eduardo, his tardiness would be the norm. That was something I could handle. A doctor who cared about his patients was a plus in my book.

Just then, the maître d', a tall man with a thick mustache shouted, "Levin, table for two." He escorted us through a number of colorful rooms to a small table in the corner of the restaurant and handed us menus. It suddenly dawned on me what a stupid choice I'd made—a high end Mexican restaurant for a Hispanic guy whose mother made great Mexican food at home.

Before I had a chance to apologize on my restaurant choice, Eduardo said, "I don't usually like to eat Mexican food out, but this place has the best red chile anywhere."

"You've been here before?"

"Many times."

I felt a sense of relief as a baby-faced waiter with a blond ponytail, appeared at our table. "Can I get you something to drink?"

I nodded. "Two more Silver Shed margaritas please."

When the young man returned with our drinks, Eduardo ordered burritos smothered in red chile and I chose the cheese enchiladas. While we waited for our food, I killed the margarita. Eduardo did the same. Then we ordered two more. After downing my third drink, I finally got the nerve to tell Eduardo the reason I had invited him to dinner. "There's something I need to get off my chest right away."

He arched a brow. "Go for it."

"There's an old custom that Orthodox Jews still practice to this day."

"Okay."

I let out my breath. "When a couple dates, they don't have sex until their wedding night. They actually don't even touch each other."

"Okay. And your point?"

"I think we should practice that custom."

"You don't want to have sex? For how long?"

"I'm not sure. We know that we are compatible in that area and, well, we need to give it time and see how we get along *without* the sex clouding our judgment. We didn't do that before and—"

"All right."

"You're willing to accept my terms?"

"As much as it's going to kill me, you have a point. Let's give it a try."

I was so grateful I reached across the table and gave him a long, lingering, overdue kiss. My body craved his more than ever. But I pulled away. "That was a mistake. We must act like brother and sister."

"If you insist." He grinned at me revealing his one immeasurably charming dimple.

When the waiter reappeared, Eduardo paid the bill and I attempted to stand up. My legs were so unsteady I almost fell down.

Eduardo placed his arm around my waist. "We should probably walk around for a while until you sober up."

"Until *I* sober up?"

"I confess, I'm a bit sloshed myself." Again, a smile and that dimple of his.

We strolled around the plaza with Eduardo's arm wrapped firmly around my waist. A cool summer breeze countered the intense heat I felt being so close to him. I was certain he felt it too.

We rounded a corner and found ourselves in front of the La Fonda hotel. I glared at him. "Did you plan this?"

"Not exactly. But if you have any better suggestions let me know."

"We could call Leo and Allison."

He checked his watch. "It's after ten. Do you want to wake them up?"

As we walked inside the hotel, I said, "Two rooms."

"Of course."

La Fonda's lobby was energetic and vibrant with its red-tiled floors and big New Mexican-style vigas running parallel to one other. As we headed toward the reservations desk, the room began to spin around. "I-I need to sit down," I said. I leaned on Eduardo as I stumbled over to an overstuffed chair.

He squinted at me. "Are you okay?"

"Not really."

"Wait here while I get our room."

"Rooms," I said correcting him. The ceiling now was spinning around like I was on a merry-go-round. Out of the corner of my eye, I saw Eduardo reach the front of the line. I stumbled up to him trying to gain my composure.

I smiled at the clerk, a tall guy with zits dotting his forehead. *Did he notice how I was leaning on the desk to keep my balance?* "How much for a room?"

"Two hundred dollars," he said.

I whistled. "Each? That's a lot of money."

"That's our standard rate, Miss." He sounded annoyed and turned toward Eduardo. "One or two rooms, Sir?"

I looked into Eduardo's eyes. "We're adults right?" Then I eyeballed the desk clerk. One big zit on his nose appeared to be growing by the second. "One room will be just fine."

"You're sure?" Eduardo asked.

"Of course."

I barely recall riding the elevator to our room. There was a kiva fireplace in the corner, an antique desk, and a beautiful hand-carved headboard on the bed. They all merged together in images swimming through my head. Eduardo found an extra blanket in the closet and placed it on the floor with a pillow from the bed. "Does this work for you?"

"It looks uncomfortable down there."

He rolled his eyes. "I'm gonna take a shower now."

As I listened to the sound of the shower in the bathroom, it felt like my body was possessed by "Alien Laila." Maybe "Bizarro Laila." Certainly not the Laila I knew for twenty-eight years. I stripped off all my clothes and joined Eduardo under the spray of hot water.

He narrowed his eyes. "What are you doing?"

"I don't know. But I can't stop myself."

He put his hands on my face and looked into my eyes. "Are you sure?"

I kissed him as the water dripped down our faces with the window and the mirrors steaming up from the moisture. As Eduardo's gentle but strong hands stroked my body, a powerful lust stirred deep inside me. Nothing made sense in those moments of passion. He knew the map to my most sensitive areas, and sweet spasms went through me as he rediscovered them.

Minutes later, we stepped from the shower and wrapped ourselves in big fluffy towels. Eduardo took my hand and led me to the bed. We lay across it diagonally, and stripped the towels off. The antique ceiling fan spun around as our naked bodies, still glistening with droplets of water, came together, as the rest of the world just vanished for a while.

When it was over, we both fell asleep without a word.

In the morning, I immediately had regrets. 'Normal Laila' had taken back my body. "We shouldn't have let this happen."

"I'm sorry," he said.

"It was my fault. I've never been that drunk."

He slipped on his Levis and stood shirtless, with his

muscular chest catching rays of sunlight through the window. "So where do we go from here?"

I shrugged. "Can we try celibacy for a while?"

He smiled. "I'll do my best, but no promises if you enter a shower naked."

CHAPTER FIFTY-SEVEN
The Engagement

Eduardo

As the nights grew cooler and the warm summer days came to an end, Eduardo continued to reside at the trailer in Sabinal while Laila lived in Santa Fe with her friends. Although Eduardo had agreed to a platonic relationship, he found the lack of intimacy agonizing. If Laila even brushed his hand, his fingers felt like they'd caught on fire. He knew there was only one way to end it, and the time had come.

One Sunday afternoon, Laila had volunteered to babysit for Allison and Leo so they could catch a matinee. She'd called Eduardo and invited him to keep her company after putting little Hannah down for her nap.

Before heading to Santa Fe, Eduardo showered and shaved then stood in front of the bathroom mirror and practiced his proposal. "Will you marry me, Laila?" *Was that too ordinary?* "I love you so very much, can we make it legal?" *That sounded too contrived.* He put on a new pair of Wranglers, a freshly ironed white shirt, and slipped the black box containing the ring he'd purchased from a Santa Fe jeweler in his pocket.

On the thirty-minute drive, he gave it a few more tries. "I love you more than life itself." *Too corny.* "You're the one I've been waiting for my whole life." *Better.*

Later, as he sat on the couch next to Laila in Allison and Leo's sun-filled living room, Eduardo pulled out the black box and opened it. A pear-shaped diamond ring sparkled inside. "You wanna—?"

She smiled. "You want to what?"

"I really want to make love to you, Laila." That came out all wrong.

"You're offering me this ring so we can have sex?"

"No, no. I mean—I do want to have sex, but I also want to spend the rest of my life with you."

Laila sat quiet for a few minutes and Eduardo feared he'd screwed the whole thing up.

Then he noticed her eyes filled with tears. "I have some news to share with you."

"I'm all ears."

She swallowed. "I missed my period."

"Holy shit. How late are you?"

"Three weeks. I took a test at a clinic in Santa Fe. I'm definitely pregnant."

"Why didn't you tell me?"

"I didn't want you to feel pressure to marry me because of the pregnancy."

"Silly girl. I knew you were it for me from our first night together." He slipped the ring on her finger. The diamond sparkled in the bright New Mexico sunlight streaming through the living room window. "Are you happy about the baby?"

"Are you kidding? I've wanted children my whole life. We talked about it on our first date," Laila said.

"Yes, I remember," he said. "What about your research?"

"It's the perfect career to do at home."

Eduardo grinned. "I'll cut down my practice so I can be there too." He placed his hand on her belly. "For our *bambino* or *bambina.*"

"You're serious?"

"Of course. We're in this thing together. Fifty-fifty."

She leaned forward and kissed him.

"I thought kissing was taboo."

"But we are officially engaged. One kiss to celebrate."

As he gravitated back toward her to kiss again, the garage door opened.

Laila pulled away.

A few minutes later, Leo and Allison entered the house. "Great movie," Allison said.

"What'd ya see?" Eduardo's voice was husky.

"*Midnight Express,*" Leo said. "This hippie dude gets caught smuggling drugs out of Turkey and thrown into prison. Based on a true story."

"We'll put it on our list," Laila said.

Eduardo finally understood that Laila needed to live in a place where she was surrounded by friends and cultural activities. He would need to change his lifelong plan to build a home for himself on his beloved ranch and find a place where they would both be happy.

Leo pulled out a bottle of Merlot from the paper bag. "Can you stay for a glass?"

"He can't," Laila said.

Allison looked surprised. "Well, ah, thanks for babysitting."

Laila followed Eduardo to the Studebaker which was parked on the street. She kissed him again.

This time *he* pulled away. He gazed at her dressed in a pair of denim overalls, red sneakers, and no makeup. Never had she looked more beautiful to him. "This needs to be a short engagement."

She smiled. "Agreed."

CHAPTER FIFTY-EIGHT
The Blood of Christ

Laila

I n mid-September, Eduardo and I purchased a three-room hundred-year-old adobe house on five acres outside of Santa Fe with a panoramic view of Sangre de Christo Mountains. Literally translated, *Sangre de Christo* means "Blood of Christ," a fact I thought best not to share with Pop and Eve.

True to his word, Eduardo remained in Sabinal, and I moved into the small house by myself. I loved waking up each morning to sweeping views of the pale blue New Mexico sky, and the colossal mountain range where some of America's earliest Spanish settlements coexisted alongside newer railroad communities. Rich in history and biodiversity, it was the perfect place for our wedding, and our future multicultural family.

Eduardo's dream of building a home on the ranch was transformed into adding an addition to our little house in Santa Fe. We set a wedding date for October 3rd and decided to get married in our backyard. Everything was falling into place. My parents and sisters bought their plane tickets and I found them a hotel near the plaza in Santa Fe.

A stack of lumber and unused adobes were piled on the side of our small adobe house. I tried to take it in stride that the addition could not be completed in time for the wedding. But no matter how much I tried to prepare for Eve's reaction, I feared the sting of her words. What would she say when she found out I was already pregnant?

A week before the wedding, Eduardo and an army of old friends laid sod in the backyard, and planted a variety of bright red rosebushes and other flowers. The front yard would have to wait.

We had kept the news of my pregnancy to ourselves, with the exception of my sisters and Eduardo's sister, Carla.

"Ma will kill you when she finds out," Amby said.

"She'll learn soon enough," Rachel said. "Best she and Pop get over their culture shock first."

The morning of the wedding, Eduardo's friends set up rows of metal chairs in the backyard, with a podium on a makeshift stage for the ceremony. Gold and blue streamers, balloons, and tiny colored lights decorated the area.

My sisters hung out with me in my tiny bedroom. As I sat on the bed in a white silk slip, Rachel blew-dry my hair and Amby gave me a manicure. In between, the two of them polished off a bottle of champagne. Since I was pregnant, I stuck to apple juice, but joined them in an endless round of giggling.

When Amby was done with my nails, I put my hand on the small mound of my belly. "Are you sure you can't see the baby bump?"

"Not unless someone's examining you," Rachel said. "Now let me finish drying your hair."

Amby looked out the window at the parade of vehicles pulling up to the house. "The caterers are here. Have a look."

Rachel turned off the blow dryer, and we checked out a van driving up the road with the logo SANTA FE GOURMET

CATERING. I glanced at the clock in my bedroom. "Right on time." I had ordered various platters of food for the reception. Four women in white uniforms stepped out of the vehicle and began setting up long tables with silver serving dishes, covered metal serving plates, fruit bowls, and flower arrangements.

Rachel shrugged and began fixing my hair again. "You want it down or half-up?"

"Whatever you think," I said.

Minutes later, Amby's eyebrows shot up. "Oh my Gawd!"

"What's going on?" I moved back over to the window. Outside, Eduardo's aunts and grandmother had arrived with homemade dishes and their own long metal table which they placed parallel to the caterer's table.

My mouth fell open. "I had no idea."

Rachel put her hand on my shoulder. "Holy shit!"

There could only be one person responsible, even though Eduardo had told her I was taking care of all the food.

The *viejas* and the caterers glared at each other as though ready for battle.

"This feels like an effing movie," Rachel said laughing. "Open another bottle of champagne, Amby."

"I don't think this is funny," I said.

"Sure it is," Amby said as she popped the cork of a bottle of Dom Perignon and poured herself and Rachel each a glass. "You gotta laugh, Laila."

"Or I'll cry." I said. "What's Eve gonna think?"

"Oy," Rachel said.

Amby shot her a stern look. "She'll have to go with the flow."

I shuddered. "That sounds like our mother."

"No worries," Rachel said. "Amby and I will take care of her."

Amby held up her champagne glass. *"L'chaim."*

We toasted to all the dishes I'd ordered on the caterers' table: roast beef and roasted potatoes, poached salmon and asparagus, fruit bowls, cut-up melons, chopped liver, and herring.

The *viejas* brought platters of enchiladas, beans, chili, *carne adovada, sopaipillas, tortillas,* cucumber salads, cookies, casseroles, string beans and more.

Carloads of people piled out of their vehicles.

Amby attempted to count everyone. "How many people did you invite?"

"About one hundred, give or take a few." I said.

"Give more than a few, honey. There's closer to two hundred people out there, and the cars keep arriving."

Rachel furrowed her forehead. "Who invited all the extra people?"

I inhaled and exhaled before responding, "My future mother-in-law."

Rachel said, "Oh, boy."

Amby's eyes popped open.

"Now you know what I'm dealing with," I said.

"Just relax," Rachel said. "Does it really matter in the scheme of things? At least we won't run out of food."

I shrugged. "You're right. I refuse to let it ruin my day."

Two of Eduardo's friends, attractive men in their thirties wearing Western suits, set up his hang-glider over the makeshift stage. A leather-bound book, a bottle of Cold Duck and two wine goblets sat on top of a podium.

I fanned myself with the latest issue of *Bride's Magazine*. "What time did you tell Ma to come, Rachel?"

"The invitation said five." She checked her watch. "It's four-thirty. Do you want me to call the hotel? Maya can be a real pain to dress."

"I hope they're prepared for a carnival," Amby said.

I suddenly felt nauseated. "Ya think?"

This time Rachel glared at Amby. "No worries, Sista. It's under control."

Eduardo's cousin, Tito, pulled up in a pickup with a muffler you could hear from New Jersey, and tires raised to the roofline.

Behind him, bronc-riding Billy zoomed up on a Harley with his buxom girl hanging on the back. Or was this a different buxom girl?

Finally, my parents arrived with Will and Maya.

Amby whispered, "Here comes trouble."

Eve stepped out of the white Ford sedan dressed in a pink sequined cocktail dress and stilettos. Her hair was now about two inches long, still streaked white in the middle. It stood up as straight as a porcupine's. As she walked toward the house, her three-inch heels sank in the dirt of our unpaved driveway.

"*Oy vey*," said Rachel. "Ya think she's a bit overdressed for the desert?"

Eve flushed as red as our new rosebushes—from her face to her décolletage—as she removed her shoes and inspected the heels covered in mud.

Pop took off his sports jacket and yanked at his tie.

The kids raced up to the house.

I hugged Will and Maya at the front door. "Run into my bedroom. Lala has toys for you." I had just put on my wedding attire. After combing traditional bridal stores in Santa Fe and Albuquerque, I had flown back to New York and spent a week with my sisters shopping for a dress in the city of my birth. Finally, I found a white-lace camisole and a long silk skirt in a small boutique in the West Village.

Eve kissed my cheek, and then wiped off the smudge of ruby lipstick with her finger. "You look beautiful, honey."

"Thank you, Ma."

She looked down at her muddy feet. "What about my shoes?"

I led her to the bathroom where she washed the dirt off in the tub. Then I found a pair of old flats in my closet and handed them to her.

She examined every inch of my tiny house, with its brick floors and colorful Mexican tile on bathroom and kitchen countertops. Wedding presents were scattered everywhere. "Nice place. A *bissel* small for a family, though."

I pointed at the construction materials in the back of the house. "We're adding a whole new wing. Come look at the architectural plans."

"Not now, honey." She opened her purse, removed a check from her wallet and handed it to me. "Here's a little something that should cover your wedding expenses."

I glanced at the check. "Wow! This is more than enough. I'll send you the balance. Thank you so much."

Pop kissed my cheek. "No need, sweetheart. Amby's wedding in New York is going to cost twice as much."

"But my first wedding—"

"What first wedding?" Pop said with a wink. "I'd like to see those house plans."

Ma started to speak, but Pop shot her a hard look and she bit her lip.

After examining the plans, Pop snapped pictures of the house and the mountains with his new Polaroid camera. "Some view you have." He turned to my mother. "Maybe we should move out here, Evie."

"Not this year," Ma said. "Do bandits and Indians still live in these parts?"

"Hello, Ma. We're in the twentieth century."

As if on cue, Brooklyn barked, followed by a knock on the front door. When I opened it, Tito stood there on crutches with two rough-looking hombres covered in tattoos. "Remember me?"

I smiled. "You're unforgettable, Tito. Looks like you're injured again."

"My girlfriend's sister got mad and—"

"Never mind. Come on inside."

My parents sat stiffly on the overstuffed couch in the living room and glared at Tito and his friends. I made introductions, fearful of what was going through their minds.

Eve's eyes twitched as Pop extended his hand.

Tito gave him a firm handshake and grinned at Ma. His gold front tooth sparkled. Turning back to me he said, "This is Pedro and Ricardo."

"Nice to meet you." I didn't remember seeing their names on the invitation list. But then half the people in the yard weren't on the list either.

Tito took my hand and gave it a gentlemanly kiss. "Do you mind if I use the *baño*?"

"Of course not. Down the hall on your left."

He hobbled back to the bathroom.

Eve's eyes were the size of *albondigas*. She whispered, "Are they *banditos?*"

"Shhh." I prayed Tito's friends hadn't heard her. "Would you like to have a seat while you wait for Tito?"

Pedro and Ricardo sat down on two of the folding metal chairs that Eduardo had set up for guests. Ricardo pulled out a pocketknife and began cleaning his nails with the blade.

Pedro opened the cap of a small canteen, took a swig, then passed it to Ricardo. He pointed at Pop. "Want some?"

"Sure, why not?" said Pop. Ricardo handed Pop the canteen and he slugged the liquid down, then coughed. "Good stuff. Is this tequila?"

"*Tapatio Añejo,*" said Pedro. "We brought it up from Mexico. *Tome un poco más.* Have a little more."

Pop downed another shot and handed the canteen back to Pedro.

The room was silent after that. Eve was usually great making small talk, but even she couldn't come up with something to talk about with Tito's friends.

I uncorked another bottle of champagne. "Who wants—?"

My offer was interrupted by the unmistakable sound of a heavy stream of water coming from the *baño*. Evidently, Tito had seen no need to close the door before relieving himself.

The color in Eve's face went from flushed to pasty white.

Pop squeezed her hand.

Minutes later, Tito hobbled back to the living room. "*Gracias,* Laila. My new cuz."

I patted his back. "Any time, Cuz."

"You'll never believe what I got you guys for a wedding present."

"You're right. What is it?"

"You'll find out soon enough." He winked then turned to his friends. "*Vamonos.*" The three exited the house together.

Ma stood. "I need a Valium. Oh dear, I think I left the bottle at the hotel."

"Calm down," I said. "Just go with the flow, mother."

"Yes, the flow coming from the john was quite lovely," Eve said.

Pop smiled. "Loosen up, honey bunny."

She walked to the open front door and shouted out to Tito and his friends. "Before you leave can I have a shot of *Tapatio Añejo*, please?"

CHAPTER FIFTY-NINE
The Chuppah

Eduardo

Up until the day of the wedding, Eduardo continued to live in the trailer. When he wasn't with Laila, he often had dinner over at Mama's. "You've got to try and accept Laila for who she is," he said to her one night as he sat at the kitchen table eating his favorite green chili stew.

"Is the chili too hot, *hijo*?"

"Did you hear what I said?"

"*Sí.* I need to make nice with your girlfriend."

"Fiancé, Mama. We're getting married in a few weeks."

"*Sí, lo sé.* Yes, I know. But why are you not getting married in the church?"

He patiently explained that they'd decided to make the ceremony non-sectarian.

She drummed her fingers on the table. "What does that mean?"

"It's when you have a judge rather than a priest marry you."

"*No comprendo?*"

"Because Laila isn't Catholic."

She nodded, but Eduardo had his doubts that Mama understood. Or that she'd ever accept Laila's differences. As long as she was nice to her though, nothing else mattered.

The afternoon of the wedding, he drove to Santa Fe in his beloved Studebaker. He was dressed in a cream-colored Western suit with a chestnut brown silk shirt and a turquoise bolo tie. Mama and his sisters followed in Carla's car. He smiled at Mama as she left the car in a red pants suit and new Tony Lama boots he'd purchased for her.

Eduardo mingled with the crowd as the two families gathered outside on a rented dance floor. A Mariachi band played on a makeshift stage.

Allison and Leo had just arrived with baby Hannah in a stroller.

After greeting them, Eduardo walked up to Laila's mother and hugged her.

"I knew you were the one," she said. "That first afternoon in the emergency room."

Eduardo winked at her, then headed over to Laila's father, who stood admiring Billy's Harley. "That's sure a fine set of wheels," Elliot said. "XLCR Cafe Racer, right?"

Billy placed his arm around Elliot's shoulder. "Sounds like you know your shit about Harley's."

"I've got an FX Super Glide. It's my new baby."

Billy nodded. "Classy wheels."

Eve pointed over at the stage. "What's that?"

"Eduardo's hang glider," Billy said.

Eve furrowed her forehead. "Huh?"

"You know, he jumps off cliffs and shit with it. Well, he used to before he became a pussy," Billy said.

Eve smiled. "He's a pussy cat?"

"It's the *chuppah,* honey," Elliot said.

Billy smiled. "What's a *chuppah?*"

"It's a canopy," Eve replied. "In the Jewish religion the marriage ceremony is performed under one."

Billy looked Eve in the eye. "Can I ask you something?"

"I don't see why not, dear."

"How do you Jews make them matzoh balls? I love those things."

Eve grinned. "I'll send you the recipe."

Eduardo smiled as he observed the two families mingling together. Everything was going better than expected. If only Papa could have been here. Eduardo felt a tightness in his chest still devastated at the loss of his father. It comforted him to remember that Papa had really liked Laila. The night she'd arrived from New York, he had taken Eduardo aside and said, "*Ella es inteligente, ella es hermosa, y ella es lo suficientemente fuerte como para manejar su madre.* She's smart, she's beautiful, and she's tough enough to take on your mother."

Will and Maya were playing with Kiki's son, Errol. Eduardo high-fived the boys and picked up Maya, who was serving as their flower girl. Then he nodded at Laila's older sister and Kiki, who stood together deep in conversation.

Rachel leaned in toward Kiki. "Your little boy is adorable. Such big blue eyes."

Kiki shook her head. "He takes after his *gringo* daddy. The son-of-a-bitch left me for a little shit from the Valley before he was even born."

Rachel squinted. "My son-of-a-bitch husband left me for a little shit from Miami."

The sisters smiled at each other.

Eduardo felt Papa beaming down at them from above.

CHAPTER SIXTY
The Ceremony

Laila

As we stood in the house waiting for word of the ceremony to begin, I began biting my freshly painted nails, a habit I had given up years ago.

Amby pushed my hand away from my mouth. "You're going to ruin your manicure."

"What's taking them so long? Rachel's been gone for over an hour." The invitations said 5:00. I looked at my watch. 5:38. "Sure you can't see the baby bump?"

"It's fine," Amby said. "Take a few deep breaths."

Finally, the band began to play "Here Comes the Bride."

Pop walked inside the house and took my arm. "It's time, sweetheart. But not too late if you have *any* doubts."

"I'm sure, Pop. Eduardo is the right man for me."

Pop's blue eyes were misty. "Let's go then."

Eduardo's brother-in-law, Rando, and Rachel, our best man and matron-of-honor, walked down the aisle as Pop and I stood in the doorway. Then little Errol and Maya followed behind, serving as ring bearer and flower girl. Errol carried two gold wedding bands on a small velvet pillow, while Maya dropped flower petals on the path.

Eduardo walked down the aisle linking arms with his mama. She sat down in the front row of chairs. Eduardo stood at the podium, where a district judge from Raton, an old friend of his father's, was waiting to perform the ceremony.

Pop took my arm and we strolled proudly down the path

adorned with flowers to the podium. He handed me to Eduardo, and took his seat in the first row next to Eve.

Eduardo whispered, "You look beautiful."

The judge spoke into the microphone. "Quiet everyone. Our dearly beloved couple would like to recite their own vows."

Eduardo and I faced each other. He cleared his throat. "Our love, born of mutual respect and admiration, has developed into this marriage. From this moment on, I devote my life to the pursuit of our dreams and the preservation of our strong family unions and traditions."

Then I said, "Those of you who know Eduardo, know what a truly special person I'm marrying, and what a close-knit family the Quintanas are. Today, in front of you all, I commit myself to a lifetime as Eduardo's partner."

The crowd clapped.

"Is there anyone here who has reason to believe that this man and this woman should not be wed?" The judge peered at the audience of our families and friends. "If so, let him speak now, or forever hold his peace."

Tito hobbled up to the front of the podium. "I got something to say."

The crowd began to whisper.

Out of the corner of my eye, I saw Eve hyperventilating.

"It's not that I don't think these two nice *personas* shouldn't get married," said Tito. "I just got some important news."

"Can't the news wait?" Eduardo said.

"It's my present to you. My honey did our family tree. She's also teaching me about astrology and the Tarot—"

"Get on with it, man," Eduardo said.

"We're fuckin' Jewish, dude. The Quintanas and Sandoval

families left Spain and hid their Jewish heritage when they moved to northern New Mexico, hundreds of years ago."

Sylvia stumbled forward, tripped on an extension cord, and fell down in the dirt.

Eduardo and I helped her up. Her face was bright red and tears spilled from her eyes.

The crowd was so silent you could hear a mosquito buzz.

Eduardo dusted some dirt off her jacket. "Mama, are you all right?"

Her voice was choked. "It's okay, *mi hijo*. Papa and I suspected this for many years."

Everyone sighed in relief.

She hugged me. "Welcome to our family, Laila. I'm sorry if I've acted badly."

"Now we're *familia*," I said. "A new beginning."

She locked eyes with me. "You will raise *su bebés* Catholic, no?"

Eve jumped up. "No way. If it's a boy, he must have a bris and a Bar Mitzvah."

Tito stepped forward. "What's a bris?"

Pop said, "It's when they cut off the skin of—"

"A circumcision," Eduardo said. "Very common these days."

"He must be baptized," Sylvia said. "Or he'll rot in hell."

"What if he's a she?" Rachel said. "Laila thinks it's a girl." Damn. My sister had drunk her share of champagne.

Eve's eyes were big as bowls as she turned to me. "You're pregnant?"

The crowd buzzed. "*Está teniendo un bebé?*"

I let out a breath and turned toward the crowd. "Yes, everyone, we're having a baby."

"*Mazel tov*," Pop said.

"The baby will need to be christened," Sylvia said.

Eduardo put his arm around his mother. "We'll work it out, Mama. We need to get married now."

Eve glared at me. "How come you didn't tell me about the baby?" She turned to Amby. "Did you know too?"

Amby looked down at her wedged sandals.

Annoyed, Eve put her hands on her hips. "You girls always keep secrets from me."

Sylvia squinted at my mother. "And don't forget a first holy communion."

"Waddaya mean?" Eve said. "You just found out you're Jewish."

"Can we finish the ceremony?" asked the judge. "It's getting late."

The crowd settled down. The judge smiled at us and continued. The scenario felt like a crazy romantic comedy. Would our marriage survive our family differences? Could any marriage survive the toxic combination of Eve and Sylvia?

But then Eduardo gazed into my eyes like I was the only one on the planet, and we both said, "I do."

The judge smiled. "By the power vested in me by the state of New Mexico, I now pronounce you husband and wife. You may kiss the bride."

Eduardo kissed me. His lips felt soft and warm. His tongue probed inside my mouth for a fraction of a second. A prelude of what would come later tonight.

A rush of heat scalded my cheeks. The reception would go on for hours. Could I wait that long?

The judge handed Eduardo one of the wine goblets and he smashed it with his foot.

Everyone in my family shouted, "*L'ch-haim!*"

The Mariachi band played "Hava Nagila."

Eduardo and I were each picked up on two chairs and marched around in the middle of people dancing the *hora* in a circle to Mariachi music.

Afterwards, as is the custom in orthodox Jewish weddings, Eduardo and I escaped to our bedroom. If we were orthodox Jews, this would have been the first time we'd been together without a chaperone.

Eduardo pulled me close to him and we kissed for the first time as a married couple.

I savored the kiss for a moment, then had a reality check. "Your mama's never going to accept me. And she and Eve—"

He placed his hand on my belly. "Nothing worthwhile ever comes easy."

I smiled. "Now, as is the orthodox custom, we must consummate our marriage."

"That's really the custom?"

I put my arms around his neck. "Does it really matter?"

"Not at all." He took my hand and led me to the bed. "Would you like a massage?"

I pointed at a giant bottle of Johnson's Baby Oil sitting on the nightstand. "You betcha!"

# # #

EPILOGUE

The extraordinary saga of settlement by secret Jews in Northern New Mexico has recently been discovered.

In 1586, King Philip II gave Don Luis Cravajal, head of a prominent family, a huge tract of land that covered New Mexico, Texas and Arizona. Carvajal was appointed governor of the territory known as New Spain, and peopled it largely with Jews who pretended to convert to Christianity during the Inquisition.

Carvajal eventually was convicted of "Judaizing." He died in prison and other members of his family were burned at the stake. In succeeding centuries, the descendants of these families either lost or concealed the memory of their origins. Often they privately maintained some Jewish traditions but outwardly professed Catholicism.

ACKNOWLEDGMENTS

This book is dedicated to the most important people in my life: Rudy, Jacob, Matthew, Marshall, Robyn, Kara, and Nikki.

And especially to the lights of my life: Madison and Taylor, and two little babies on their way into this world.

Special thanks to the cadre of author friends for their honest critiques: Tosh McIntosh, Patsy Shepherd, Brad Whittington and John Jones.

Thanks to Ellen Sklarz for the incredible job she did as my proofreader.

Also, thanks to my independent editing team: Paul Lynch, Rita Singer, Lidia Pabon, Susan Rockhold, and John Jones.

A special thanks to my cover designer and book formatter, long time writing mentor, and friend, Tosh McIntosh.

And *mucho gracias* to my best cheerleader and forever supporter, my sister Rita Singer.

DISCUSSION QUESTIONS

1. Who is the antagonist in this story? Are there more than one?
2. What could Eduardo have done to make Laila's life better once they got to New Mexico?
3. Who is your favorite character in the book? Why?
4. Did you think Dave, the Son of Sam copycat, was at all sympathetic?
5. Why didn't Laila go back to New York when she and Eduardo split up?
6. What role did Laila's sister Rachel play in the book?
7. What is the real reason Eduardo's mother does not like Laila?
8. Was Laila's approach to pregnancy prevention by encouraging sex education the most effective choice for Española, New Mexico, with its large Hispanic Catholic population?
9. Laila had issues with both her mother and future mother-in-law. Were the mothers likable? How could Laila have dealt with them better?
10. What was the biggest surprise in the book?

ABOUT THE AUTHOR

A native New Yorker, author Lara Reznik escaped to New Mexico in the 1970s in a Karmann Ghia that she jump-started cross-country. As an English major at the University of New Mexico, she studied under esteemed authors Rudolfo Anaya and the late Tony Hillerman. She also attended a summer program at the prestigious University of Iowa's Writers Workshop.

In 2012 Lara published *The Girl From Long Guyland,* a psychological suspense novel that struck a chord as a ride down memory lane for baby boomers. The book has garnered over 330 Amazon customer reviews and powerful editorial reviews from Kirkus, Publisher's Weekly the executive producer of *The Late Show with David Letterman*, and the former President and COO of the *New York Daily News.*

Following the breakout success of *The Girl From Long Guyland*, Lara retired from her day job as an I.T. executive at a Texas utility to write full time. Her second novel, *The M&M Boys,* published in 2015, is the coming-of-age story of a troubled little leaguer from Queens, who learns valuable lessons about love, honor, and friendship when Roger Maris and Mickey Mantle move next door to him during the home run race of 1961. The book achieved #1 in multiple Amazon genres such as coming-of-age, sports fiction, and historical fiction, and received outstanding editorial reviews and over 180 Amazon customer reviews.

Bagels & Salsa, evolved from a screenplay Lara wrote in 2001 that was a finalist in a *Writer's Digest,* Austin Heart of Film and Southwest Writers screenwriting contests. Since numerous fans of *The Girl From Long Guyland* wanted to learn more about the relationship of Laila Levin, *Guyland's* Jewish protagonist, and Eduardo Quintana, her Hispanic husband, Lara decided to adapt the semi-autobiographical screenplay into the love story of how Laila met Eduardo.

Bagels & Salsa, the novel, recently was a finalist in the Texas Writers League 2017 fiction contest

OTHER BOOKS BY LARA REZNIK

The Girl From Long Guyland (prequel/sequel to *Bagels & Salsa*)

MEMOIR MEETS THRILLER: Set against a 1969 psychedelic love-in backdrop, *The Girl From Long Guyland* is shared through the eyes of Laila Levin when decades later, an unsolved murder pulls her reluctantly into her past. A dramatic collision of then and now entwining family, marriage, profession and ethics.

The M&M Boys

Marshall Elliot's joy of making the All-Star team evaporates when his father misses his triumphant opening game, and his mother spirals into a bed-ridden depression. Then, Roger Maris and Mickey Mantle move next door as they battle to break Babe Ruth's home run record. The three find solace in each other's triumphs, frustrations, celebrations and disappointments.

CPSIA information can be obtained
at www.ICGtesting.com
Printed in the USA
LVHW031915080720
660120LV00002B/189